A DOMESTIC SLAVE

A DOMESTIC SLAVE

A B Given

Text Copyright © 2019 A B Given
All Rights Reserved

ISBN: 9781086545401

To my good friend Robert Windsor.
I am indebted to him for his ongoing support and assistance.

CHAPTER 1

Tears streamed from Mary's eyes. She'd never laughed so much. It was difficult to walk with a balloon held between your knees and even more difficult when you were laughing so hard. It was Nancy's hens night and all the women were in a silly mood. The phallic symbolism of the balloon wasn't missed by anyone and a steady stream of ribald comments flowed as the two rows of women raced to be the first to pass their balloon to the end of the line.

Mary wiped her eyes as she thrust her knees forward. Bev Wilkins did the same and somehow they managed to pass the balloon between them. Her job done Mary stepped aside to watch its progress. Who won or lost didn't really matter. Winning wasn't the point of the game. The only point was to have fun and it was working.

The women were cheering now. The balloon was being passed to Nancy and then the game would be over. The Bride-to-be's team won all the games but it didn't stop them congratulating her. Mary waited until last. 'We won!'

Nancy rolled her eyes. 'Yeah, what a surprise!'

Mary began to fidget. 'It has been a wonderful night.'

'Oh no, please don't say you're going already!'

'It is a bit late.'

'What are you talking about; it's only half-past-nine! The stripper hasn't even been yet.'

'Geoffrey will be waiting. He doesn't like to be home alone.' Mary felt herself blush as Nancy's eyes moved to the ragged scar cutting through her right eyebrow. But when she spoke it was about something else. 'At least stay for the stripper. He's due any minute.'

'I thought you didn't want a stripper?'

Nancy shrugged. 'You know what Megan's like! You can't tell her no.' Nancy winked. 'Besides, I'm not supposed to know. It's meant to be a surprise.'

At the mention of Megan, Mary's good mood slipped a little. It wasn't that she didn't like Megan, she did. But there was a time when she, not Megan, would have been asked to organise Nancy's hens night. They had been so close before she married Geoffrey. To shake herself free of any bad thoughts, she smiled. 'Alright, but only until he's done.'

Nancy found her a drink and Mary dutifully took a miniscule sip. Geoffrey didn't like her drinking.

Ten minutes later a man wearing a cheap imitation of a policeman's uniform entered the room. The shirt was stretched at the seams to accommodate his huge muscles. Not that it stayed on him long. As the stripper eased out of his shirt, Mary slipped quietly to the back of the room. While it made sense that the stripper would focus in on Nancy, she'd heard stories of other nights. It seemed strippers had a knack for spotting shy women and would single them out. From the safety of her corner she watched and laughed with the others as he showed off his body. He got down to a tiny G-string that bulged impressively at the front. Tucking several lolly snakes into the narrow waistband he coaxed Nancy use her teeth to extract them. Several ribald comments made Mary blush, but it was all in fun.

Placing her untouched drink on a table edge she made her way to Nancy. 'I really do have to go this time.'

Nancy hugged her and kissed her cheek. As they parted she noticed Nancy's eyes go back to the scar. 'He does love me!' She'd spoken more forcefully than she'd intended and Nancy looked taken aback. 'I'm sure he does.'

To recover the situation Mary quickly leant in and gave Nancy's cheek a peck. 'I'll call you.' Before Nancy could reply, she turned and fled. It was only once she was outside she realised she should have called for a taxi first. It was dark and lonely out in the street. She didn't own a mobile phone now. She couldn't remember exactly when she'd stopped having one. She'd always owned one. She rarely used it but it was always in her handbag, ready if needed, for situations like this one. Only now it wasn't.

The main road was north so she turned right and walked to the end of the street. Her old car would have come in handy too now. She hadn't drunk more than a sip of alcohol the whole night. But she didn't own her little car now either and Geoffrey didn't like her using his fancy new BMW.

At the corner she turned left and kept walking.

Her legs were getting tired by the time she flagged down a taxi. She sat in the back and fretted. It must be getting quite late by now! The house looked dark when the taxi stopped at the end of the drive. She hoped Geoffrey had gone to bed. He might never know what time she got home. She paid the taxi and crept down the driveway. Sliding the key silently into the front door she opened it. Her heart sank. She could see a faint light at the rear of the house. It was the new room Geoffrey added when he had the house completely renovated. It was his games room. She hated it.

Putting her handbag down she forced a smile and walked towards the light. 'You're still up?' she said brightly.

Geoffrey only stared back at her.

That was when she noticed the glass at his elbow. It was his whiskey glass. It was made from cut crystal and had a heavy base so it wouldn't easily tip. After the last time he'd promised her he'd thrown the glass away. But there it was, at his elbow.

'Where the fuck have you been?'

'You know it was Nancy's hens night; I told you all about it!' she said in a pleading tone.

Geoffrey was sitting in his chair: the one directly in front of the massive TV screen. But the TV wasn't on. His polished Italian shoes were next to the chair. The jacket of his Italian suit was draped neatly over the padded arm and his tie was slightly loosened. Mary knew this was Geoffrey's idea of relaxing. He reached for his glass. He held it in front of his face for a long time, as though challenging her to say something. She didn't and he eventually took a long swallow. 'What did you bitches get up to?'

He was drunk. He'd promised her he wouldn't drink whiskey again, not after that last time. She wished she'd come home when she first planned. Nancy was her closest friend but she cursed her. Geoffrey wouldn't be as drunk if Nancy had just let her go! She hadn't enjoyed the stripper anyway.

As though he'd read her mind, he suddenly demanded, 'I bet there was a stripper! You bitches never get together unless you have some guy parading around for you!'

She hated it when he was drunk. Normally Geoffrey behaved so sophisticatedly but he could be coarse when he was drunk.

'Go on,' he challenged her, 'Deny it!'

She knew better. Nancy worked at the bank and so did most of the other women. So did Geoffrey. It was where they met. She'd worked at the bank too, before they were married. If she lied she knew Geoffrey would find out. 'Just one,' she said meekly. 'And he wasn't very good.'

'I bet he had all those stupid sluts panting over him!'

'It wasn't...'

'What about you?' he demanded, cutting her off. 'Were you panting over him? Did he make you wet between your legs?'

She held out her hand to him. 'Why don't we go to bed?'

He looked at her before picking up his glass once more. 'I don't want to go to bed.' He took another long swallow. 'I want to hear how hot you got watching some stranger flashing his dick at you.'

'I didn't even see it. He kept his underpants on.'

Geoffrey laughed, spilling whiskey over his trousers. 'I bet you were disappointed.' He leered at her. 'But don't worry, I've got something for you.'

'I really think it would be best...'

With his free hand Geoffrey stabbed angrily at the floor in front of his feet. 'Get down there!'

Mary jumped. Bracing herself, she stepped closer. Forcing a smile, she said, 'Please, Dear, why...'

Geoffrey lashed out with his fist, slamming it into her unprotected stomach. 'I said, kneel on the floor!'

Mary was bent double, struggling for breath.

'Do I have to tell you again!' he roared at her.

'No, Dear,' she managed to say. Using the arm of the chair to help support her, she lowered herself to her knees.

'That's better.' Putting his hand under her chin, he lifted her face higher, so they were looking into each other's eyes. 'Why do you make me do things like that?'

Tears were watering her eyes, making his face waver. 'I'm sorry, Dear.'

The anger drained from his face. Looking contrite now, he told her, 'You know I love you and that I don't like hurting you...but sometimes you make me so angry. If you just did as I told you, when I told you, things would be much better for you!'

'I'm very sorry, Dear, I promise I'll try harder in future.'

He nodded, satisfied. 'Show me just how sorry you are for upsetting me.'

Mary reached out and unfastened his belt. Swallowing her fear, she unbuttoned the top of his trousers and slid the zipper down. Pulling the flaps wide apart she reached inside. He was already semi-hard, which puzzled her. It was as if hurting her somehow excited him. With a shake of her head she pushed that thought aside. Knowing what he expected, she made herself smile as she pressed her lips to his long shaft. 'Mmm,' she murmured as she kissed it.

'You bitches are all the same,' he said, as he sat comfortably back in the large padded chair. 'Some guy shows you his dick and it's all you can think about!'

Mary kissed him all over before opening her mouth wide and taking him between her lips. He tasted of sweat and urine but she forced herself to slide more and more of him into her mouth. Fighting the urge to gag she worked her lips over his quickly stiffening shaft. She knew from experience it was going to be a long night. Geoffrey didn't cum quickly when he'd been drinking. Her stomach hurt terribly and tears mixed with her saliva as she did her best to please her husband.

She heard Geoffrey take another swallow. 'Be a sweetheart and get me another glass?'

Freeing herself, Mary used the arm of the chair once more to push herself to her feet. She winced with pain and grabbed hold of her stomach. When she reached for the glass, Geoffrey pulled it back. Glaring at her, he demanded, 'What was that little show for?'

'It's nothing, honest.'

'Bullshit! I know what game you're playing but I'm not falling for it!' Suddenly grabbing her arm, he pulled her face close to his. 'If you were a better wife I wouldn't have to punish you, would I?'

She knew better than to struggle even though his fingers were digging deep into her arm. 'No, Dear.'

'No, Dear,' he said mimicking her. 'Is that all you can say?'

There was no reply to that so she waited patiently. Eventually he released her arm and she walked to the bar. A newly opened bottle of Black Label was sitting on top of it. The bottle was two-thirds empty. Mary thought about skimping but not for long. Filling the glass, she carried it carefully back to him.

He snatched it from her, spilling some of the expensive liquid. 'Now get back down there and finish what you started!'

'Yes, Dear.'

'Yes, Dear...yes, Dear. You're a fucking broken record!'

Even when she heard his snores, she didn't stop. She was too frightened of waking him. It was only when she felt him begin to soften in her mouth that she finally allowed herself to relax. Pushing herself back, well away from her husband, she crawled silently from the room. She ignored her bed. She didn't want Geoffrey to wake later and find her there.

Wincing with the pain she rose to her feet and made her way to the spare bedroom. It wasn't much of a hiding spot but she didn't think Geoffrey would come looking for her. All the same, she turned the key in the lock.

Slipping out of her dress she pulled back the quilt and climbed into bed. She was dead tired but sleep evaded her. Her stomach hurt but that wasn't what was keeping her awake. It was her guilt that kept her from sleep. Geoffrey was right; she knew that. He did love her. If only she'd come home when she'd first intended; none of this would have happened!

Everything was her fault! She knew Geoffrey was right. If she could be a better wife then he wouldn't get so angry with her. It was her fault!

She hated to admit it but her mother was right too. Her mother told her she was lucky to have a husband like Geoffrey. 'You're such a plain girl; I don't know why someone as handsome and as clever as Geoffrey Parker would be interested in you!' Her mother had never been kind to her so Mary ignored her, at the time. Then later, when they were married, Geoffrey came home one Friday night and he'd been drinking. He was also very angry. His boss, Mr. Roberts, had conducted a surprise audit. Mary didn't see why this bothered her new husband. Surely Mr. Roberts had the right to conduct an audit. She had worked at the bank herself and her work had been audited many times. She made the mistake of pointing it out.

'What the fuck would you know? You were never higher than a Grade Two. Of course they audited your work!' At the bank, there was a ranking of all employees. New starters began as a one. Fifteen was the highest and only the Chief Executive Officer was a fifteen. Geoffrey was an eight and very proud of it.

'I only meant...'

'Bloody Roberts,' ranted Geoffrey over her. 'How dare he audit me!' He seemed to settle himself and a smug look came over him. 'It's not like he'd even know what I've been up to anyway.'

Without thinking, she blurted out, 'What have you been up to?'

He looked at her like she'd slapped his face. First he looked surprised. Then he looked angry. Very angry. 'What do you mean? What exactly are you accusing me of?'

'I...I didn't mean anything. You said...' She didn't get the chance to finish explaining. Geoffrey pulled back his fist before slamming it into her face. She collapsed to the floor, stunned. He took hold of her by her hair and pulled her back to her feet. Waving his arm to encompass the kitchen, he shouted at her, 'This house is filthy! What the fuck do you do all day?'

Still stunned from the unexpected punch to her face, she made the mistake of saying, 'But, Geoffrey, the house isn't dirty.'

He still had hold of her hair. Pointing at the benchtop with his left hand he said, 'What do you call that?'

She looked at the spotless benchtop. 'I don't see anything.'

Using his hold on her hair, he slammed her face against the edge of the bench. Her eyebrow split open spraying blood across the bench. Pulling her back, he held her face over the bench. Pointing at the blood splatter, he said in a triumphant voice, 'If it's so clean, what do you call that!'

Defeated, she said, 'I'm sorry. I'll clean it up.'

Geoffrey stood over her and watched as she scrubbed every inch of the kitchen. It was hard for her. She had only her right hand; her left was holding a piece of cloth to her eye to hold back the bleeding. With both her hands busy there wasn't anything she could do for her tears. They flowed and flowed.

When Geoffrey was finally happy, he told her, 'I'm going to bed.'

Mary sat on the floor and cried.

The next morning, when Geoffrey saw what he'd done to her face, he told her to get in the car. Neither of them spoke as he drove her to the hospital. He waited in the car. The doctor was polite but told her she'd taken too long to come in. He wanted her to have an x-ray but Geoffrey was waiting in the car so she declined.

The doctor sighed deeply. 'I should make a police report.'

'But whatever for?' she'd replied. 'I walked into a door.'

He didn't look happy but he did the best he could with her eyebrow. He was right though, the cut healed badly, leaving her with a nasty scar.

Geoffrey ignored her all weekend.

On Monday, when Geoffrey went to work, she drove over to her mother's. She still had her car back then. She went looking for sympathy and support. She got neither.

'You must have done something to deserve it.'

Mary stared back at her mother. It was as if her entire world had crumbled in three short days. Pointing to the plaster covering her eyebrow, she said, 'Can you see this?'

Sheila turned away. 'He must have had a good reason!'

'He said the house was dirty...'

Sheila spun back around. 'There you go! You can't expect an important man like Geoffrey to live in a dirty house, can you?'

Mary began to cry. 'But the house wasn't dirty. I work really hard, all day!'

'It must have been,' Sheila pointed out, 'or Geoffrey wouldn't have said it was. He works at a bank!'

Mary was about to point out she had worked at the exact same bank but she no longer had the strength.

Sheila made them both a cup of tea. Mary's sat untouched. Sheila looked at her. 'Are you taking care of him in the bedroom?'

'Mum?'

'I'm being serious here. Geoffrey is a very good looking man. You don't want to give him any excuse to stray.'

All Mary knew was her father had left when she was still young, too young to really remember him. 'Is that what happened with Dad?'

Sheila's face turned stony hard. 'Don't you dare throw your Father in my face!'

'I'm sorry, Mum.' She stood up. 'I think I should go.'

'Just promise me one thing. Promise me you'll do whatever it takes to make him happy!' That night Geoffrey came home with a massive bunch of flowers and pearl bracelet. He told her he loved her and she promised to try to be a better wife.

Mary woke feeling awful. Her stomach still hurt but she didn't think she needed to go to the hospital. Not this time. She had become quite good at self-diagnosis. She showered and dressed using the clothes she kept in the spare room for just this sort of occasion.

Feeling slightly better, she went in search of Geoffrey. She found him asleep in their bed, lying next to a drying pool of vomit. While he showered she pulled the bed apart and made breakfast.

'Good morning,' said Geoffrey, quietly.

'Good morning,' she said, with a smile she didn't feel.

Placing a cup of coffee and a plate of eggs on toast in front of him, she discreetly put two plain white tablets next to his coffee cup. He read the Sunday morning paper while she fussed about the kitchen.

Turing the last page of the paper over, Geoffrey finally looked up. 'Do you have anything to say?'

Mary stepped closer. With her head bowed, she said, 'I'm sorry I was out so late last night.'

He was smiling now as he wrapped an arm around her trim waist and pulled her onto his lap. 'Then we'll say no more about it.'

She felt relieved. During the night she'd convinced herself she was the one to blame. After all, she knew what Geoffrey was like. She also knew what he liked and what he didn't like. All she had to do was work within those boundaries and everything would be fine. She smiled and kissed him. His mouth tasted of toothpaste and coffee. His hand found her small breasts. She moaned, this time with pleasure. Geoffrey picked her up and carried her to the bedroom. The room smelt of air-freshener and clean sheets. He laid her on the bed. Mary giggled. He made slow tender love to her and she wished their life could always be like this. But she knew what she had to do. She had to be a better wife. If she could just be better she was convinced there wouldn't be any further unpleasantness or any more trips to the hospital. She would just have to try harder!

CHAPTER 2

Chantelle shrieked,. 'Not like that!'

The undisguised disgust in his wife's voice made Robert cringe.

'You'll bruise it. Just stir it slowly.'

Even though Robert knew it was absurd advice, he slowed the rate he was whisking the batter to please Chantelle. While Robert was the chief cook and bottle washer for their household, his wife always knew how to do everything better than he did. This superior level of knowledge didn't inspire her to actually get off the sofa and help. Instead, Chantelle reserved her knowledge for issuing instructions on where her husband was going wrong.

Chantelle was sitting on the sofa filing her already perfect nails, while keeping half an eye on Robert to make sure he was following her instructions properly. He was so useless. She wondered how he would possibly manage if she wasn't around to help him. After a moment's silence, she said, 'Have you checked the potatoes lately? Remember how you ruined them last time?'

'I'll check them now, Dear,' said Robert, remembering how he had wanted to take them out of the oven but his wife had insisted he leave them a little longer. From where she was sitting in the other room, they had looked a little undercooked. When he served her meal, she merely looked at the potato bake and sighed. 'You've burnt them now!'

'But you said to leave them in longer,' he said, in his own defence.

Chantelle gave him a withering glare, as she informed him, 'I didn't say to burn them, did I?'

'No, of course not, Dear,' he quickly slipped in before she became angry. God, he didn't want to make her angry.

So tonight he kept a close eye on the potato bake as he finished the rest of the meal.

'Why is it that I have to do everything?' she asked herself, just loud enough for her husband to hear as she put down her nail file. Picking up her glass of wine she settled back comfortably into the sofa.

Serving the fragrant food onto two plates Robert slipped the pudding batter into the oven to cook as they ate. 'It's ready,' he announced, as he carried the two steaming plates through to the dining room table. Chantelle sat down in her usual chair and began to eat while Robert poured her a fresh glass of wine.

The house was magnificent with an unobstructed view of the water. Robert loved the view because he loved the sea. Chantelle loved the view because, in Sydney, a view of the harbor was a status symbol. Any view of the water was good; an unobstructed view, such as theirs, was something you could really rub in other people's faces. Chantelle made full use of that fact whenever she could.

The house had been built on the side of a steep hill. Usually this would have created difficulties however, with the right architect it turned into a positive. The architect Chantelle found had designed a piece of art that moulded itself perfectly to the hill-face. Chantelle, herself a self-styled artist, had personally approved the design. Robert had cringed at the projected cost. Chantelle put her foot down.

The projected cost of a building such as this could and usually did blow out but there was another side to Chantelle. While she saw herself as an artist, she was also a hard-headed businesswoman. She hounded the builder and his tradesmen mercilessly, ensuring that every single aspect of the house met or exceeded her expectations, all without costing them any extra money.

Robert had been an engineering student at the same university where she was studying art. As a student Robert was well known and considered moderately handsome, yet it had been a shock to everyone, including Robert, when the glamorous Chantelle began to make her interest in him obvious. She was a member of the glamour set. She was classically beautiful with the tall, willowy body of a model. She moved with an easy, self-assured grace and heads turned as she floated across the grounds of the university. She could have the choice of anyone and she chose Robert, though not for the reasons anyone suspected. Robert's family wasn't wealthy but she had an unerring nose for money and her nose told her that he would soon be rolling in it. He had the brains; all she had to do was point him in the right direction.

Her own family had been wealthy until her father gambled it all away. It had been such an embarrassment for her. She never forgave him for forcing her to live in an ordinary house in an ordinary suburb. While many of her old friends snubbed her, there was enough of her former circle left to exploit, if only she could come up with the right plan. She hadn't known exactly how Robert would fit in but she sensed he was the one. So she fluttered her long eyelashes at him and he, filled with lust and love, married her.

A DOMESTIC SLAVE

Robert always had a love of boats and the sea. Although his engineering studies hadn't been directed towards his hobby, he was clever enough to utilise what he learnt. It soon became obvious he was a brilliant and intuitive boat designer. His concepts were as innovative as they were inspirational. Robert didn't care about money; he only wanted to build better boats. It was Chantelle who made sure his ideas made money. It was Chantelle who guided him into building leisure craft. He started with simple runabouts, quickly building a reputation for the latest in design and quality. It was Chantelle's ability to tap into her old social connections that allowed him to gradually move into designing and building luxury cruisers only the very rich could afford. For Robert, it gave him the ability to expand his imagination. His new clients could afford anything he could dream up and Chantelle made sure his clients paid handsomely for their highly individualised craft. In seemingly no time at all she was welcomed back into her former circle and her former way of life. She revelled in her return, shunning her parents and what she considered their squalid existence in the suburbs.

The business was going so well now she had time to return to her former love: art. The lowest level of the house had been built as her studio. Here she could paint or simply gaze out at the panoramic view of the harbour. Chantelle still kept a close eye on the books, only now with time to do what she wanted, she treated herself.

It was a perfect arrangement. Robert didn't understand anything about art and she didn't encourage him to become interested. That allowed her time and freedom to express herself fully. Some days she painted, others she spent with one of her many lovers. She had never intended her marriage to be monogamous. Over the years she had taken scores of lovers, discarding them whenever she tired of them. In the early days she had been very careful. The last thing she wanted was to upset her gravy train. Now she had the freedom and the time to do as she pleased. So she did.

'The chicken is better tonight. It only takes a touch more paprika to bring out the flavour.' Robert looked over at his wife eager to accept her praise, only to see her disapproving stare as she pushed her potato around her plate. 'Mind you, I don't know how you could have made such a mess of a simple recipe again?'

'I am sorry, Dear,' he said, not seeing anything wrong with the potatoes. His tasted fine.

With an impatient sigh she held out her half-empty glass and he hurried to fill it for her. Chantelle took a minuscule sip before returning the glass to the table. 'How is the boat for Jack Hodges going? I hope you were able to incorporate the expanded lounge without too much fuss.'

Robert's mind flicked over the many problems the late change had created, before replying, 'All taken care of.'

'I hope you recorded any extra time taken. They will have to pay for that of course,' she said, as she mentally calculated how much she could charge regardless of what figures her husband produced. In her mind, the main problem with Robert was he was basically honest. Despite his brilliance he would never have made any money without her. She had no scruples when it came to charging money. She actually encouraged her clients to continually alter their plans as they went along, knowing full well she would charge extra for any alterations to the original design. To Chantelle these changes were the cream. To Robert they were his worst nightmares. Some of the absurd demands his clients made left him pulling his hair out trying to figure out a way to incorporate them without detracting from the functionality and performance of his beautiful craft.

'Oh, did I mention your brother and that dishcloth wife of his are coming for dinner Saturday?'

'Why do you call her that?' he said, trying not to sound too reproachful.

'Well honestly, I've seen more animation in a stuffed doll than that woman has.'

'You are too hard on her. Mary is alright.'

'That's right, take her side. I'm beginning to wonder about you two,' she retorted cattily.

Robert returned to silence, finding it safer.

'I must put some thought to the menu. Geoffrey has such excellent taste.'

Robert understood what his wife meant by *excellent taste*. She reserved that particular praise for people who liked her paintings. Robert wasn't enthusiastic about them himself, which he thought partly explained the scorn his wife appeared to hold for him lately. For something to say, he asked, 'When were you talking to Geoffrey?'

'Oh, I don't know. I suppose he must have rung or something!' She glared at him. 'Does it matter?'

Not wanting to upset his wife over nothing, he quickly replied, 'No, of course it doesn't. I was only making conversation.'

'I'm thinking pork. There are some wonderful new recipes for pork these days.'

Robert wondered if it was the wonderful new recipes or the fact his sister-in-law wasn't fond of pork that inspired Chantelle. 'Maybe I could make a couple of different dishes,' he suggested, hoping to ease Mary's suffering at his wife's hands.

'I'll think about it and tell you what I decide.'

***

Monday morning Mary rose early and prepared Geoffrey's breakfast. Except for her sore stomach she'd managed to put her misbehavior behind her. Geoffrey had forgiven her for leaving him alone and that was what mattered.

On Monday mornings Mary usually went shoppin.to top up on things they'd used over the weekend. Without her little car shopping had become more difficult. Strangely though, Geoffrey didn't mind her spending money to take a taxi to the shops. As he didn't ask to see the receipt she started walking and pocketing the money. It began as a bit of a game. She didn't need money for anything in particular but as she no longer worked it felt odd not having any money to call her own.

She gave the house a quick once over before gathering her purse. This morning she considered going by taxi but it felt right to make herself walk. It would be her penance for upsetting Geoffrey. Gritting her teeth she headed off.

It wasn't too far and her stomach wasn't hurting any worse by the time she arrived. Collecting a trolley she headed inside. Luckily she didn't need much today. Taking out her list she began to wonder up and down the aisles. At the biscuits she hesitated. Biscuits could be such a dilemma. Geoffrey only liked the expensive types but they could quickly make a hole in her budget. He only gave her so much money each week and she was expected to manage without going over.

Sometimes she could get away with buying home-brand items, if she hid the packaging. Deciding Geoffrey deserved a treat she picked out a packed of his favorite Tim Tams while tossing in a packet of home-brand plain biscuits for herself.

Moving to the meat section she looked longingly at the T-bone steaks. Geoffrey loved T-bone and she needed him to be in a good mood, if not tonight, then shortly. The electricity bill had come in and there was no way she could cover it out of the housekeeping money. Selecting an extra big T-bone for Geoffrey she picked out a cheap piece of meat for herself. She continued on, balancing her desire to please Geoffrey against the need to keep expenses low. By the time she finished she felt pleased. She'd bought what she needed to make her husband happy while substituting enough cheaper items to balance her books. The fifteen dollars she was allowed for the taxi fare, each way, she would add to her secret stash. Not bad for a morning's work!

She was forced to stop three times on the way home. She was starting to wonder at the wisdom of saving fifteen dollars against catching a taxi with her shopping. But the house was only around two more corners; surely she could make in back now!

Flopping onto a stool she massaged her aching arms. The bag handles had begun to cut into her fingers and they tingled as the blood flowed back into them. But when she pulled down the old fashioned recipe jar and slipped thirty dollars under her collection of recipes she cut from magazines, she knew it had been worth it.

Mary put the jar back on the high shelf without counting the money it contained. She'd never counted it. Somehow it felt like it would be bad luck. She put the money inside the jar and then did her best to forget about it.

After a refreshing cup of tea she unpacked the shopping, making sure to discard the home-brand packaging where Geoffrey would never find it. She passed the rest of the day away cleaning already clean rooms and doing some more laundry.

Every night, except Friday nights, Geoffrey arrived home promptly as seven o'clock. She liked Geoffrey's punctuality; it gave her a reliable timeframe to plan around. Placing the electricity bill where she could lay her hand on it if needed, yet where Geoffrey wouldn't easily stumble across it, she laid out one of her best dresses. She liked to look nice for him when he came home. Brushing her hair she touched-up her makeup. The T-bone wouldn't take long to cook so she left it for last. The vegetables went on first and then her piece of meat. While they cooked she checked the refrigerator to make sure there was a frosted glass sitting next to a cold bottle of beer in case Geoffrey wanted a drink.

She even cleaned his whiskey drinking glass and put it back behind the bar. For a fleeting moment she considered smashing the cursed thing but realised that would be childish. It wasn't the glass's fault she'd stayed out too late. That had been her own doing!

With the T-bone half-cooked she made a dash into the bedroom and slipped on the fresh dress. By the time she heard the motorised door to the garage going up, she was ready.

At exactly seven o'clock Geoffrey entered through the access door from the garage. In his immaculate Italian suit, his leather shoes polished to a mirror shine and his hair combed with minute precision he looked so incredibly handsome. Her heart fluttered each time she looked at him. It didn't seem right that he could have picked her when he could have had any number of women. Mary didn't know a single woman at the bank who didn't have her eye on him. When he saw her and smiled any lingering concerns over Saturday night were instantly forgotten. With the art of a magician he produced a huge bunch of flowers. 'For the most beautiful woman I know!'

Mary blushed and giggled like a schoolgirl. 'Are they really for me?'

He flashed another charming smile. 'Come over here and give me a kiss.'

She dashed to him. Geoffrey didn't bother to bend down so she was forced to stretch up on tippy toes so he could kiss her. Taking the flowers, she told him, 'I'll find a vase for these.'

He gave her backside a playful slap as she turned around. 'Don't take too long.'

She giggled again. 'I won't, I promise.' She filled her biggest crystal vase with water before gently placing the flowers inside it. Carrying it to the dining room she positioned it proudly in the center of the table. Geoffrey was opening a bottle of wine. When he turned around he stared at the vase. He didn't say anything but by the way he sighed she knew she'd done something wrong. 'What is it, Dear?'

He frowned as he said, 'You don't just throw the flowers in; they should be arranged.' Putting the open bottle down he began to fiddle with the flowers. 'There,' he said, stepping back.

Mary couldn't see any difference but she dutifully told him, 'That is better.'

'All it takes is a bit of thought!'

Sensing her evening was quickly taking a change for the worse, she offered, 'I'll get us some glasses.' When Geoffrey didn't reply, she dashed from the room.

Returning with two of his best wine glasses, she handed them to him. When he smiled as he handed her one of the filled glasses, she sighed with relief. She wasn't sure what she'd done wrong but she was glad Geoffrey wasn't holding it against her. 'You sit down and I'll get your dinner.'

She fussed over him while he sat and sipped his wine. Fortunately he was so engrossed in his steak he didn't notice she had something different.

'Thank you again for the flowers; they truly are beautiful!'

Geoffrey merely nodded in acknowledgment.

After a period of silence, she asked, 'How was your day?' Geoffrey loved to talk about himself.

'Something odd did happen today. The bank started someone new in our Department.'

'What is he like?'

Geoffrey frowned to show his displeasure. 'I'd happily tell you if you stopped interrupting.'

Feeling suitably chastised, she muttered, 'I'm sorry, Dear, please continue.'

Geoffrey paused for a moment or two to emphasis his point before continuing. 'Apparently he's been working down in the Melbourne branch for the last four years. I'm not even sure why they transferred him to Sydney. Old Roberts seemed as mystified as anyone.'

She waited to make sure he'd finished, before asking, 'What is his name?'

'Frank Dobson.'

'Is he married?'

'God, I don't know. We men don't gossip the way you women do!'

Feeling flustered, she blurted out, 'I just wondered, that's all.'

'Well, I don't know if he's married and, to tell the truth, I couldn't care less.' He paused before adding in a more thoughtful tone, 'He is older though. I'd guess he is about forty-five, which makes him as old as Roberts.'

'That's interesting.'

'Why is that interesting?'

She hadn't meant anything by the comment but under Geoffrey's intense stare she racked her brain for something clever to say. 'It's just that the rest of you are all so young. You yourself have always said trading in futures is a young man's game. Why would they send over someone older?' Geoffrey didn't immediately reply. To Mary it seemed he was actually giving thought to her comment. 'You might have a point. It does seem odd now you have mentioned it.' Mary preened. It was rare for him to make such a concession.

With a shake of his head, Geoffrey dismissed the new man.

She feigned attention as he gave her a recital of his day. The matter of the electricity bill came back to haunt her. She was so distracted she nearly missed it when Geoffrey slipped in an important comment. 'I had a small windfall today.' Fortunately she heard enough to catch his meaning. Her head snapped up excitedly as she eagerly asked, 'Tell me all about it.'

Reaching inside his jacket he pulled out a thick wad of rolled up notes and tossed them on the table. 'Just a few shares I sold for a modest profit.'

Mary's eyes opened wide in genuine surprise. She had no way of knowing how much money was in the roll of notes but she could tell by Geoffrey's manner it was a lot. 'I know this isn't the best time to raise the subject but the electricity bill came in today and I've run out of money.' The moment the words were out of her mouth she cursed herself for her stupidity. Why couldn't she have waited while she allowed him to tell her how clever he'd been? To her amazement, Geoffrey laughed. A nice laugh too, not his nasty laugh. Reaching for the wad he tossed it across the table to her. 'Help yourself.'

Mary slipped off the rubber band before counting out five of the hundred dollar notes. The bill was for four-hundred and thirty dollars but seeing as he'd so generously allowed her to count out the money herself, she took the liberty to adding to her secret stash. Wrapping the rubber band back around the still thick wad she carried it back to him. Wrapping her arms around his neck, she kissed him. 'Thank you so much, Darling. You don't know what a worry that bill was to me.'

Geoffrey shrugged off her concerns. Taking the rubber band off he counted out four more hundreds. Tossing them onto the table, he said, 'Use that to buy yourself a new dress. You'll need one shortly.'

'I know,' she said, her excitement growing. 'Nancy's wedding is only two weeks away.'

'You'll need one before then. We're invited to my brother's this Saturday and I want you looking nice.'

'Oh,' she said, as her heart sank.

'Don't pout. Anybody would think you didn't want to go to Robert's.'

'Oh no, it's not that,' she assured him. She quite liked his brother. Robert was such a lovely man. It was his wife she dreaded. Chantelle had taken an instant dislike to her and never missed an opportunity to put her down. As the wine bottle was empty, she offered, 'Let me get you another.'

Geoffrey tightened his hold on her. 'Not so fast.' Fear gripped her but when she looked down he was smiling. He pulled her down onto his lap. 'Do I deserve another kiss?'

He was so incredibly handsome. She felt herself melt. She kissed him. Her breath caught in her throat as he unbuttoned her dress. When she stood it dropped to the floor leaving her dressed only in her lacy underwear. Geoffrey eyed her over before standing too. Without speaking he headed towards the bedroom. Mary gathered her dress and trotted after him.

She hadn't been a virgin when they married but it soon became obvious he had much more experience than her. As a new bride she was willing to learn from him. She was in awe of him. At the bank he was a rising star while she was a base level clerk. He was tall, handsome and very sexy. She was, in her own estimation, pretty without being special. She had no idea what had attracted him to her. When he suddenly appeared and swept her off her feet, she'd been as surprised as anyone. Just glad to be his, she readily agreed to perform the special things he taught her. Her one desire was to please him. Her own need for pleasure was irrelevant.

Tonight she had extra reason to please him. He'd forgiven her for Saturday night and he'd given her money for the electricity bill. Using her mouth she did that thing he liked so much. At times she gagged but she forced herself to continue. She wanted to continue. She wanted to show him how much she loved him.

When she was finished, Geoffrey dressed and went to his games room. Mary went to the kitchen and put on the coffee machine. Checking Geoffrey was settled, she took down her recipe jar. While she never counted the money inside it, there were times when she exchanged some smaller denomination notes for larger ones, to make more space. Playing with the money like this made her happy. Even without counting it she could see there was a reasonable collection of hundreds in there now. Replacing the jar on its shelf, she told herself there wasn't a reason she collected the money and kept it hidden.

A B Given

CHAPTER 3

When she woke the following morning it was as if the weekend had never happened. Life was good again. Geoffrey loved her; she knew it. She had money for the electricity bill and more for a new dress. The only downside was she would have to wear it to Robert's before she wore it to Nancy's wedding but at least she would now have a new dress for the wedding.

She rose early, as she normally did. After showering she dressed and prepared Geoffrey's breakfast. She only woke him when it was nearly ready, leaving him time to shower before she served him. Geoffrey only dressed for work once he'd eaten. He didn't want to risk spilling anything on his suit.

He didn't like to eat a big breakfast. He was conscious of his weight so she made him two pieces of toast and a boiled egg. Coffee was mandatory. Very occasionally he might ask for tea so she kept a small stock of Russian Caravan just in case.

The flowers were now on the bench, where she could see them as she worked. They were very beautiful and must have been very expensive. Surely they proved how much he loved her!

Geoffrey read the morning paper as he ate.

'How was everything?' she asked, as he folded the newspaper.

He wiped his mouth on a napkin. 'The egg was a touch too hard but otherwise acceptable.'

She made a mental note to reduce her cooking time down by a couple of seconds. He disappeared into the bedroom only to return fifteen minutes later looking immaculate. 'Thanks again for the flowers,' she called after him.

'I'm glad you like them,' he said, without turning back.

She cleaned away the breakfast things and wiped the kitchen over so it sparkled. She would have to go shopping for her dress but she could put that off for a day or two. Her little garden had been neglected all weekend and yesterday so she changed into old clothes and slipped on her rubber boots. Mary loved gardening but Geoffrey forbade her to work in the front yard. He hated gardening himself and never went near it but he didn't want the neighbours to think he needed his wife to do menial labour. He hired a gardener for the front. The back he had paved. She had begged for a little patch and he grudgingly agreed she could use the land behind the garage, where no-one could see it.

Mary wasn't interested in growing flowers: not that she wouldn't have if she had more room. She grew vegetables. Some time ago she'd stumbled on a radio program. It played every Saturday morning. Geoffrey was usually hungover Saturday morning so she was quite often able to listen to it. Two lovely men talked about nothing but gardening. People could ring and ask questions but Mary never did. But she'd discovered if she listened often enough someone would eventually ask the question she was curious about herself.

She began by marking out a small square of land in the sunniest position she could find. Grudgingly taking some money out of her recipe jar she bought a garden fork. She turned the soil over and planted carrots and dwarf beans. She wasn't really expecting a result. It was more a way of filling in some time. But the most amazing thing happened. Her little vegetable patch grew. Some of the carrots were a funny shape but once she'd cut them up Geoffrey never noticed. And the beans were the same as she bought at the supermarket.

The next season she expended her patch and added new varieties. Now the whole of the area behind the garage had been taken over. Some of it was too shaded for a good result so she grew things like lettuces there. She loved her little garden and was very proud of it. She once asked Geoffrey if he wanted to come and see it. He only laughed. 'Why in God's name would I want to do that?'

'I thought you might want to see what I'm growing.'

'I don't think I'd be very interested in a bunch of half-dead plants.'

She felt hurt now. 'They're not half-dead. They're beautiful!'

'When you win a prize at the Royal Show, you let me know.' He laughed at his wit and turned on the TV.

If he didn't want to see her garden so much the better, she told herself. Now she could do whatever she wanted out there without worrying if Geoffrey would approve. And she did.

The only restriction she placed on herself was how close she brought her garden to the edge of the garage. So long as it couldn't be seen from the back door, which was about as far as Geoffrey ever ventured, then she felt safe. When she heard on the radio about these bamboo screens she went out and bought one. If Geoffrey even noticed he never mentioned it. Now she could garden right up to the edge of the garage wall. Her garden had grown considerably from her first tiny square. It was now an irregular L shape that filled the entire strip between the garage and the side fence, which, while being narrow, was quite long. The area behind the garage was a lot wider but not as long.

Today she weeded. Her crop was already in place so there wasn't anything much to do but wait for her plants to grow. It was so peaceful out here. She spotted a tiny weed and plucked it. Mostly she just wandered through her plants, admiring them. Using a little trowel she scratched around the edges of her beds. This didn't actually achieve anything but it gave her an excuse to linger. The sun was shining and the sky was a perfect shade of blue. It was far too nice to be inside.

The hose was long enough to reach right around her garden but Mary preferred to use a watering can. Initially her garden was funded out of her recipe jar but since then she was able to cut down on buying vegetables. She made a mental note of what she thought her contribution to the pantry would cost if she bought them from the supermarket and put that money back in her jar. She figured she was in front now.

It was with a sigh she put her tools way and headed back inside. She planned a roast for tonight and it would take time to cook so she needed to get started on it. Mary liked cooking roasts. She got to use so many of her vegetables without Geoffrey even suspecting.

***

It was Friday and the events of the previous weekend were a distant memory. Besides, Fridays presented their own challenges for Mary. Geoffrey frequently went drinking after work with his colleagues leaving her with no idea what time he would be home or in what state. If he didn't go drinking he expected to find his dinner waiting for him. If he went drinking he had often eaten by the time he arrived home and didn't want what she'd cooked. If she cooked something simple he'd be angry if he came home early. If she cooked something grander, it would be wasted if he didn't come home. These days she tended to cook something that would keep and she ate it the following night.

In the end she cooked a Chicken Kiev with roast vegetables. She opened a packet of sausages earlier in the week and she cooked the last of them for herself. She tried watching TV but gave up. She opened a book but couldn't get interested in it. She thought about doing some housework but the house already sparkled and there wasn't any laundry left to do. With a sigh she found the knitting she'd tried to learn but had given up on. That lasted for about half an hour. Desperate for something to do she turned the TV back on. She nearly cheered when she found a David Attenborough special.

In the end she decided to go to bed. If Geoffrey was hungry when he got home she could get back up and re-heat his dinner for him. She changed into a nice nightie she was climbing into bed when the doorbell rang. The doorbell never rang. Worried something bad might have happened to Geoffrey she tossed on a robe and sprinted to the door. Flinging it open she was confronted by a stranger who leered at her.

'Hello, Mrs. Parker.'

Mary was about to ask how the man knew her name when she spotted Geoffrey lying on the middle of the front lawn. 'What's happened to my husband?'

The man's smile grew. 'He's alright, just can't hold his liquor.'

To Mary it was obvious the man had been drinking too but he wasn't as drunk as Geoffrey. 'Can you help me bring him in?'

'I've carried him this far, I suppose I could carry him a little further.'

She didn't like stepping outside in only her dressing gown. It was a light satin one and didn't offer as much protection as she would have liked. The good news was Geoffrey wasn't as bad as he'd seemed. He laughed jovially as she took one of his arms and pulled him up into a sitting position. 'Hello, my Darling,' he said in a slurred voice.

'Did you have a good night?' she asked, tugging on his arm.

'Yes.' With his free arm, he waved airily in the stranger's direction. 'You know that new man I told you about? Well, Frank and I have had a wonderful night, haven't we Frank?'

Frank laughed as he grappled to take hold of Geoffrey's waving arm. 'That we did but it's time to go inside now.'

Ducking under her husband's arm she wrapped her own arm around his waist. With Frank's help she managed to get Geoffrey onto his feet. She wanted to manage the rest on her own but Frank wrapped his arm around Geoffrey too. When his hand brushed against her breast she told herself it was only an accident. When it happened a second time, only more forcefully, she knew it wasn't accidental. But what could she do? She had to get Geoffrey inside and the front yard wasn't the place for a confrontation. If Geoffrey ever heard about it he would be so angry.

Fortunately once they reached the doorway there wasn't enough room for them all to go inside together and Frank was forced to release his hold. Mary thought the best place for Geoffrey would be the bedroom but she didn't want to go there with Frank still here so she half-carried, half-steered him down to his games room and pushed him into his big leather chair. Straightening, she looked at Frank. She did her best to smile, as she told him, 'I think I'll be alright from here, but thank you for bringing him home.'

Frank's smile never faltered as he strolled casually to the sofa and sat down. 'Hey, Geoffrey old boy, what happened to that beer you promised me?'

Geoffrey's head was lolling to one side, but he managed to say, 'Yeah, that's right. Mary, get us a beer.'

Geoffrey wasn't in any state to be drinking but she knew better than to argue with him. Hopefully he'd take a sip or two and pass out. Then she could get rid of Frank. The way he stared at her the whole time was making her very nervous. 'Are you sure you want one?' she asked Frank. 'It is getting pretty late.'

He settled himself back more comfortably on the sofa. 'I never knock back being served a beer by a pretty woman.'

Mary was very conscious of her light robe over her tiny nightie. She'd dressed for her husband, not some leering stranger. She desperately wanted to tell Frank to leave but what would Geoffrey say. These two worked together and it appeared they were now friends. He would be livid if he thought she'd been rude to him. She'd made trips to the hospital for much less.

Mary went to the bar and took out a cold bottle of beer. Pouring two glasses she gave one to Geoffrey who accepted it but didn't drink. Instead he balanced it precariously on his thigh. Reluctantly moving closer to Frank, she stopped at a safe distance and held out the frothy glass to him. Frank stretched out his arms and laid them on the top of the sofa. 'Why don't you hold it for me?'

Mary was puzzled now. Uncertain what to do she stood holding Frank's glass.

'Do you always do as you're told?'

His eyes were roaming slowly over her, making her skin crawl. 'I'm not sure what you mean?'

'If I told you to come closer and hold the glass to my lips so I could drink, would you?'

Mary shook her head.

'Do it!' he snapped at her. He was no longer smiling and she was frightened now. 'Come on, just one little sip.'

'And then you'll go?'

His smile returned as he shook his head. 'Oh no, you're not getting rid of me that easy.'

She had no idea what he was up to but she didn't like it. She had to get him out of her house. 'Can't you just go? Geoffrey isn't going to be any company like this.'

'It's not your husband's company I desire.'

Desire! The strangeness of the word frightened her. Her mind raced, searching for an answer to her dilemma. 'I think I should wake Geoffrey and put him to bed.'

'If you wake him, before I give you permission, I'll tell him you offered yourself to me.'

'But...but that's a lie! I never did any such thing!'

Frank shrugged. 'Shall we wake him and see who he believes?'

'No!' The word was out before she had the chance to stop it. Frank's smile turned to a smirk. 'I mean...he wouldn't like to be woken like this. It would embarrass him to think he'd fallen asleep with a guest in the house.'

'Come closer and hold the glass to my lips so I can have a drink.'

She wanted to throw the beer over him. She wanted to run. She wanted to do many things but what she did was step closer and hold the frosted glass to Frank's lips so he could drink. He took a satisfied swallow and she pulled the glass back.

'There, that wasn't so hard, was it now?'

She didn't reply. She only stood with her head bowed, her face burning with shame.

Frank nodded to the small table at the side of the sofa. 'You can put the glass on there.'

She obeyed, hoping this was the end of her torture.

'My feet are feeling tired; take off my shoes.'

She glanced at Geoffrey. He was snoring softly. With her mind in turmoil it was difficult to think. Would it be worth the risk of waking him? He would certainly be angry if he knew what Frank had been saying to her. Frank had a dangerous look to him but Geoffrey was at least six inches taller. Even drunk as he was, he wouldn't be frightened of someone as short as Frank.

But what of Frank's threat? She'd learnt how unreasonable Geoffrey could be at times. She had the scars to prove it. What if he believed Frank? Surely he wouldn't. He knew how much she loved him. It was unthinkable...but what if? He would be so angry! He'd put her in the hospital for much less.

Mary slowly lowered herself to her knees. Taking hold of Frank's right ankle, she slipped his shoe off.

'And the sock.'

She'd come this far, a sock was nothing. She peeled it off and draped it over the shoe. Then she did the same with his left shoe and sock.

'Now, kiss my feet.'

She'd known he was going to say it even before she knelt at his feet but hearing him say the words still sent a shiver of disgust down her spine. What must he think of her? They'd barely met yet here was he demanding she kiss his feet. With her husband sitting no more than three feet away. Poor Geoffrey! He'd taken this man in as a friend. He would be so hurt to know how Frank had betrayed his trust. Tears sparkled in her eyes as she looked up at Frank. 'Please don't make me do this!'

He looked back at her with a pleased expression. 'Are you going to cry?'

She sniffed wetly. 'No.'

'That's a shame, I do love tears.'

'What kind of man are you?'

With a speed that surprised her, he whipped out his hand and took hold of her by her hair. He shook her as he told her, 'Enough questions, bitch. Kiss my feet!' Using his hold on her hair he tossed her to the floor. Her scalp hurt where he'd pulled on her hair and her tears spilled over and ran down her face as she pressed her lips to the top of his right foot and kissed it.

'That's better. I like a bitch who learns quickly.'

She kissed his smelly foot all over before switching to his left. Unsure what else to do she alternated between his feet, smothering each in turn with kisses before moving back to the other.

'Stand up.'

Mary stood, her head bowed to hide her humiliation and her shame.

'Take off your robe.'

This time she didn't even bother to try and resist. Slipping the knot in her sash loose she shrugged the satin robe off her shoulders and allowed it to pool around her feet.

'Look at me.'

With a sigh of resignation she raised her head just enough to see his face.

'Are you wearing panties?'

The question shocked life back into her. 'Yes,' she said with more defiance than she thought possible. 'And they're staying on.'

'I don't like my bitches wearing panties. The next time I come, I don't want you to be wearing any. Is that clear?'

She was beyond caring. As long as he didn't expect her to take them off right now, what did it matter what she said. 'Yes.'

'I want another drink.'

Dressed now in only her pretty nightie she walked to the small table and picked up his glass of beer. She held it out to him but he didn't drink any.

'Sit on my lap and offer it to me.'

'I think this has gone far enough. You've had your fun, but now I think it's time to leave or I'm going to wake Geoffrey.' The words had tumbled out hurriedly but she felt very pleased with herself for saying them. She thought Frank might be angry but he didn't look angry. His eyes only shifted to the scar running through her eyebrow and she felt herself blush.

'Tell me; what did you do to deserve that?'

'That's none of your business!' Her tone had been even firmer this time and she felt some of her old self returning.

'I've met men like your husband before. I'd guess it didn't take much.' He tipped his head to one side as he studied her. 'How many other scars do you have?'

'He loves me!'

Frank laughed. 'I'm sure that's what he tells you and I'm sure you believe it. The world is full of stupid bitches like you who believe their husbands love them...even while he's beating your brains out.'

'He loves me!' she repeated, though not with the same force as before.

'Sure he does. That's why you're standing in front of me, wearing just your nighty, and he's still sound asleep. The real truth is you're shit scared of him!'

'No I'm not.'

He shrugged. Then making as though he was going to stand, he asked, 'Want me to wake him?'

'No!'

'Sure? It wouldn't be any trouble. I could wake him up and explain how you were trying to seduce me. I could tell how shocked I was and what I'd do if you were my wife. I bet you'd end up with more than just a few scars this time. Hell, he might even kill you! Wouldn't that be fun?'

She didn't speak. Tears trickled down her cheeks as she sat on Frank's lap and offered the glass to his lips. He took a single small swallow. 'You can put the glass down again now.' She did but she knew the rules of this game well. She didn't climb back off his lap. She hadn't been given permission yet.

Frank slipped his arm around her waist as he said casually, 'Show me your tits.'

Mary hated herself for not trying to resist. She silently unfastened the buttons that ran down the front of her nighty and pulled it wide open. Frank didn't speak as he looked her over. She'd known this was coming from the moment he asked her to sit on his lap so she wasn't surprised when he leant forward and pressed his mouth to hers. She'd done things for him and she might do more yet but she wasn't going to kiss him. She knew what people thought about Geoffrey but she knew he loved her and she wouldn't betray him like this. She'd made a vow and she'd meant it. She belonged to Geoffrey, not this hideous man.

When she refused to respond he gripped her nipple and twisted it. She held her ground. He twisted it harder. A cry of pain escaped from between her pursed lips. Geoffrey stirred. She held her breath and he settled once more.

'We wouldn't want him to wake up now, would we? Not with you in such a compromising position.'

This had to stop and it had to stop now. Looking straight into Frank's eyes, she told him, 'He'd kill you if he saw us like this!'

'I believe he would try, but only after he killed you. Are you ready to die?'

'Are you?'

'You don't have to worry about me; I can take care of myself.'

She believed him. Geoffrey might occasionally take his frustrations out on her but she didn't think of him as a fighter. Frank might be a lot smaller but he was basically sober and he looked a dangerous type. When he pressed his mouth to hers this time she kissed him back. When his fingers reached for her nipple he was gentler. Not kind but gentler. When he forced his tongue into her mouth she wrapped her lips around it and sucked, the way Geoffrey had taught her.

Suddenly he pushed her off his lap and she landed in a heap on the floor. On his feet he looked down at her. 'Do you remember what I told you?'

'Yes.'

'Repeat it!'

'The next time you come, I'm not to be wearing any panties.'

'See, even a stupid bitch like you can learn.' With that he strolled casually to the front door and left.

As soon as she heard the door close she ran to it and locked it.

A B Given

CHAPTER 4

She straightened her nightie and wrapped her robe back around herself. Shivering as though she was cold she rescued Geoffrey's untouched glass before it spilt. He cursed her as she gently shook him awake. She apologised as she took a firm hold of his arm and pulled him to his feet. He lurched unsteadily to the bedroom and waited while she undressed him. Naked he lay on the bed while she covered him with the quilt. With Geoffrey settled for the night she began to cry. She cried for Geoffrey as much as for herself.

That terrible man left her feeling soiled. She'd felt his eyes on her bare breasts as a physical touch. Her nipple still tingled from where he'd toyed with it and used it against her. The taste of his mouth was still in her's. She felt like vomiting. With her stomach rolling she dashed to the second bathroom. Ripping off her clothes she jumped into the shower. Before anything else she loaded a toothbrush with lots of paste and scrubbed her mouth clean. Only when she could no longer taste beer fumes and sweat did she take up the soap and scrub her body. She scrubbed every inch of it. When the memory of kissing his smelly feet returned she gagged. Loading the toothbrush a second time and cleaned her mouth again.

She knew she'd never be able to wear the nightie again without thinking about what Frank had done to her. It was a favourite of Geoffrey's but she tossed it in the bin along with her panties and the robe. In the spare bedroom she found fresh clothes and dressed. It was late now but she didn't feel like sleeping. She boiled the kettle and made a cup of tea.

'Poor Geoffrey!' Tears threatened to spill over and she fought them back.

Some of what Frank said was true but that didn't make what he'd done right. And it didn't change the fact that Geoffrey loved her. She knew he loved her. Not because he told her so or because he was always so sorry after he'd hurt her. She knew because he'd been faithful to her. There had never been even the slightest hint he'd looked at another woman. The bank was one huge gossip hall. If there had been any to hear, she'd have heard it. She knew he'd been with other women before they met, but so what? She'd dated other men too. She'd even slept with a couple of them. She wasn't a virgin when they married. Who was these days? Since their wedding she hadn't looked at another man and Geoffrey hadn't looked at another woman. The fidelity of their marriage was the rock she clung to when times were tough.

Only now she'd done things with Frank.

She hadn't wanted to and she hadn't enjoyed doing them, but she had done them. She'd exposed herself to him and kissed him. She'd kissed him the way she kissed Geoffrey. As she sipped her tea she relived every moment of that terrible evening in her head. It had been degrading and humiliating then and it was degrading and humiliating now but she gave a sigh of relief. She could say with positiveness she hadn't had even the slightest flicker of enjoyment. Not once. She knew there were people like that, people who got pleasure from being treated that way, but she hadn't. It was such a relief. She'd have gone insane if it had been different. How could she possibly live with herself knowing she enjoyed been treated like a piece of meat, a plaything only to used only for someone else's pleasure.

It was true that she did things for Geoffrey, things she'd prefer not to do, but she did these things willingly. She did them out of love, not fear. She wanted to please Geoffrey and that was what made the difference. Frank had taken her love for Geoffrey and used it against her. He'd twisted her love into something loathsome and for that alone she would never be able to forgive him.

It was very late when she finally went to bed. She undressed in the dark. Stripping naked she climbed into bed. Geoffrey always slept in the nude but she usually wore a nightie. Tonight she wanted to feel him. He was lying on his side with his back to her so she slithered closer and spooned herself around him. His skin felt soft and warm against her own. She pressed her beasts to his back and placed gentle kisses on his shoulders. Guilt at what she'd done wracked her. In response an outpouring of love, so deep it made her body tremble, gripped her. She reached for him. He stirred slightly as she stroked her fingertips over his flaccid penis. His breathing became a little heavier but he didn't respond in the way she wanted. When his penis remained soft she took it as a rebuke. She tried to tell herself there was no way Geoffrey could know of her guilt but it didn't stop her thoughts. His flaccid penis felt like an accusation. Her love for him was fiercer now than ever, but would he still love her? How could she tell him the things she'd done and still expect him too. But how could she keep it a secret? She could already feel it eating away at her core. Their mutual fidelity was what had kept her sane. It was the pillar of their marriage. It was what enabled her to get through the bad times. When the doctors and the nurses at the Hospital pestered her to make a police report it was the knowledge of Geoffrey's deep sense of commitment to their marriage that allowed her to look them in the eye and say: no! And now she'd gone and spoiled everything!

She could look the doctors and nurses in the eye but how could she ever look Geoffrey in the eye again?

What if he could tell just by looking at her? What if Frank said something? Could she trust him to keep his silence? Fear gripped her. Frank didn't even need to tell Geoffrey. She knew how gossip travelled through the bank. If he so much as hinted to anyone he'd been intimate with her, the whole bank would know within a week. Nancy would hear it too and all her other friends. The shame of it would kill her, even if Geoffrey didn't do it first.

Oh, how did she ever get herself into a situation like this!

She woke feeling terrible. Her eyes felt like someone had rubbed sand in them and her head was as thick as when she had the flu. Knowing she had to act as if nothing had happened she dragged herself out of bed. She didn't want to give Geoffrey any cause to be suspicious. She showered and made him breakfast.

Geoffrey sat reading the morning paper as he ate. 'Is everything alright?'

Mary nearly jumped out of her chair at the sudden question. 'Why do you ask?' To her ears, her shrieked reply cried of guilt but Geoffrey only said, 'You don't seem yourself this morning?'

'I'm fine,' she said, as brightly as she could.

He put down the paper and studied her more closely. 'You don't look fine. You look positively haggard!' When a tear spilt onto her cheek he rushed to her. Wrapping a comforting arm around her shoulders, he said, 'I'm sorry, I didn't mean it the way it sounded. I only meant that you seem...not yourself.'

'It's just that time of the month,' she said, knowing how all men hate to discuss that subject.

'Right!' He gave her back a rub before returning to his chair. 'Why don't you have a little lie down?'

'I might later,' she said, trying to force herself to cheer up.

'I have some work to do this morning.' He looked at her intently. 'Will you be alright on your own?' He paused for a moment, before saying, 'I could do it later...'

His concern for her wasn't helping as it should. Normally she longed for moments like this one but today it only served to heighten her feelings of guilt. She forced a smile she didn't feel. 'No, I'm fine, really. You go and do what you need to do.'

'It will only take me an hour or so.'

'I'll be fine. '

He left her and Mary cleaned the breakfast dishes and cleaned the kitchen until it sparkled. She hung his suit and washed his clothes from yesterday. Geoffrey hadn't reappeared so she went out to her garden. It was here she finally found some peace. It was here she managed to rationalise what had happened. She wasn't the guilty one. That was Frank! He was the one who should be ashamed, not her! It didn't wipe away her fear of someone finding out what had happened but it did allow her to live with herself. Now she could face her husband, if not with a clear conscience, at least without a deep sense of dread.

When Geoffrey reappeared he seemed distracted. She made them coffee and while he munched on a Tim Tam, he asked her, 'What did you think of Frank?'

Doing her best to still her racing heart, she said, 'He's OK.'

'I'm sorry I fell asleep and left you with him.'

Mary was shocked. He rarely apologised for anything. Her heart flooded with love for him. 'He didn't stay long.'

'What did you two talk about?'

The question was asked casually but she studied him closely, searching for a hint of accusation. Not finding any, she shrugged. 'Just the bank. But he's new to Sydney so he didn't know any of the people I mentioned.'

Geoffrey nodded. 'I'm not sure he's my type.'

A glimmer of hope shone through the gloom of her day. Geoffrey was like that. With him either you were in or you were out. There was no middle ground. 'He did seem a little dull,' she said, hoping Geoffrey wouldn't take offence.

He merely nodded again.

They sat in silence for a time, before he said, 'I suppose we should be getting ready.'

Mary was puzzled for a moment until she remembered. It was Saturday. Today was the day they were going to Robert's. How was she ever going to cope with Chantelle after last night? For a brief moment she thought about claiming some mystery illness but Geoffrey would probably get angry. Besides, she thought she owned him a level of obedience as penance for last night. She wouldn't enjoy it but she'd go and try to smile for his sake.

The only blessing was that they were going to Robert's house. The only time Robert and Chantelle came to here ended disastrously and Mary had the scars, both physical and emotional, to prove it. Geoffrey had been in a flap for a fortnight before, checking this, demanding that, while actually not helping in any way. Mary scrubbed the house until it shone like it had never shone before. Geoffrey showered her with money so, with no restrictions on what she bought for the menu, she bought the best of everything.

Robert and Chantelle arrived an hour and a half late. Geoffrey was beside himself with worry. When their guests finally arrived Mary thought her worries were over. They were only just beginning. Geoffrey showed them around while she did her best to save the perfect meal she'd spent all day preparing. As they sat down to eat Chantelle turned to her and, in a low confidential voice everyone heard, said, 'If this house is too much for you, I could recommend the name of a good housecleaner.'

Looking around her with disgust written across her face, she added, 'I've heard she enjoys a good challenge!'

Mary was so taken aback she didn't know how to respond. She could see Geoffrey was seething so she let it go. What she didn't realise was he wasn't seething at Chantelle's rudeness.

Throughout the entire evening Chantelle did her best to undermine her at every turn. Not that she openly criticised her. Chantelle was far too subtle for that. It was the way she overemphasised her chewing action to suggest her beef medallions were tough as old boot leather. It was the way she screwed her face up as she tasted her coffee and the way she ran her finger across the top of the sideboard as she passed it before taking out her handkerchief and wiped her finger as though removing a year's worth of grime.

The moment their guests left Geoffrey turned on her. She couldn't believe how he took Chantelle's side in everything. There wasn't anything she could say or do to defend herself. Geoffrey simply refused to listen.

Things were just starting to quieten down when the phone rang. It was Chantelle warning Geoffrey she was suffering with possible food poisoning and to watch out for symptoms. He apologised profusely and even offered to drive over and take her to the hospital himself. Apparently, even though Chantelle thought she was in risk of dying, she wasn't so bad she needed to go to the hospital: yet.

When he shouted at Mary, telling her she'd made Chantelle sick, she couldn't make him see logic. They'd all eaten the same food and no-one else was ill.

'Are you accusing her of making it up?'

Mary wasn't given a chance to respond. She came to the following morning in a hospital bed. Geoffrey was at her side, explain to the nurse how Mary had fallen again. The explanation of a fall didn't explain her concussion, the broken ribs and the two black eyes but they were used to her *falls* now and didn't bother to ask any questions. No-one even offered to contact the police for her.

Mary was home when Robert called to apologise. He hadn't known about Chantelle's phone call until much later. He laughed as he told Mary it was no wonder his wife was feeling queasy with the amount of red wine she and Geoffrey had drunk. When he said he hoped it hadn't caused any trouble, she told him, 'Don't worry about it, everything was fine.'

When she hung up she'd cried. While Chantelle was at home nursing a hangover she'd been discharging herself from hospital early so Geoffrey didn't feel uncomfortable with the way the nurses looked at him.

She spent two days searching for this dress. Knowing she'd be judged by Chantelle she refused to settle for anything less than stunning. She knew she didn't have a model's figure but she was petite and the Fuchsia coloured dress hugged her in all the right places. The halter neck was cut deep and showed more of her small breasts than she normally liked but the matching belt tucked tight, accentuating her tiny waist.

She spent a long time on her make-up. She had never been one for lots of make-up and she knew Geoffrey didn't like women who were overdone. He called it a slutty look. As she studied herself in the long mirror she felt ready, even for Chantelle. Knowing she'd done the best job she could she brushed her hair once more and went in search of Geoffrey. 'How do I look?'

He glanced at her. 'You look fine...I guess.'

If he'd left it at his unenthusiastic, *You look fine*, she thought she could have coped. It was the added, *I guess*, that killed it for her. She felt her new found confidence leaking away. Finding an excuse she dashed back to the bedroom. She studied herself once more in the long mirror as she wondered what it was he saw that she didn't or vice versa.

She gloomily trudged behind him as he started the BMW. The drive was completed in silence. Geoffrey didn't like to be distracted when he was driving and she didn't feel like talking.

With the house perched precariously on the side of a hill there wasn't much room for parking, so a small platform had been constructed that extended out over the sheer drop. Mary hated driving out onto this. It felt as though the car should suddenly drop over the side at any moment. She knew Geoffrey shared some of her misgivings, even though he'd never admit it. He clung to the steering wheel so tightly his knuckles turned white. Today was no different. If anything it was made worse by the fact there was already another car parked on the platform, forcing him to park close to the edge on his side.

Mary didn't recognise the car, so she asked, 'Will there be others here tonight?'

'Not that I knew about.'

His tone had been churlish and her spirits rose fractionally. Geoffrey hated surprises. Maybe it would be Chantelle's turn to feel his wrath. He locked the door with a beep from the remote before leading her over the short footbridge to the ornate front door. The door was at the top level of the unique house.

A breathless Robert greeted them before Geoffrey had a chance to ring the bell. 'Spotted you on the security monitor,' he said, with one of his usual apologetic, boyish grins.

While the family resemblance was obvious so were the differences between the two brothers. Geoffrey was tall and handsome with a carefully cultured air of sophistication about him. Even dressed in his casual camel coloured slacks and knitted polo shirt he looked anything but casual. Robert, on the other hand, looked as though he had been doing the housework, which Mary thought was probably the case. She couldn't picture Chantelle risking one of her nails.

Looking at the two, she decided it was their hair as much as anything that defined their characters to a casual observer. Geoffrey's dark hair was cut short, with a side part of military precision. Robert had a thick mop that stood up in spikes at random angles. Geoffrey looked like a high level bank employee, which he was. Robert looked like a beach bum, which he probably would like to be.

'Do you know Nadia?' asked Robert cheerfully, as he led them down the circular stairway to the next level.

Geoffrey didn't reply, which both Robert and Mary took to meant he didn't.

Robert tripped off the stairs and into the large entertaining area in his usual fashion. Although Geoffrey had been right behind him, traveling as quickly as his brother, he slipped gracefully into the room making the type of entrance few people manage to achieve. Sliding passed his brother, he wrapped his arms around Chantelle giving her a hug as she kissed his cheek. Mary always thought it odd. Usually Geoffrey wasn't into acts of intimacy but he always gave his sister-in-law a hug and a kiss whenever they met.

Chantelle smiled brightly into his eyes as she said, 'Hello, stranger.' The pair locked eyes for a fraction of a second before Chantelle swept him over to the other couple. 'Nadia, Rupert, this is my favourite brother-in-law, Geoffrey.'

Nadia's bottle black hair was trimmed incredibly short. Her makeup was dramatic, dark purple lipstick heavily applied with matching eyeliner. She wore a pair of torn jeans and an oversized windcheater, yet still managed to look cultured and sexy. Rupert was a perfect caricature of what a sixties bohemian might have looked like. His pencil thin moustache, his green corduroy pants and shapeless jacket somehow suited his pale chubby face.

It was only after hellos had been exchanged that Robert slipped in, 'Don't forget Mary, Dear.'

Chantelle looked about her as though surprised to find Mary in the room with them. Mary was still standing at the end of the stairway looking embarrassed and a little lost. 'Oh of course, Geoffrey's wife, Mary,' said Chantelle, in an apologetic tone that seemed to say to her friends, *It isn't my fault, I didn't invite her!*

'Hello,' Mary said softly, already feeling incredibly uncomfortable. Her sense of displacement wasn't helped when Geoffrey said in an irritated tone, 'What are you doing over there?' as though it was her fault he and the others had completely ignored her. She now felt like a truant schoolgirl who'd been told off in front of the whole school assembly. Conscious of every eye on her, she stumbled to her husband's side.

'You look very nice tonight,' Robert said, to break the awkward silence.

'Thank you,' said Mary, feeling pleased he noticed.

Chantelle didn't look happy about the exchange. She looked Mary over. 'Yes, that dress looks...' Chantelle hesitated as though she was searching for the right words. 'Positively you,' she finished off with a sweet smile.

Nadia smiled in a supercilious way that infuriated Mary as much as Chantelle's comment. Any hope she might find an unexpected ally had already disappeared. With everyone staring at her she felt her face redden and she wished she could say something awful back. Chantelle was dressed as only someone twenty years younger than her deserved to dress. Her blonde hair, with its long loose tresses, was highlighted with streaks of reddish-orange, then piled on top of her head in an untidy bun with curly tendrils hanging to her shoulders. She had on a pair of aquamarine satin three-quarter pants that were cut low at her hips. The soft buttercup yellow crop top barely covered her large breasts, exposing more tanned skin than it covered. Her pierced navel sparkled with a large diamond suspended on a short gold chain. The term *mutton dressed up as lamb* would normally come to mind. Unfortunately for Mary, Chantelle looked fantastic. Chantelle had the gift of always looking seductively beautiful no matter how she was dressed and tonight she had gone to some effort to look sexy. Mary was restricted to giving Chantelle a cold stare.

The stare appeared to amused Chantelle, confirming her barb had hit home. Turning away she took Geoffrey's arm and led him closer to her other guests, leaving Mary isolated once more.

Robert came over and saved her by taking her arm and leading her to the sofa. 'I'll get you a drink.' With an apologetic wink, he added, 'I don't know about you but I think I could use one right about now.'

The tears that threatened to spill over miraculously retreated, saving her the embarrassment of shedding them within the first minutes of arriving. It would have been a new record. It usually took Chantelle longer than that. Geoffrey had been no help either and Mary wasn't happy with him. He always acted so strangely around Chantelle.

Chantelle was holding the floor as she usually did. 'Nadia is a sculptress; you wouldn't believe some of the things she does with old scrap.'

Mary rolled her eyes, now she really didn't like the other woman. It turned out Rupert, her partner, was a self-appointed art critic. He described himself as self-employed, which Mary took to mean he was unemployed. *Probably unemployable*, she thought to herself, accurately assessing the foppish little man.

Robert returned shortly with a tray loaded with glasses of champagne. Mary took a crystal glass from the offered tray before Robert moved over to the small knot of people several feet away.

'Are we celebrating something?' asked Geoffrey.

Chantelle unsuccessfully attempted to look modest, as Robert announced, 'Chantelle's new painting is finished and it has been selected by the Seymour Gallery for their next showing of local artists.'

There was a general round of compliments and Geoffrey bent low and gave her another kiss. 'Can we see it?' he asked eagerly.

'Of course,' she said, taking his arm. At the head of the stairs leading down to her studio, she said to her two friends, 'Follow us.'

The four headed off and Robert held out his arm. 'Come on, you too!' he called to Mary.

She would have preferred to stay where she was; however, Robert always tried so hard to make sure she was included, so she didn't want to reject his offer. By the time they reached the lowest level of the house the others were already gathered around a large painting hanging on the feature wall. Three spotlights shone down from the ceiling illuminating it.

'This is definitely your best work yet,' cried Nadia, sounding genuinely excited.

Geoffrey was admiring the painting, his arm wrapped around Chantelle's slender waist. 'You can feel the power just looking at it.'

Rupert had gone closer and, with his nose only inches from the canvas, was intently studying it. After a time he turned back and grandly threw his hands in the air and cried out loudly, 'You are a genius!'

Mary looked at the large rectangle of canvas covered in splotches of dark green and black paint and frowned

Robert gave her a look that said, *Don't ask me, I don't understand it either!*

'It is a pretty frame,' she whispered.

Robert chuckled, before announcing loudly, 'You'll have to excuse me, there are a few things that need doing upstairs.'

Only Mary seemed to notice and she offered, 'I'll help.'

'Oh no, guests don't do chores in this house. You stay with the others; dinner won't be long.'

Mary watched his disappearing back and a feeling of depression settled over her. The others were discussing the painting and Mary discovered it was supposed to represent the sea. She didn't know why Chantelle hadn't simply painted the scene outside her window. One whole wall was made completely of glass and a large section of the harbour lay spread out below her. Drawn to it, she moved over to the glass and looked out at the view.

In the daytime the harbour would be littered with tiny triangles of sail. Now night was closing fast. A few larger motor boats, with their red and green lights blazing, moved slowly across the dark water. In the distance the long trail of taillights mapped out the roads surrounding the coast.

Mary wished she was out there. She wished she was anywhere but here.

A B Given

CHAPTER 5

Chantelle sat at the head of the table with Geoffrey on her right, followed by Mary. Nadia sat on Chantelle's left with Rupert next to her. Robert's chair was at the far end of the table, though he rarely used it. Chantelle kept him busy, spitting out a continual string of instructions on everything from how to stir the sauce for the pork to how to open the wine.

Mary ate as much of the pork as she could before Robert rescued her by carrying her plate away. Not that it mattered; dinner consisted of six courses, each more exotic than the last. Robert sped back and forth to the kitchen bringing in trays of food or taking away trays of dirty dishes. In between he kept everyone's glasses topped up while Chantelle chatted with Geoffrey and her friends.

As the meal drew to an end, Chantelle asked, 'I hope everything was satisfactory?'

It was a blatant attempt to extract compliments and it worked a treat. Nadia, Rupert and Geoffrey showered her with compliments she accepted with mock graciousness. Mary only shook her head wondering how they didn't know she had nothing to do with the wonderful meal. Robert had done everything yet Chantelle happily accepted all the glory. In fact she had done more than that; she had demanded the glory.

Nobody was paying her any attention, so she slipped away from the table and joined Robert in the kitchen. He was elbow deep in suds, cleaning a mountain of dirty dishes while his wife entertained. She took up a tea towel and stepped over to his side. 'Need some help?'

'You don't have to do that, I'm alright,' he said cheerfully.

'Trust me; I'd rather be in here.'

Robert smiled. 'She can be a bit much at times but she isn't all bad.'

'When?' Mary blushed brightly when she remembered they were talking about Robert's wife. Despite what she might think about Chantelle, she shouldn't voice her thoughts to Chantelle's husband. Robert had always done his best to make her welcome and she wouldn't deliberately insult him for the world. 'I'm sorry; I shouldn't have said that.'

'Don't worry about it.' To change the subject, he asked, 'Did you like the dessert? It was a new recipe.'

They chatted happily for a time, both pleased to be away from the others. All too soon the dishes were done and put away. Robert drew out their time together a little longer by brewing coffee. When they couldn't delay it any longer they each carried a tray back to the others.

'One sugar and a little milk,' Chantelle said to Mary as though she was a servant. Mary wished she had the courage to ignore her or tip the coffee in her lap. Instead she added a level teaspoon of sugar and a splash of milk to Chantelle's cup before placing it on the table in front of her.

Chantelle lifted her cup to her lips and sipped a minuscule amount before wrinkling her face. 'You didn't stir it!' she said to Mary, as though she was accusing her of trying to poison her.

'I'm sorry!' It came out before Mary had a chance to think. She wished she had said, *Stir it yourself, bitch!* Of course she never would. She rolled her eyes when Geoffrey took up a spoon and vigorously stirred Chantelle's cup, saving Chantelle the indignity of stirring her own coffee.

Giving Mary a disapproving stare he went back to his story. Apparently he was attempting to explain to Rupert the unemployable and Nadia the welder of junk, the intricacies of the Futures Market. It looked like it was heavy going so Chantelle broke in, 'Of course his boss understands nothing, does he, Geoffrey?'

Geoffrey rolled his eyes and began his recital of woes against Mr. Roberts. This Rupert and Nadia understood. Believe it or not, they too had come across people who didn't appreciate what they did. Mary seemed to be the only one who wasn't surprised.

The conversation rolled along for a little while longer before Chantelle realised she was no longer the centre of attention. 'Geoffrey has outsmarted them though, haven't you dear?' Her hand settled on Geoffrey's, as she said, 'Some time ago I suggested to him that he simply ignore these old fat fools and do what he thinks is best.'

'Isn't that a little dangerous,' interrupted Robert from the end of the table. Chantelle looked annoyed as she searched for the person who had interrupted her. She seemed surprised to find her husband still there. 'Apparently your brother isn't a frightened, headless chicken!' she said caustically, before turning away.

Feeling suitably chastised Robert remained silent for the rest of the night. Mary wished she had the courage to demand Geoffrey answer Robert's question. She wanted to know if it was dangerous and, if it was dangerous, in what way was it dangerous.

As she pondered the possible consequences she did her best to follow his explanation. She soon realised he was being deliberately vague. She knew enough about the operations of the bank and his work to know he wasn't telling them anything important. She wondered if he was simply avoiding making things too complicated for them or whether he didn't want them to know what he was up to. Mary hoped it was the second alternative because it might mean he was angry with Chantelle for raising the subject in front of strangers. The thought Geoffrey might be upset with Chantelle brightened her night.

What she did glean from his explanation worried her. Apparently, at Chantelle's coaxing, he had taken it into his hands to ignore the guidelines set out by Mr. Roberts and the bank and had begun to speculate in areas that gave greater return. These areas were also accordingly greater in their level of risk. Geoffrey, of course, was supremely confident in his ability to minimise this risk. What was worse he had roped in a couple of others to assist him. Apparently it needed a small group to be able to cover up the transactions sufficiently so they wouldn't be discovered. If only one person was doing it, the unauthorised transactions would stand out more readily. If a number of them spread these transactions out amongst them there was less chance of them being discovered. Geoffrey said he wasn't worried about being discovered. He was making the bank more money than if he did it their way. He felt confident they would view his actions positively once he explained it to them.

Rupert congratulated him on his foresight and his courage but Mary knew Geoffrey had left out a number of import facts. The first being, how was he explaining the extra earnings? If he was declaring them that would mean they already knew what he was up to, which made no sense. From her time at the bank she knew Bank Executives didn't have a reputation for rewarding renegade employees who acted outside their level of authority.

All the way home she longed to ask him about it but after suffering a night with Chantelle her courage had deserted her.

* * *

Over the next two days, to rid herself of Chantelle's hurts, Mary spent as much time as she could in her little garden. It was working. At the time she had been insulted by the way everyone, except Robert, completely ignored her but she now realised it had been a blessing in disguise. Less contact with her sister-in-law meant less insults to forget. It was Robert she felt truly sorry for. He had to live with her!

As Mary picked a dead leaf from one of her prized dwarf beans she wondered how two brothers could be so different. Robert was so kind and understanding while Geoffrey was...? Mary's thoughts trailed off. What was Geoffrey? How would she describe her husband? She knew he loved her but what did that actually mean? Up until now she simply accepted her life with Geoffrey. This was the first time she tried to think rationally about their relationship.

He loved her: so what! Was that enough?

Now she thought about it she felt his attitude towards her had gradually changed over time. At first he had been full of compliments, giving her flowers and gifts at every opportunity. Mary wondered why she hadn't noticed this before. His attitude towards her had changed, almost from the moment they were married. Once the honeymoon was over, he'd been less attentive.

She knew she sometimes annoyed him. Generally he was tolerant, explaining the way he liked things done. There were other times though, usually when he was drunk, when he could be abusive. True, he was always sorry afterwards. But, if he was truly sorry, why did he do it in the first place? Mary had no answer and it bothered her.

Why did Geoffrey hit her? More importantly, why did he think he had the right to hit her?

She knew all the excuses. He was drunk or she hadn't done as she was told, etc. If he truly loved her, how could he hurt her like that? And why did he let Chantelle treat her the way she did without saying or doing something?

There was one thing she knew for certain. She knew he wouldn't put up with Chantelle's antics if he was married to her. Amused with the thought, Mary tried to picture Chantelle and her husband living together. *They would kill each other on the first nigh!*

Unbidden, her asked herself, *What would it be like being married to Robert?*

When a feeling of niceness flooded her, she quickly forced her mind down a different track. Some things shouldn't be even thought about. Her choice had been made and she would have to live with it. As the vow said, *For better or for worse*.

Searching for safer ground she switched to thinking of her friend's wedding. Nancy was her best friend when they both worked at the bank. It seemed strange not to be more involved in Nancy's wedding. Apart from being Mary's bridesmaid, Nancy was involved in every step of the planning. It was Nancy who organised Mary's hens night. It was Nancy who went with Mary when she picked her wedding gown. It was Nancy who helped with the guest list and most of the other thousand and one things that had to be organised. Now it was Nancy who was getting married and she hardly knew any of the details of her friend's forthcoming wedding. She hid it but she'd been bitterly disappointed when she wasn't asked to be in Nancy's bridal party. 'Still,' she had reasoned to herself. 'After three years I should be pleased I'm invited.'

Geoffrey had been no help. He was the one who opened the invitation as he did with all the mail. Tossing it casually aside he made a number of excuses why they couldn't go. Mary was devastated. She had to go. In the end she begged him to think about it. All that week he made her sweat. She cooked all his favourite meals and at night she did special favours for him. She willingly performed all the kinky acts she usually was hesitant about. On the last night, Geoffrey came home with a new outfit for her. It was a kinky parody of a maid's outfit: mainly black lace and not much more. Tucked away in the back of her wardrobe were the naughty nurse and cowgirl outfits he had previously bought. Geoffrey forced her to parade around in it all evening while he played the role of Lord of the Manor. The night ended as she suspected it would, with a good spanking. It usually did when she wore any of these silly outfits. When he finally agreed to go to the wedding she felt like she had earned it.

As the week progressed the more excited she became. She made sure she didn't do anything silly and upset Geoffrey so he didn't have any excuse to not go. It was spring and the air seemed charged with vitality. Her little garden was bursting forth with green leaves and the sun felt warm and invigorating. Spring was such a perfect time of year for a wedding. It was to be an afternoon wedding in a park. Nancy had shown her the wedding dress at the hens night and she couldn't wait to see her friend in it. Nancy would make such a lovely bride.

When she married Geoffrey she hadn't realised how it much it would change her life. Naively she'd assumed it would carry on as it always had. Sure, there would be changes, but she hadn't expected to lose her job and her friends. If she had known, she would still have chosen Geoffrey but at least she would have known what to expect. When it did happen it happened so gradually she really didn't notice until it was too late. She was cut off from her old friends and her old life, leaving Geoffrey as her main contact with the outside world. There were times when she felt terribly lonely, times when she wanted to reach out to someone else. But there were other times too, times when she couldn't be happier. All the same it had been nice to catch up with Nancy and the others. She felt as though she hadn't completely lost contact. You never know, Geoffrey might even hit it off with Nancy's new husband and they could all become friends. She doubted it but you just never knew.

* * *

Mary was dressed in the same outfit as last week as she studied herself in the long mirror. She honestly couldn't find anything wrong with it. Geoffrey was in his dressing room so she walked over and asked, 'How do I look?'

Geoffrey was yet to put on his shirt. Dressed only in his trousers he winked at her. 'You look good enough to eat.'

She knew she should be pleased by his response but the memory of last week's lukewarm response to the very same question still lingered with her.

Geoffrey came closer and made a show of peering down her cleavage. 'Very nice!'

Mary felt her frustrations slip away. She leant against him as he slipped his arms around her waist and kissed her throat. 'You just wait until we get home,' he breathed into her ear. She felt her knees go weak. She couldn't help herself. Geoffrey always had this effect on her. He searched for her mouth and they kissed, slowly at first, letting their passion grow. Mary felt him slowly untie the straps at the back of her dress. Then his warm soft lips were on her shoulders and she moaned softly. She didn't want to be late but Geoffrey was gently licking her nipples now and there was no way she was going to ask him to stop. She loved the thought such a gorgeous man was excited by her.

By the time they showered and Mary re-did her make-up they were running seriously late. By the time they arrived at the park the ceremony had already begun. They snuck to the rear of the small crowd with Mary hoping their late arrival went unnoticed.

The ceremony was simple, though beautiful, as all weddings are. Mary cried as she kissed her old friend and wished her well. Then all too soon the bridal party was whisked away for the usual round of photos.

As Nancy and Ricky both worked at the bank many of the guests had a connection with it too. While most of the guests were not friends of Geoffrey's, he didn't let that stop him from being his most charming self. As they waited for the time to move off to the reception he circulated through them as though he was the host.

She thought he looked spectacularly sexy today. Tall and dark, his Armani suit fitting like a glove to the contours of his body, he was charming, confident and witty and she felt proud just to be at his side, his arm through hers.

She noticed the way many of the women looked at him. Their envy and their lust were obvious in their eyes. She knew Geoffrey must be able to see the same thing, yet he never allowed his eyes to make contact with theirs. She had never seen him even so much as flirt with another woman since their marriage. While Geoffrey had his bad points, Mary was unshakable in the trust she placed in his fidelity. It was this trust that was the cornerstone on which she built her marriage. It was the anchor that held her hopes, her dreams and her sanity in place. There were times when she put up with a lot, yet she had no complaints. She willingly put up with it all to be Geoffrey's wife. He was a very handsome, charming man and she knew he could have his choice of women. The fact he had chosen her above all others made her incredibly happy. She felt so happy she wanted to cry out; *You can look all you like ladies but this one's mine!*

At the reception she was delighted to find she was seated with many of her old friends. She knew from her own wedding that one of the hardest tasks was the seating arrangement. It didn't matter how hard you tried, you always upset someone. She was glad this time it wasn't her. It was almost like old times. The only blot was the fact she wasn't up with all the latest gossip so she couldn't always be included in the conversation.

Geoffrey's good mood held and he chatted sociably all through the night. The highlight of course was when Nancy and Ricky came over. There wasn't any time to actually catch up but at least she had the chance to wish her friend well and cry once more. Mary noticed Geoffrey talking in his friendliest manner to Ricky. They even shook hands as they parted. You just never knew.

The bride and groom left in a flurry of cheers and catcalls. They were to stay in a nearby motel for the night before leaving for New Zealand the following day. Once they had departed the guests gradually filtered away. Mary and Geoffrey were one of the first to leave, though Mary didn't care. She'd had one of the most wonderful nights of her life.

'Thank God that's over,' said Geoffrey, as he pointed his car out of the carpark.

'What do you mean?'

'Weddings are always so boring and that was one of the worst.'

'I thought you were having a good time,' she said, as her sense of joy began sliding away.

'I should have known. After all, he is only a Grade Five.'

Mary was painfully aware of the status Geoffrey placed on his rank of eight but it hardly seemed relevant here. 'Does it matter what rank he is?' she asked, more in hope than anything else.

Geoffrey snorted; it was all he had to do to tell her it meant everything. 'All you have to do is look at where they're going for their honeymoon,' he said, as though it proved his point.

'What's wrong with New Zealand?'

Geoffrey looked at her with one raised eyebrow which told her he was getting tired of this conversation. 'What's right with it!' was all he said, before turning back to face the road.

Her dreams of them all being friends seemed a forlorn hope unless Ricky had a sudden and meteoric rise up the rankings. It didn't seem likely.

A B Given

CHAPTER 6

When she heard the soft footsteps on the stairway leading down to her studio Chantelle draped her naked body over the leather sofa and waited, while hoping to make her pose appear natural. She had taken care in the placement of the sofa .It was positioned so it was the first thing you saw as you came off the stairs. It was also one of her favourite places to have sex. She loved to look out over the harbour while she was with one of her young men. The glass wall gave her a feeling of being exposed to the boats on the water even though they couldn't actually see her. If she was feeling particularly naughty she would go up to the next level and out onto the balcony. Here she could be seen by passing boats. It was potentially dangerous but that was what made it so thrilling. While it added a whole new dimension to her sex life she didn't do it too often just in case someone worked out who the house belonged to.

She heard the sharp intake of breath and turned as though surprised to find someone looking at her. 'I was just admiring the view,' she said, turning her eyes back to the glass wall.

While Geoffrey wasn't deceived he was pleased to think she had gone to this much effort. He'd slipped away from work for the afternoon, confident Mary wouldn't ring. Even if she did, one of the guys would put her off. They didn't know where he'd gone but they had a fair idea what he was doing and would cover for him. 'So was I!' he said, in his sexiest voice as he drank in her nakedness. He was aware of Chantelle's exhibitionist nature. She enjoyed being naked or close to it in the presence of others. Her long loose limbs were invitingly arranged on the sofa while her blonde hair was casually flung over her left shoulder covering her breast. Her body belied her true age. Even like this she could pass for years younger than she really was. It was only when you got close that some of the tell-tale signs could be detected. There were faint lines at her eyes and around her mouth: lines she spent a small fortune trying to conceal.

Turning back to him, Chantelle felt her body tingle as her brother-in-law's eyes travelled over her. She could see the desire and the lust in his eyes and it drove her wild as it always did. They had been lovers from even before her marriage to Robert. Chantelle was committed to Robert, though not from love. Rather it was the money she sensed in him. Geoffrey had only been a seventeen-year-old boy when they were introduced. She was twenty-five. She thought Geoffrey was the most handsome boy she had ever met and instinctively they were drawn to each other, all the time knowing they could never be together. Robert wasn't the problem. The problem was their natures. They were both too much alike. They both knew they wouldn't last more than a year together; yet apart, they could enjoy each other as often as they wanted. Neither saw any problems with this. Robert didn't have to know and so the longest they were ever apart was when Chantelle and Robert were on their honeymoon.

Even on her wedding night she'd been unable to do without him. When she was supposed to be changing out of her wedding dress, preparing to leave on her honeymoon, the bridesmaids covered for her while she snuck out and met Geoffrey. She led him into the dark garden and they had sex on the grass. When Chantelle turned her head she could see Robert talking to the guests through the brightly lit windows of the reception house. It was such an incredible turn-on, knowing her new husband and all the others were so close.

'Why don't I get us a drink?' teased Geoffrey knowing she didn't like to be kept waiting.

It was this about Geoffrey she hated and loved at the same time. Chantelle liked to control the encounter and usually did. With Geoffrey it was a constant battle. Any other man would have rushed to her and it would be her who would be making them wait. Having made herself available, she loved to make her lover stop and move at her pace, knowing the sense of frustration they felt made them easier to manipulate.

She heard the cork pop and soon Geoffrey was coming to her, a smile in his lips. God she loved his mouth. Geoffrey was so talented with it. Mostly from her tutelage.

He gracefully placed himself next to her, his leg close though not actually touching hers. Chantelle moved her leg to his, seductively rubbing it against him, knowing it forced her to part her legs even wider than they already were. It was this sort of thing that never happened to her normally. It was only Geoffrey who could manipulate her like this.

Handing her a glass, he toasted, 'To the most beautiful woman I have met today.'

Despite the backhanded compliment, she smiled as his eyes travelled down her body to where her neatly trimmed patch of wispy blonde pubic hair lay exposed by her parted legs. She felt a shiver pass up her spine as she sipped her Champagne. 'I've missed you,' she said as she threw an arm over his shoulder and pulled him to her. Their mouths meet and she eagerly explored his body, removing his clothing as quickly as she could. 'God I hate that bitch wife of yours,' she breathed, pressing her body to his. She never used Mary's name. Both naked now, their bodies entwined as they writhed on the sofa.

He took a handful of her hair and pulled her head back. As he licked her exposed throat, he laughed. 'Why is that?'

'Because she has you!'

'You have me now,' he said, his tongue snaking up towards her ear.

'But it was easier before you married that bitch. I could come over and see you whenever I wanted.'

He still held her head tipped back as he moved his tongue to her nipples.

'I don't know what you see in that sad dishrag,' she cried out through her lust and her desire.

'She has her uses,' he said, teasing her by drawing out the talk, knowing she wanted to move on to other things.

'But I want you all to myself.'

'Don't you have enough lovers to keep you busy?'

'I'd get rid of all of them if you wanted me too!'

He only laughed again. 'No you wouldn't.'

When she tried to move, his hold on her hair hurt her. If any other man had dared do that, she would have ordered them out. Knowing it was Geoffrey only fanned the fires of her desire. He took a hold of one of her wrists and forced her arm behind her. Knowing what he wanted, she brought her other arm around and allowed him to wrap a large hand around both her wrists. With her arms pinned behind her and his hand holding her head painfully by her hair, she was at his mercy. She groaned loudly as he continued to run his tongue over her body. Nobody could make her feel this way expect her husband's younger brother. 'Now, Geoffrey!' she begged, 'Do it now!'

He only pulled back and smiled a charming smile. Without warning he slid off the sofa. Using her hair he pulled her down onto the floor. She was lying on her back with her arms pinned underneath her. He released his hold on her wrists. Even though she could have pulled her arms free, she left them where they were.

Her eyes widened as she watched Geoffrey take up his glass. He took a sip of the sparkling fluid before deliberately tipping the rest over her breasts. Chantelle writhed as the ice-cold liquid ran over her stiff nipples. Still holding her by her hair, he lowered his mouth to her breasts and licked them clean. Only then did he climb on and take her.

Later, he sat on the sofa and looked out over the harbour. After an afternoon of sex they were both feeling sated, though Chantelle continued to caress his naked body. She was naked too, of course. The only time she wasn't these days was when she was with her husband. She felt contented but it had been murder for her on

Saturday night, being so close to Geoffrey and not able to have him. She meant what she said; she hated Mary for being his wife. She knew it was illogical but it didn't change her view.

Without looking at her, he said, 'I really don't think it's wise to spread around what I'm doing at the bank.'

His soft tone didn't fool her. She knew he wasn't happy. Hoping to placate him, she purred in a low sexy voice. 'I know but I so wanted them to know how clever you are. I am so proud of you and I wanted them to know it!'

'Just don't do it again.'

She felt her hackles rising. She wasn't his dishrag wife. He couldn't give her orders. Even the knowledge she was in the wrong couldn't alter that. 'If you say please, I'll think about it!'

It was Geoffrey's turn to smile. 'Don't go and get all fired up. You know how dangerous it is. They would fire me if they found out what I was up to. All I'm asking is you keep it a secret until I can convince them it is the way we should be going.'

Chantelle felt her anger subside as quickly as it had risen. 'Alright, I won't mention it again.'

The pair fell into a silence for a time.

'So, how are things,' she said, to break the silence.

Geoffrey knew she didn't mean with Mary so he said, 'There is a new man who turned up last week.'

Unlike Mary, Chantelle knew every detail of what Geoffrey was doing at the bank. After all, it had been her idea. The thought of all the money at his control made her head spin. It had taken a long time for her plan to manifest itself: even longer to convince him to try it. At her instigation he started trading some of the bank's money in forbidden areas, areas that were normally considered too risky, though areas Geoffrey felt confident in. So far he had been proved right. The really clever part was getting Geoffrey to siphon off the excess profit so the bank wouldn't notice it. It sounded logical, only she hadn't told him the best part of her plan. When the money got enough she intended leaving Robert and letting Geoffrey take care of her. That way they could spend more time together.

So far the plan was working perfectly. Even with them keeping small amounts as play money, there was a huge nest egg building. She didn't like lying to Geoffrey but lying came naturally enough to her to make it palatable. Besides, didn't the ends always justify the means?

The money didn't mean as much to Geoffrey. To him it was a way to prove he was right and they were wrong. He only wanted to show them he was cleverer than they were. In his mind he would one day produce this additional money and say, 'See, this is what can be achieved if you are brave enough!'

Only now there was someone new at the bank. 'Who is he?'

'Just a man from the Melbourne branch.'

'You didn't mention anything about him coming,' she accused.

He didn't like her tone. 'None of us knew he was coming until he arrived.'

'It seems odd, don't you think?'

'There is one funny thing about him. He is a lot older than the rest of us. I reckon he is about forty-five.'

'Do you think it means anything?'

'I don't know but I guess it wouldn't be too hard to check him out.'

'Maybe you should, just in case.'

His smile didn't hide his growing nervousness. 'In case they've discovered what I'm up to, you mean?'

'You never know. It wouldn't hurt to be safe.'

He was confident his manager didn't have a clue of what he was doing but, as Chantelle said, it didn't hurt to be safe. 'OK. Tomorrow I'll call someone I know in Melbourne and see what they say.'

While Chantelle felt a little easier, Geoffrey's mind was beginning to wander. All night his mind remained active and by the time he arrived at the bank the following morning, he was feeling worried. He debated with himself over talking to his colleagues about Frank. Finally he decided to wait until he received something concrete. His opportunity arrived just before lunch. Roberts left for a meeting, saying he wouldn't be back for a couple of hours. Geoffrey snuck into the manager's office and locked the door behind him. Using the office phone he placed a call to a select line in the Melbourne branch.

'International Banking.'

Trying to keep the concern he felt out of his voice, he said, 'Hello, Ryan, it's Geoffrey Parker.'

'Hello, Geoffrey, good to hear from you.'

'So, how have you been?'

'Good, yourself?'

'Going very well.'

Ryan gave a friendly laugh. 'So, now we've got that out of the way, what do you want?'

'Actually there was something I thought you might be able to help me with.'

'No problems, what do you want?'

'Do you know Frank Dobson?'

'The name rings a bell but that's all. Who is he?'

Trying to make his question sound casual, he said, 'Just some guy who moved here from your branch. I just wondered if you knew anything about him.'

'I could ask around if you like?'

'Only if it isn't any trouble. He arrived here a bit suddenly so we're just a bit curious about him.'

'I'll have a bit of a sniff around and see what I come up with.'

'As I say, only if it isn't too much trouble. It isn't very important.'

Ryan only laughed. 'Don't worry, I'll be discrete. I'll email you anything I find in the morning.'

Feeling better he returned to his work, putting Frank out of his mind.

***

The bank's Internal Security Department conducted a search of the personnel records. Ryan Donaldson worked with Geoffrey before transferring to Melbourne. He showed as most obvious person for Geoffrey to contact. There were a couple of other possible people and they spoke to all of them. They were all given the same ultimatum. If they didn't do as they were told they risked losing their job at the bank. Along with their job, they would have their reputation ruined and there would be the distinct possibility of court action–even a jail term.

They all buckled.

They were told to expect a call from Geoffrey Parker. If they received a call, they were to act normally and promise to do whatever he asked. Then they were to contact the head of the Security Department. If they spoke to anyone other than Wilson Blake about this, they would be instantly dismissed.

Ryan liked Geoffrey and they had been friends in Sydney but friendship only went so far. He didn't owe Geoffrey enough that he would risk losing his job to try and protect him. He didn't like lying but what choice did he have? He sat with his head in his hands. 'Geoffrey, what have you got yourself into?'

With a heavy sigh Ryan picked up his phone and dialled the number he'd been given. 'He called, sir.'

'What did he want?' came the brisk reply.

'He asked about someone called Frank Dobson.'

'What did you tell him?'

'I told him the name sounded familiar but I didn't know who he was. I hope that was alright, sir.'

In his office in Sydney a short balding man paused as he thought it over. Nodding, he said, 'Yes, I think that will fit in nicely.'

'I said I'd ask around, discretely of course, and email him anything I found in the morning.'

'You have done very well so far, Ryan, and your involvement will soon be over. Before the end of work today you will receive some information from me. All you need to do is, in the morning, pass this information to Parker.' There was a significant pause before Blake added, 'You realise your activities will be closely monitored by me so I would strongly advise you don't do anything silly. You have done very well so far. All that remains is to pass on my information in a way that won't bring about any suspicion and you can get back to work and forget all about this.'

'I can assure you, sir, I don't have any idea what is going on and I don't want to. I worked with Parker a couple of years ago but that's all. We're not friends.'

The bald man relaxed and sat back in his chair. 'We at the bank won't forget your dedication,' he added, as a sweetener.

'Thank you, sir.'

Ryan hung up wondering if this might turnout ending in his favour.

In Sydney, Blake sat and thought for a while. As the Head of Security, Blake received intel from various sources on a regular basis. Most of this intel proved to be nothing but he never ignored it. When he first started hearing rumours about unusual transactions, he wasn't worried. But the more he looked into them the more concerned he became. Being a very cautious man he began investigations on the quiet. Blake had been the head of the bank's Security Department for over ten years and he knew there were faster ways of dealing with this type of problem but the bank didn't like to air its dirty laundry in public. The quiet way may be slower but it was the bank's way.

Not wanting to wait too long he planted a man in the Futures Department while his other lines of inquiry progressed. If there truly was something amiss, Geoffrey Parker seemed the most likely suspect. He hoped Geoffrey wouldn't place a call to Melbourne but Blake didn't work on hope. He was a man who covered his tracks. While making the call to Melbourne didn't conclusively prove Parker's guilt, added to everything else, it did look very suspicious. He would have to contact Frank and tell him to be extra careful.

He made a phone call to a number only he knew. 'How is it going?'

'Slow! We've been accessing the computer records and trying to put them into some sort of order, but it all takes time.'

It wasn't what Blake was hoping to hear but it was what he'd been expecting. 'I suppose it can't be helped. We need this to be done right.'

'Plus, these people all have their own codes. We're breaking them down but, as I said, it takes time.'

'Hopefully the man I put in there will be able to send through something soon..'

'Anything he can send us will help.'

As Wilson Blake hung up the pone he pressed his fingertips together and pondered what cover story he should have Ryan send Parker.

A B Given

CHAPTER 7

Geoffrey arrived at the bank looking his resplendent best. Only a very astute observer would have noticed the tiniest of worry lines at the corner of his eyes. Rebuffing his manager's attempt at a friendly greeting he took his place and fired up his computer. Without trying to look too interested he searched through his emails. There were three from various brokers and one from the BMW dealership, reminding him his car was due for its twenty thousand kilometre service. There was nothing from Ryan. While he was disappointed he knew it didn't mean he wasn't going to receive a message later in the morning, which had always been the most likely time.

When nothing arrived by ten o'clock he was tempted to call Ryan but he didn't want to seem too interested. He decided to give Ryan until three before he called again. Just as he turned back to his work the tiny symbol appeared in the bottom right-hand corner of his computer screen. An email had arrived. Bringing up the email he quickly read it.

Your new friend worked down here for a number of years. Seems someone felt he showed good initiative. They were so pleased they thought his talents could best be utilised elsewhere.

People I spoke with said he's a nice guy. They said they trusted him.

Hope this helps.

Geoffrey read between the lines and smiled. Frank didn't mind bending the rules, which had annoyed his boss but his workmates liked him. It still didn't mean Frank could be brought into their little circle. If for no other reason, Frank was probably still being watched pretty carefully but at least Frank wasn't someone he had to worry about. Frank was one of them and that made Geoffrey breathe a little easier. After all, it explained why he had arrived so suddenly and that was what had been worrying him the most. Under normal circumstances it seemed a very strange thing for the bank to do. In light of what Ryan had sent him, it was now understandable.

The bank liked to be discrete about such things. They wouldn't want to advertise they were moving someone they weren't happy with.

He pondered whether to tell the others but finally decided it might only worry them. He would keep this to himself unless one of them raised a concern over Frank's sudden arrival. Then would be a better time to reassure them everything was fine.

The only person he would need to discuss this with was Chantelle. He didn't want her worrying needlessly. Besides, he enjoyed hearing her voice and any excuse would do.

***

Mary sat and read the postcard for the third time. There and then she made a promise to herself. She wasn't going to let Geoffrey stop her being friends with Nancy. She didn't care if Ricky was only a Grade Five at the bank; she liked him. More importantly, she liked Nancy and Nancy was her friend.

Now she had resolved to defy her husband, Mary wondered how she was going to manage it. As she thought it through, she couldn't remember Geoffrey ever actually saying she couldn't meet up with any of her old friends. It was more that he made it difficult and she had submitted. To meet with Nancy at night might still prove to be difficult, but there was always lunchtimes.

Geoffrey never said she couldn't go out during the day. All he asked was she did the housework set out for her; other than that, the day was hers. It had been her unwillingness to upset Geoffrey that had held her back. That was about to change.

According to the postcard, Nancy was due back on the weekend. She knew the newly married couple had booked a further week's holiday to set up their house before returning to work. That fitted in perfectly for her. She could go to their house and meet them.

She wondered whether she should tell Geoffrey her intentions. Would it be better to be honest and up front with her decision, or would it be better to be a little less honest? After all, not telling wasn't exactly the same as lying, was it? If she deliberately lied to Geoffrey, that would be different and she would understand if he got angry. However, if she wanted to see a friend, what business was it of his? If she didn't let her duties at the house slip, did it really matter?

She knew she was fooling herself. Of course it would matter to Geoffrey. 'Tough, he'll just have to get used to it!' she said, out loud to herself. Her defiant words, spoken with feeling, didn't shed her sense of impending doom. Sitting a little straighter in her chair she decided it was still worth doing. After all, what could he do that he hadn't already done? They had been married for only three years and Mary had already made several trips to the hospital. Three times she'd had to stay overnight. At worst she would make another trip to the hospital and at best she could convince him her friendship with Nancy didn't threaten their marriage or whatever his problem was.

Mary thought to herself, *It's funny what you can get used to!* The first time Geoffrey beat her, she had been terrified. She would have done, and did do, anything to stop it happening again. Yet, despite her best efforts it had happened again. It happened again and again. Now she was no longer terrified. Not that she looked forward to it happening or anything silly like that; it was more she had experienced it enough times now that she no longer doubted it would happen. She had come to accept, at some point, that Geoffrey would snap and beat her. The knowledge it was inevitable somehow lessened her fear. Regular beatings for little or no reason other than her husband was drunk or found an imaginary fault with her duties as his wife had somehow become a part of her life. Not a part she liked, but she loved Geoffrey enough to accept the beatings. So, if that was what it took to stay friends with Nancy, then so be it. Mary had taken Geoffrey's worst before, she could take it again. Nancy was worth it.

* * *

Geoffrey stared at his computer screen and frowned. He had requested a search for the record of a transaction he enacted twelve months ago and the stupid machine only flashed an error message. He hated these error messages; they never seemed to make any sense. Angry, he dialled the Help Desk and prepared to wait. To his disappointment he was switched straight through. He had been hoping to add the wait to his list of complaints.

'Help Desk.'

The muffled, nasally reply grated on Geffrey. 'Geoffrey Parker. I have an error message, #396 flashing on my screen. Can you tell me what it means?'

The man with a nasal complaint laughed. 'It means you've got a problem.'

Geoffrey rolled his eyes. He hated funny people, especially when he had a problem. 'I worked that much out on my own. What I was hoping was you would be of some assistance to me. What I didn't want, or need, was a comedy routine from a half-witted computer geek.' Geoffrey's voice rose with every word he pronounced in his clearest tone.

'All right, pal, hold on. I was just trying to add a little bit of humour to your day,' said the nasally voice, sounding as annoyed as Geoffrey felt.

'Well you didn't. Do you know what #396 means?'

'Easy: you're attempting to recall some old records, right?'

'Yes.'

'You can't because those records are already being accessed by someone else.'

'Who would be doing that?' demanded Geoffrey.

'That, pal, I can't tell you!'

The man sounded happy about not being able to help and Geoffrey was tempted to give him a piece of his mind but other thoughts pressed themselves into importance: namely, who was accessing his transaction records and why?

When an idea came to him, he stepped over to Frank's cubicle. Walking up as quietly as he could he peeked over the other man's shoulder to look at what he was doing. Frank was working some basic transactions which had nothing to do with Geoffrey. With a sense of relief he placed a hand on Frank's shoulder. 'You up for a drink tonight?'

Frank swivelled around and smiled. 'I'm always up for a drink.'

'What have they got you doing?' he asked, trying to sound casual as he nodded in the direction of the computer screen.

Frank frowned and pointed at the screen. 'Just some stuff I could handle in my sleep. I get the feeling Roberts doesn't trust me with anything important yet.'

Geoffrey was confident now it wasn't Frank who was searching through old files. With his suspicions fully allayed, he grinned as he whispered conspiratorially, 'Take it from me, Roberts has no idea.'

'I'm starting to know what you mean!'

'I'll catch you tonight.'

He knew it wasn't Frank but that didn't answer the question of who was looking into his old files or why. The problem he faced was it could be perfectly innocent. If he made a fuss over it, someone might start to wonder why. He wanted to know what was going but he had to do it in a way that didn't raise suspicions.

He tried to think of what he would do in this instance if he wasn't trading illegally with the bank's money and skimming off the profits. He decided to be bold. After all, he couldn't go on with his work without these records.

Without bothering to knock, he entered Roberts's office. 'Do you know if someone is doing a routine check on our files?'

'I'm sorry?' said Cliff Roberts, looking startled by his sudden appearance.

Geoffrey took a breath and prepared to clarify his question. 'I'm working on that Russian wheat deal and I need to look at what I did with a similar deal twelve months ago.'

'And?' said Cliff Roberts, still none the wiser as to Geoffrey's problem.

'When I tried to bring up the records all I got was an error message. Apparently the message means someone else is accessing the records so I can't.' Geoffrey frowned. 'Oh, by the way, there's a moron with a nasal problem working at the Help Desk. He's completely incompetent. You should contact someone down there and have him sorted out.'

Cliff ignored the last part. It was only the first bit that interested him. 'Why would someone be looking at our old records?'

'That's what I came in here to find out?' said Geoffrey, feeling exasperated. 'You're in charge; don't you know anything about it?'

'No I don't, which is odd, because I should!'

Geoffrey waited while Roberts thought things through. 'Let me make a few phone calls and I'll get back to you.'

It wasn't what Geoffrey wanted but it would have to do. He was trapped. He didn't want to make too much fuss and attract unwarranted attention to himself. 'Can you make it quick? I need to have that Russian deal stitched up by tonight.'

Cliff looked annoyed, as he said, 'I'll do my best but you might just have to move on without it.'

Geoffrey groaned his disapproval and left. On the way back to his desk he ran through the encounter in his mind. Satisfied he had acted as he would have done if he had nothing to hide, he settled down to work on finishing the twelve million dollar Russian wheat deal so he would be ready in time for the pub.

Cliff's first point of call was the Computing Department. 'Hello, Gary, it's Cliff Roberts over in Futures and Risk. One of my men just tried to access some old records and he couldn't because someone else is already doing the same thing. What I need to know is who is doing it and why. Can you help?'

Cliff Roberts hadn't been taken into the bank's confidence but Gary Watson had. The bank didn't think Cliff was involved in any way; they were just annoyed because he should have discovered what was going on under his nose and he hadn't. He may not be involved but his head was on the chopping block.

Gary had a line worked out for such an inquiry. 'No problems: I can tell you exactly what's going on. We had a problem with some of the back-up tapes so we are going through them all, checking for faults. Some information has been lost but at this stage we think it is minimal.'

'OK,' said Cliff, easily convinced. 'So how long before my man can access the records?'

'How far back is he trying to go?'

'Twelve months.'

'Give me a second.' While he was on hold Cliff listened to Frank Sinatra singing *My Way*. Old Blue Eyes was just reaching the end of the song when the line suddenly clicked back. 'If your guy only needs to go back twelve months, he should be OK in an hour or so.'

'Sometimes my men need to look at what they did on other deals. Is this problem with the back-up tapes going to take long to fix?'

'That's hard to say. We don't know what we have to fix until we find a problem. We're systematically going back through all the tapes looking for problems.'

'Can you give me a ballpark figure so I can let them know?' asked Cliff, feeling pleased with himself that he'd thought to ask.

'We're hoping to have things pretty well fixed by the end of next week.'

'It must be some sort of a problem,' said Cliff, sympathetically.

'You're not telling me anything. Upstairs are tearing my balls out over this!'

'Oh, by the way,' said Cliff sheepishly. 'Have you got someone on the Help Desk who sounds a little nasally?'

'I think I know who you mean; why's that?'

'Nothing really. Just tell him to take care if he ever speaks to Geoffrey Parker again. He can be a right royal pain in the arse but the bank thinks a lot of him. I'd hate to see your man get into trouble over nothing.' He hung up feeling convinced he had gotten to the bottom of the problem. Stepping out of his office, he called out, 'Can you all drop what you're doing and come over here please.'

There was a collection of groans and sighs as slowly everyone came over to within earshot.

'Geoffrey came up against a problem accessing an old record. I've just spoken to Gary Watson in the Computing Department and he assures me they are working on the problem and, while we might have some difficulties, everything should be back to normal by the end of next week. Oh, and Geoffrey, they said you should be right in about an hour for what you want.'

Geoffrey forced himself to remain silent so he was relieved when someone else asked, 'What's the problem?'

'There is a stuff-up with the back-up tapes and they need to go over them to find out what went wrong.'

Geoffrey studied Cliff intently and he was convinced Cliff believed what he was saying. He didn't think his boss could carry off a lie that well. Neither did the bank management, which was another reason Cliff hadn't been brought into the loop. Geoffrey still wasn't totally convinced but he was breathing easier so he risked speaking. 'What about the moron on the Help Desk. Are they going to sort him out?'

'I put in a complaint and that is being taken care of.'

The way Cliff avoided looking at him told Geoffrey his Manager was lying, which reinforced his belief Cliff hadn't been lying earlier.

* * *

While Cliff was talking to his department, Gary Watson was on the phone to Wilson Blake.

'Are you sure it was Geoffrey Parker who was checking his old records?'

'I didn't want to push it but from what Roberts said, I took it that it was Parker.'

'No, you did right not to push for information.' After a slight pause, Blake added, 'And thank you for calling so promptly.'

'No problems, sir.'

'I'll keep in touch,' said Blake. Parker wanting to assess one of his old records wasn't something they had foreseen. Still, they had taken precautions should something like this come up. By the sounds of it, they may have gotten away with it. All he could do now was wait to hear from Frank and see what he thought.

A B Given

CHAPTER 8

Mary sat, as she did on every Friday night, trying to watch TV while listening for her husband to come home. His arrival was harder to pick on Friday nights because he didn't always take his car. Usually she would hear the sound of the automatic garage door opening and closing. On Friday those nights he caught a taxi and could suddenly appear without her realising he was home.

Frank's name hadn't been mentioned for a couple of weeks now and Mary was beginning to hope she could put the terrifying experience behind her. She hadn't known how to handle his attentions then and she didn't think she had any better idea now. Frank gave her the creeps yet somehow he knew how to manipulate her. She still couldn't believe she'd kissed him while sitting so close to Geoffrey. She shuddered with self-disgust every time she remembered how she'd opened her nightie and displayed her breasts for him. The thought she'd allowed him to fondle them, so close to Geoffrey, caused her break into a sweat of fear. But there wasn't anything she could do. True, she had asked him to stop but it hadn't helped. Frank only stopped when he was ready to stop.

It was very late and she wanted to go to bed. Only the thought of putting on her nightie before Geoffrey come home stopped her. Fear gripped her when she heard voices at the front door. She recognised Geoffrey's instantly. It took a little longer to pick Frank's voice but she knew it was him even before he came into view.

'Here she is,' said Geoffrey, looking pleased to see her. He smiled one of his best smiles and she moved quickly to him. After she gave him a kiss, he added, 'You remember Frank, don't you?'

'Hello, Frank,' she said without warmth.

'I am pleased to see you again, lovely lady.' Frank's smarmy tone made her skin crawl. He was standing a little behind Geoffrey so Geoffrey didn't see the way he ran his eyes over her, but she did. Despite the disgust she felt, Mary didn't feel as vulnerable this time. While Geoffrey had obviously been drinking he wasn't anywhere near as drunk as he had been the last time he invited Frank into his house.

Pretending she hadn't noticed Frank's attentions she gave Geoffrey another hug and a kiss. 'I have your dinner ready if you want it and I'm sure I could stretch it out if your friend is hungry too,' she said, deliberately not using Frank's name.

'Thanks, but we've already eaten,' said Geoffrey, before turning to Frank. 'At least, I'm not hungry. What about you?'

With a knowing wink, Frank said, 'I'm not hungry but I'm a little thirsty.'

'Coming right up.' Geoffrey headed for the bar. 'What would you like?' he called over his shoulder.

'A beer will do nicely,' said Frank, lingering behind. As soon was Geoffrey passed through the doorway to the games room Frank reached out and squeezed Mary's buttock. 'Did you miss me, gorgeous?' he said in a low tone before running his tongue over his lips. Mary cringed and Frank laughed.

'What's so funny?' called Geoffrey.

'I was just thinking what Roberts would be doing right now. Probably doing a crossword while sipping tea.'

'He's such an old woman!' agreed Geoffrey, with feeling. 'I can't believe the crap work he has you doing!'

They both spent the next hour getting stuck into their boss and the rest of the bank management while Frank made sure Geoffrey's glass remained topped up. Then Frank looked at his watch and announced, 'It is getting late; I should be going.'

'Are you sure? I was just getting started.'

'I should go. I'm not used to drinking this much.'

'I suppose we have had a few,' conceded Geoffrey.

Frank swayed as he rose to his feet. Reaching out he gripped the edge of the bar to steady himself. With a grin in Geoffrey's direction, he said, 'Whoa, maybe I've had more than I thought.'

'Why don't you just stay here, there is plenty of room.'

'I wouldn't want to put you to any trouble?'

'No trouble at all,' said Geoffrey, before calling out, 'Mary!'

When Mary appeared at the doorway, he told her, 'Frank's had too much to drink so he is going to stay the night. Can you see he has everything he wants?'

Her mouth opened but she closed it again without saying what she wanted to say. She wanted to offer to call a taxi for Frank but Geoffrey wouldn't like her contradicting him like that. He didn't know what his new friend was like, and she couldn't tell him, so he wouldn't understand her desire to get Frank out of the house. Instead, she simply said, 'I'll make sure the spare bed is ready.'

She was bent over the bed, turning back the quilt when she sensed someone was there. Mary looked over her shoulder to find Frank was standing in the doorway watching her. Startled, she stood up straight. His eyes travelled over her. 'Is there anything I can get you before I go to bed?' she asked, without any emotion in her voice.

An amused smile spread across Frank's lips. 'There's nothing at the moment but I'll let you know if anything comes to mind.'

She hated the way he leered at her; it made everything he said sound dirty. 'I'll leave you to settle in,' she said, stepping towards the door.

He gave her a wink. 'Don't go on my account.'

Mary ignored him and kept walking. It was only as she approached the door that she was forced to stop. Frank hadn't moved. He was still blocking her exit from the room. 'Why not stay and keep me warm.'

'I'd rather not!' she said, as she tried to push passed him. Frank didn't stop her, but he'd positioned himself so she had to rub her body against his to get past. Once clear she headed straight to the safety of her room and Geoffrey. It was amazing how Geoffrey made her feel. In his presence she was safe yet she was too scared to tell him about Frank in case he made the wrong assumptions.

She wasn't in the mood to be romantic but Geoffrey had other ideas. She didn't bother to fight it. Fortunately Geoffrey had drunk enough alcohol to feel randy and too much to be able to do much about it. After a short session he rolled over and went to sleep.

She tossed and turned for over an hour, jealous of her husband's ability to drop off the moment his head hit the pillow. A niggling ache was starting to make itself felt behind her left eye. She was too tired to be bothered getting up to take an aspirin. That was when Geoffrey started to snore. She gave in to it all and climbed out of bed.

Normally she would have taken up residence in the spare room but with Frank in there she couldn't do that tonight. Tonight she would have to resort to taking a couple of aspirin and hoping for the best.

She slipped a light satin robe over her cotton nightie and snuck as quietly as she could to the kitchen. Confident she hadn't made a sound she opened the top draw under the sink and pushed out two of the little white tablets. From the refrigerator she took out a plastic jug of filtered water. Pouring a little of the cold water into a fresh glass she tossed the tablets into her mouth before gulping some of the water. She paused for a moment to make sure the tablets had slid down her throat. Sometimes they refused to go no matter what she tried. She decided to take another swallow of the water just to make sure. Confident she'd successfully swallowed the tablets she re-opened the refrigerator. The light blinked on as she placed the jug back on the shelf.

Before she could shut the door two arms wrapped around her. One hand was placed firmly over her mouth preventing her from crying out. The other took a hold of the front of her robe and held her tight. She instinctively knew this wasn't her husband so it could only be one other person. His body warmth passed through her thin clothing. Even without being able to see him, she knew he was naked. Naked, in her kitchen! How dare he be naked in her kitchen! Terrified Mary struggled to free herself. She felt hot breath against her ear. She heard his hoarse breathing as he strained to hold her.

'That's it, gorgeous; wiggle your little arse just like that. It feels so nice.'

She became aware of the ramrod stiffness of him pressing against her buttocks. The thought he was enjoying her struggles made her stop but her whole body trembled with horror when his hot, wet tongue licked her ear. His breathing rattled throatily making her skin crawl.

'I heard you two before,' he whispered. 'I don't think your husband was up to the task but you're in luck, Gorgeous. I'm happy to finish what he started.'

Mary's mind screamed out for her husband to save her as Frank's tongue licked deep inside her ear. Hot, wet and searching, it repulsed her like nothing she had ever experienced before.

'I'm going to take my hand from your mouth now. If you scream or do anything silly, I will tell Geoffrey you came to my room and threw yourself at me.' He paused for a moment, before adding, 'Do you understand?' He released his hold a fraction and Mary was able to nod. She felt the pressure gradually slacken off and she was able to breathe through her mouth again. Shivering in fear, she gulped in air.

'That's better,' he whispered. 'There's no reason to fight me, is there?'

'If you touch me, Geoffrey will kill you!' she whispered back.

Frank only laughed a soft, ugly laugh. 'True enough, my lovely, but only after he's killed you!'

She tried hard to think of a comeback but she couldn't. She was afraid Frank was right. Geoffrey probably would kill her. He had beaten her to the point where she needed to be hospitalised because Chantelle claimed she had given her food poisoning, which had been plainly ridiculous. What would he do if he found her, in his own home, in the middle of the night, with a naked man? He wouldn't be asking too many questions or listening to too many protests of innocence. Mary knew from bitter experience being innocent didn't stop Geoffrey taking out his frustrations and his anger on her. While she loved Geoffrey, she was convinced he would kill her if he found her like this.

'We're going to have some fun, you and I,' he whispered into her ear.

She shuddered at the thought but she didn't bother to protest. Nor did she struggle. She knew this was madness but she couldn't stop it. Frank knew how to twist her fear of Geoffrey against her. She hated being forced to submit to this man but she felt powerless to prevent it. All she could hope was that Frank would soon take her back to the spare bedroom where Geoffrey would be less likely to discover them. To remain standing in the kitchen like this was madness!

She didn't resist as Frank turned her around to face him. She stood motionless as he untied the sash of her satin robe. She was like a rabbit caught in a spotlight. She knew she was trapped and there was no way out. Geoffrey, her only possible saviour, lay sleeping just a short way down the passageway. He'd wake if she screamed but she didn't dare.

Frank was smiling as he slipped the robe over her shoulders. It whispered down her body to the floor. 'I'm not the monster here.' Frank paused but Mary held her silence. He reached out and ran a single fingertip over the scar in her eyebrow. 'I'm not the one who beat you into submission.' His grin broadened. 'I'm only taking advantage of Geoffrey's good work.' He sighed as he dragged his fingers down her cheek. 'All my life I've searched for a woman like you.' His fingers stroked her trembling throat. 'A bitch I can own.' His hand cupped her right breast. 'I do own you. You know that, don't you?'

She refused to speak or to look at him.

'Do you remember my instructions for you?'

She felt herself blush. She'd forgotten all about it. He'd told her to not wear any panties the next time they met. She wasn't wearing any but not because of his instructions. Geoffrey had pulled them from her and she hadn't thought to put them back on when she went to take the aspirin. Now she was caught. She didn't want him to think she deliberately removed them to obey him but she didn't want to anger him either. She had a feeling there would be punishments for disobedience. She nodded.

'Did you obey me?'

She hated herself for her weakness. 'Yes.'

His hand continued to fondle her breasts. 'Tell me what you did to obey me.'

A tear trickled down her cheek. 'I removed my panties as you told me to do.'

His forefinger and thumb gripped her nipple. Giving it a firm squeeze, he told her, 'Show yourself to me.'

She finally forced her eyes to meet his. 'Please!' The single word contained all her anguish. It was a plea for respect and a cry for mercy. His reply was to tighten his grip on her nipple. She squirmed with the pain of it. Frank moaned. Knowing protest was useless she reached for the hem of her nightie. Taking a deep breath she raised it high enough to expose her lower stomach.

Frank paused to savour the moment. He had full control over her. He knew it and what was better, she knew it. He dipped his head to one side as he studied her. Mary knew better than to lower her nightie without permission...even when he stretched out his left hand towards her. A shudder of revulsion rippled through her as his fingertips lightly brushed against her neatly trimmed patch of pubic hair. 'You learn quickly.'

Sensing he wanted her to speak, she said, 'Thank you.'

'Spread your feet wider apart.'

She obeyed him, hoping he would soon tire of this game and take her somewhere more private. She gritted her teeth as his fingers explored her most sensitive areas.

'Take everything off and let me see you properly.'

Frank released his hold on her nipple so she could pull the light cotton nightie over her head. Reaching out she dropped it to the floor to join her robe.

His was an ugly smile as he ran his eyes over her. Occasionally he would reach out and touch her somewhere, just to show he could.

'Kiss me.'

'No, please don't,' she begged. Being forced to display herself like this for him was one thing but kissing him seemed betrayal of her vows to Geoffrey.

Frank grabbed a handful of her hair and pulled her head back, forcing her to look into his eyes. He sneered at her. 'I don't like telling sluts twice.' As he let go of her hair he shoved her head back so it banged against the edge of the refrigerator. It was hard enough to make her almost cry out with the pain. Yet she knew this had been but a *love tap*. There would be more painful punishments if she disobeyed him. The threat of pain frightened her but it wasn't why she obeyed him. It was the worry he'd think of something even more disgusting for her to do if she didn't.

Mary was whimpering softly now as she wrapped her arms around his neck. Puckering her lips she pressed them to his. This was madness and she knew it. They were both standing naked, in the kitchen, illuminated by the open door of the refrigerator.

As they kissed Frank ran his fingertips over her soft, warm skin, all the way from her shoulders to her buttocks and down along her thighs. His moan was full of want and desire as he thrust his tongue between her quivering lips. She fought back the urge to gag. Bile lurched in her stomach.

The man in her arms was a disgusting pig but she forced herself to appear as though she was responding to his attentions. Consumed with self-loathing her fingers moved over the skin of his neck. Her lips closed around his tongue as she sucked seductively on it. When he pressed himself firmly against her, she swayed her hips, rubbing herself over his stiffness. 'Turn around.'

This time she didn't bother to beg. She knew it was useless. She longed to cover herself but didn't. There was no point! He would only punish her and then make her display herself anyway. She closed her eyes, not wanting to look at his face or any other part of him as she slowly turned around to face away from him.

'Bend over.'

She obeyed him.

'Use your hands to part your buttocks. Show me what you have hidden in there. I want to see every inch of your body.'

Hot tears flowed now as Mary pried her buttocks apart so this sick bastard could ogle her anus. Frank didn't do or say anything for a long time. He just ran his eyes up and down her naked body. He liked what he saw. The bitch was no model but she was pretty enough to excite him. Her body wasn't like any he had seen in a porno, yet there was an appeal in her slender lines. Somehow she seemed so much more vulnerable than if she had been very beautiful or had a curvy, voluptuous body. She was terrified and his head swam with the power of it. 'Pick up your clothes and follow me.' He turned and walked away from her without looking back.

Mary hated herself now more than at any other point in her life. Here was her opportunity. She could run to her room and the safety of her husband but what she did was meekly stoop down and pick up her clothes and follow Frank back to the spare bedroom. She knew how bad it made her feel but she couldn't gather the strength or the courage to resist.

'Close the door,' he ordered.

She obeyed.

As she waited by the door for further instructions Frank climbed onto the bed and propped himself up with a couple of pillows. He watched her for a moment or two before saying, 'Come over here and let's see what kind of a whore you make!'

A B Given

CHAPTER 9

Geoffrey was puzzled by Mary's behaviour. She seemed distracted and...weird, even for her. If he didn't already have enough on his plate he'd have taken her to task.

Now he thought about it the entire weekend seemed strange. He woke Saturday morning to the sound of Mary in the shower but when he felt her side of the bed it was cold. He knew she hadn't slept in the spare room because Frank was in there. He assumed she must have slept on the sofa. He shrugged. So long as she hadn't disturbed his guest, he supposed it didn't matter where she slept.

Frank acted strangely too. Geoffrey heard the sound of the front door closing just as he was about to replace Mary in the shower. When he looked out the window he saw Frank climbing into a waiting taxi. Frank hadn't even waited for Mary to cook him breakfast. Geoffrey chuckled to himself. Frank must be embarrassed about having drunk so much last night he couldn't make it home.

As he was showering his thoughts changed. He decided it was rude of Frank to not say his goodbyes. He had been generous enough to offer Frank a bed. Surely it wasn't asking too much for a little politeness?

He dressed and walked to the kitchen. He sat and picked up the morning paper.

'Would you like your eggs scrambled, poached or fried this morning, Dear?'

He was reading an interesting article on the Stock Exchange and didn't reply immediately. When he did, he turned to find Mary leaning against the counter staring out into nothingness. He snapped his fingers. 'Come on, woman.'

Mary jumped like a frightened rabbit. 'Yes, Dear!'

He watched for a few moments as she whirled around the kitchen. She really could be strange at times. Bored with her antics he returned to his paper.

Halfway through his eggs he looked at her again. She was sitting with her head bowed, staring into a bowl of untouched porridge. She looked awful. There were lines around her eyes as though she hadn't slept all night. 'What's up with you?'

She jumped again, nearly upsetting the bowl. 'Nothing.'

'I'm not in the mood for any of your silliness this morning. I have important matters at the bank to deal with and you're not helping, so whatever it is, snap out of it!'

'Yes, Dear.' She jumped up and went off to clean something. At least she wasn't annoying him now with her moping and he went back to his breakfast.

It was only later he membered to tackle her over Frank's sudden departure. 'Did you know he'd called a taxi?'

'Yes, Dear.'

When she fidgeted with the hem of her dress, he demanded, 'What?'

'Actually, I called it for him.'

'I think it was rude of him not to say goodbye!'

'I suppose...'

He waited but she didn't finish her sentence. She could be so annoying some days. 'You suppose what?' She jumped again. What was wrong with her this morning? It wasn't as though he'd had to punisher for anything lately.

'I suppose...he had somewhere he needed to be.'

He stared at her. What in hell was that ridiculous statement meant to mean? 'Did he say anything to you?'

'No, Dear.'

'What, nothing at all?'

'Just that he wanted me to call him a taxi.'

It was a puzzle but his head was staring to hurt now and he couldn't be bothered with it. 'Get me some aspirin. Putting up with all your nonsense is giving me a headache.' He swallowed them down with the water she handed him. 'By the way, where'd you sleep last night?'

'Sleep?'

'Yes, your side of the bed was cold this morning.'

'I...well...'

He cut her off. If she couldn't even answer a simple question with a straightforward reply he wasn't going to waste time with her. Holding up his hand, he told her, 'I'm going to do some work.'

'Would you like a coffee to take with you?'

He didn't bother to answer her. He didn't really have any work to do this morning; he simply needed some time alone to think. Strange coincidences were happening and he didn't like them. Ryan's information had been reassuring and it would have settled things for him if it wasn't for the computer record business. He didn't like that they had happened together, but then they had both been explained satisfactorily enough. Just as a precaution he invited Frank out drinking, to give Frank the opportunity to ask him about his work. If Frank had been sent to investigate him, surely he would. Frank hadn't, which seemed to prove his innocence, but a nagging doubt lingered. If only Frank had waited a little longer before sneaking out like that. It made him look guilty over something. Or was it only his imagination running overtime. He ran his hand across his brow. Sitting here worrying was only making his head hurt more. 'Mary!'

She ran in sounding breathless.

'Get me a coffee and some stronger tablets. Those stupid aspirins you gave me aren't doing a thing.'

Tossing two tablets into his mouth he washed them down with a gulp of coffee. He nearly spat it out again. Thrusting the cup at her, he said, 'You stupid woman; there's no sugar!'

'Are you sure?'

He stared back at her unable to believe his ears. Was she questioning him? 'Am I sure? You stupid fucking bitch; don't you think I'd know whether my coffee's been sugared or not? Of course I'm sure.' Mary grabbed for the cup. In her haste she spilt a little on his leg. 'What in hell is wrong with you this morning!'

'I'm so sorry; I'll clean everything up straight away!' She dashed away only to return in seconds with a damp cloth which she rubbed briskly over the small wet patch on his trousers.

Brushing her hand aside, he demanded, 'What is wrong with you today?'

'I don't think I slept well last night.'

'I hope you didn't annoy Frank, wondering around the house at all hours!'

'Frank? Why would I have annoyed Frank?'

'For God's sake woman, get a hold of yourself! I didn't say you had, I only said I hoped you hadn't.'

She picked up the coffee cup. 'I'll get you another one.'

He was becoming so annoyed with her he nearly told her not to bother, that all he wanted was for her to stay out of his sight, but his head was hurting and he hoped a coffee would help. 'Just try to get it right this time!'

'I'm very sorry, Dear, I'm not sure how I could have made such a simple mistake.'

'As I'm continually telling you, you need to concentrate more.'

She left muttering apologies he didn't bother with. It was as though there were days when she deliberately set out to annoy him. When he decided he needed a wife to take care of him, Mary seemed such a good choice. She was as timid as a rabbit, which meant she would be trainable. She wasn't beautiful but she was pretty enough to look at and her figure was trim. He couldn't have been bothered with a beautiful, sexy wife. He'd have spent the rest of his life wondering what she was up too. Mary was atrocious in bed but he knew he could do something about that. Besides, he only needed her to fill in between his visits with Chantelle. He considered he was a good catch for a woman like her...and he was a good provider. Surely it wasn't too much to ask that she made a drinkable coffee once in a while?

She brought in a new cup and waited demurely for him to taste it. He fussed with some papers on the desk, making her wait. Eventually he picked up the cup and sipped. Without looking at her, he said, 'Yes, you've done wonderfully. You've finally managed to make a drinkable cup of coffee. You can go now!' Mary shuffled away. When she was gone, he wondered if her strange mood this morning had anything to do with Frank. He was starting to suspect she was upset because he hadn't told her he was bringing Frank back with him. Why it bothered her, he didn't waste time thinking about. Hell, this was his house and if he wanted to invite a friend to stay over, he would, and his wife had better get used to the idea. Either that or he might have to teach her who was in charge, again. You'd think she would have learnt by now, but apparently not. Something was the matter with her and if she didn't stop moping about the house, she'd soon get another lesson!

Geoffrey pushed thoughts of his wife to the back of his mind where they belonged and concentrated on himself. Even though he had been trying very hard to convince himself there wasn't a problem at the bank he couldn't quite do it. Reluctantly his thoughts turned to what might happen if the bank discovered what he'd been doing.

Two scenarios seemed the most likely. If it became known he was trading in areas in which he wasn't authorised he felt he had a chance of talking his way out. After all, he hadn't lost any money and none of the deals had fallen through on him. If they challenged him he would brazen it out. He might even be able to turn their attack around and challenge them. If he could prove his point, they might even let him continue. At worst he might receive a reprimand.

However, if they discovered he was siphoning off the extra money, he was gone for sure. There was no way he could justify taking that action. At best they would have him escorted off the premises. At worst they would have him arrested. He could end up in jail!

With these prospects looming large over him he didn't bother to ask Mary what was wrong and she didn't volunteer any information. Ignoring her, he spent the weekend working out different defences and lines of attack depending on what they might discover and challenge him with. By the time Monday morning came around he felt ready for them, no matter what they threw at him.

***

For Mary it was the worst weekend of her life. She thought the previous encounter with Frank had been bad but it didn't even come close to this one. She hated herself and she hated Frank for making her feel like this. He used and abused her and that wasn't the worst thing he did to her. The worst thing was he made her submit to it all without even trying to fight back. She felt so helpless! There was nowhere and no-one she could turn to.

She felt so dirty. The disgusting things he had her do for him made her want to cry every time she thought about them and they were all she could think about. When Geoffrey was drunk he sometimes made her do things for him, but that was different. He was her husband and he was drunk. It was a very different matter when the man wasn't your husband and it was so much more degrading when he was sober. Knowing Frank did this to her for his pleasure, making her humiliate herself, just because he enjoyed it, made it so much worse than anything Geoffrey ever did.

Frank made her stay with him most of the night. The whole time she was terrified Geoffrey would wake up and come looking for her. If he found her in Frank's room, doing those disgusting things, he would have killed her for sure. Her only compensating thought was, Geoffrey would kill Frank too.

Only Geoffrey didn't wake and come looking for her. At times she wished he would, at least her humiliation and her terror would end. Frank's sick, twisted mind kept coming up new, vile acts for her to perform. Terrible, shameful acts of humiliation and perversion: things no man had a right to ask a woman to do for him, and she had done it all, without question. After a while her mind had gone numb and she acted as though by remote control. In this state of mindlessness she refused him nothing. She submitted to his will completely.

In the morning he forced her to get down on her knees and kiss his feet while she begged to be allowed to leave. When he finally agreed, he refused to allow her to dress. Standing naked she'd phoned for a taxi for him. Terrified, she snuck passed Geoffrey to reach the shower. She'd hardly begun to remove Frank's stink when Geoffrey woke.

All morning she was a nervous wreck. She couldn't do anything right and she knew she was making Geoffrey angry. She desperately needed his support but how could she tell him? He would be so angry with her. If he chose to punish her, she wouldn't blame him. It was Geoffrey she felt truly sorry for. None of his was his fault. She was the weak one. She was the one who couldn't stand up for herself!

When he asked her where she slept, she nearly died. She'd muttered something and he moved on but every single cell of her body strained to detect a hint of suspicion in him. Geoffrey genuinely seemed only curious. Last night she wished he found her and killed her. Now she knew she didn't want to die, no matter what. She tried to calm herself, while her knees knocked together. To her, her every action screamed out her guilt. Yet Geoffrey didn't appear to notice anything wrong.

The rest of the weekend he spent locked away in his study working on something, only appearing for meals. Normally she would be annoyed but this weekend she was grateful. She spent most of her time in her little garden trying to calm her shattered nerves and to regain some of her lost self-respect. Her nerves calmed a little but her self-respect would take longer than a weekend to return.

When Geoffrey returned to work on Monday she locked herself in the house and refused to go outside. She knew it was irrational but it didn't matter. She felt safe locked in the house. She didn't even venture out into her garden. Without the security of Geoffrey's presence the outside world turned into a scary place where men like Frank roamed at will. It was a place she wanted no part of.

∗ ∗ ∗

Geoffrey felt particularly nervous as he drove to work Monday morning. He couldn't rid himself of the possibility he might be under investigation. It was probably only his guilty conscience playing tricks on him, but he felt uneasy all the same.

Keeping a brave face he smiled as he greeted his fellow colleagues on the way to his desk. The Russian wheat deal was completed before he finished on Friday so there wasn't anything pressing waiting for him. Out of curiosity he pulled up the report he hadn't been able to produce on Friday. Today it loaded onto his screen without any hesitation. He quickly scanned it, looking for any evidence someone had been scrutinising it. Not knowing what he was looking for, he gave up.

He brought up two other old reports before trying another one of his funny deals. Not wanting to spend too long with this on his screen he scanned the report to see if anything stood out as different. He had gone to great lengths compiling these reports, making them appear as though they were his normal work. Of course there were lies built into them but you had to know what you were looking for to detect them. The money he siphoned off never showed in these reports. There was a completely separate program in place that allowed him to accomplish this. He was confident his work would stand up to all but the strictest scrutiny.

He brought up three normal files before bringing up another doctored one. Geoffrey followed this process all morning, randomly recalling one of his doctored reports and scanning it. By lunchtime he was feeling quietly confident. No-one had attempted to speak with him and nothing out of the ordinary had happened. He couldn't see anything that stood out as obvious in the files he looked at.

He considered sending Brett an email, then decided the old fashioned way might be better. Scribbling a short note on a piece of paper he walked casually by Brett's desk, discretely slipping the paper in front of him as he passed. Twenty minutes later Brett stepped out of the building's lobby and walked outside. At the corner he turned left and walked to the little coffee shop. Geoffrey was already there, sitting at a table with two cups of coffee in front of him. Discreetly looking around him, to see who else was in the shop, Brett asked, 'What's up?'

'Nothing, I hope.' He fixed his stare on Brett as he asked, 'Have you noticed anything unusual going on?'

'Like what?'

'That is the tricky part,' explained Geoffrey. 'I don't know exactly, just anything unusual?'

Brett thought for a moment before shaking his head. Then his face turned serious. 'The new guy, Frank. It seems a little weird the way he just appeared like that!'

'Yes, I thought so too, so I contacted a friend of mine in Melbourne. Turns out they suspected Frank of being inventive with some figures. They couldn't prove anything but they thought a change would do him good.'

'You mean they moved him out before he embarrassed them?'

'Sounds about right.'

Brett looked deep in thought, before saying slowly, 'But that doesn't make sense.'

'Why not?' demanded Geoffrey.

'If they thought he was being a bit funny with the figures, why would they send him to the Head Office? Usually it is the other way around. Normally they ship you out to some God-forsaken branch where you can't do any damage.'

Geoffrey was stunned into silence. Why hadn't he made that connection? He blamed Mary's strange behaviour. She had been so disconcerting it had derailed his usually impeccable thought processes. Besides, he'd felt so relieved when he received Ryan's email he hadn't questioned it.

'And why would they send him to our department?' continued Brett. 'You don't catch someone with their hand in the lolly jar and then send them to the lolly shop to work, do you?'

'Christ!' Geoffrey's mind was working overtime now. How could he have been so stupid? Why hadn't he seen any of this? Brett was right, it made no sense. The bank wouldn't send someone they were suspicious of to the Head Office and then set them to work in the Futures Department. It suddenly all clicked into place. They wanted him to think Frank was suspect in the hope he would try and enlist him. That was why Frank was being so friendly. The prick had even spent the night in his house.

Geoffrey suddenly turned cold. Frank had all night to search his house. Was there any incriminating evidence there? He thought not. By nature he was a very cautious man. Besides, Mary had been up wandering around at strange hours. Surely she would have seen him. He would have to question her more closely tonight!

'I have a terrible feeling about all this. I can't talk to the others in case they are watching me. You'll have to speak with Kevin and Philip, tell them to stop everything immediately: try the best they can to make sure there aren't any loose ends. And, for God's sake, don't talk to Frank or anyone else about anything!'

'Do you think they'll figure out what we've been up too?' asked Brett, sounding concerned. Like Geoffrey he had been married for three years, only he had a baby to worry about as well.

'I'm sure everything is fine. Just stay calm,' reassured Geoffrey, not liking the sudden rise in Brett's tone. 'I'll handle everything. They might not even be able to figure out what we did and, even if they do, I have a couple of contingency plans.'

Brett was looking decidedly worried now.

'Hey, it will be all right. I can handle Roberts.'

'Yeah, I know you can.'

'You'll talk to the others?' checked Geoffrey.

'Yeah, I'll do it straight away.'

'Just stay calm, OK!'

'Yeah, no worries.'

As Geoffrey walked away, he muttered to himself, 'Yeah, no worries.'

For the first time he wondered if Chantelle wasn't right. Maybe he should have kept this to himself. The others were useful in spreading the fake deals around, only now he had to worry about how they would stand up under the pressure of a possible investigation. He knew he would handle anything the bank threw at him, but the others?

At least Brett and the other two didn't know the full story. They didn't know how much money he had siphoned off. He'd given them enough to keep them interested and quiet but that had been a mere fraction of the money he collected. He convinced them they were only proving a point. They were the experts, and the bank and, more particularly, Roberts, shouldn't be restricting where and when they traded. The money he slipped them had only been an added bonus.

Geoffrey calmed a little as he realised it might even work in his favour. If one of the others broke and spilled everything to the bank, they could only tell them the version Geoffrey had told them. If he kept to the same story, at worst the bank might reprimand him. At best they might let him continue trading the way he wanted. Everything would be all right so long as they didn't discover how much he'd actually siphoned off. If he could keep that hidden, he would be saved from disgrace.

As he sat behind his desk another thought interrupted him and sent his mind into a spin. How did they know to send him the wrong information about Frank? He'd called an old friend and asked him confidentially. There was only one explanation; Ryan was a part of it. But how could they even know he would call him? And how did they make Ryan turn against him?

Suddenly this had a bad feel about this. Geoffrey wasn't prone to paranoia but he could feel a net closing in around him. Who could he trust? No-one by the looks of it!

He desperately needed to see Chantelle! She was the only one who could comfort him!

***

In a small office on the fifth floor a man in a crumpled grey suit dialled the telephone on his desk.

'Yes?'

'He's getting nervous.'

'How do you know?' demanded Blake.

'We fitted a key-stroke reader to his terminal. It reproduces everything he does up here. He's spent the morning bringing up old files and then closing them down again after about fifteen minutes.'

'Has he just,' said Blake. 'He may have just narrowed our search down for us. I want all those files printed out and I want our auditors to go through them with a fine-toothed comb.'

'Already onto it.'

Wilson Blake sat back comfortably into his chair. He had a feeling the clever Geoffrey Parker would be his by the end of the week.

A B Given

CHAPTER 10

The days passed slowly and by Thursday Mary was beginning to see some light at the end of the long dark tunnel her life had become. She made herself a coffee and sat down to think this through. She'd thought of nothing else all week but only now did she feel ready to try and put some sort of perspective to it.

Yes, a terrible thing had happened to her. She had been raped. There was no other way to describe what happened to her. It was degrading and humiliating and she would carry the mental scars with her the rest of her life. Worse still, she had meekly submitted to another's will. She'd allowed herself to be used in ways she never before imagined. Yet, these were not the worst things she did. She didn't kept her marriage vows to Geoffrey and that was what she hated about herself the most. She knew she wasn't a raving beauty. There weren't lines of men wanting to have sex with her as there were lines of women ready and willing to have sex with Geoffrey. Yet, it was she who had broken their vows to each other. It was she who had had sex outside of their marriage.

These were the downsides and, while they were pretty damning, there is always an upside if you looked for it. She was still alive and that had to be a good thing. She hadn't been physically hurt. While she did have scars, they weren't physical ones. It was rape; so far though, Geoffrey didn't know anything about it. While this didn't diminish the guilt she carried, it did save her having to defend herself against an enraged and violent husband.

The question Mary struggled with was: could she really claim it was rape when she'd gone some way to consenting to it? She hadn't tried to fight him off! She hadn't encouraged him either or asked him to even touch her. In fact she had let it be clearly known she didn't want to be touched by him. After all, *No* was supposed to mean *No*, wasn't it? Did it matter that she didn't have bruises from where she'd tried valiantly to fight him off? Frank knew she didn't want to do any of those things he made her do. Did it matter that he made her do those things by the strength of his will alone rather than by physical strength? Rape was rape, surely!

And, if it was rape, could she really blame herself for breaking her marriage vows? In fact, did rape even constitute a breaking of her marriage vows? Surely only consensual sex constituted a breaking of such a vow. Rape was beyond her control. And what happened with Frank was completely beyond her control!

She knew she would have a hard time convincing others that stripping in front of a stranger in your own home in the middle of the night, while your husband slept in his bed, was beyond her control. Especially when all he did, was tell her to do it. Mary knew most people would never understand how she felt, how totally powerless, how completely terrified she had been. Sitting here in her kitchen, in the bright light of day, she even had trouble with it herself.

When he'd turned around and walked back to his bedroom, why didn't she simply run in the other direction? She'd known, if she followed him, what his intentions were. So why did she meekly lock herself in with that perverted bastard! She'd done whatever he asked. She obeyed every instruction, complied with every request and allowed herself to be subjected to ever greater levels of humiliation. It was so hard to explain but at the time there hadn't seemed any alternative.

Mary searched her soul. Had she enjoyed any part of it?

At least that was easy; the answer was a clear...*No!* She knew there were women who enjoyed being treated like a piece of warm meat, gaining a perverted sense of pleasure by being made to feel powerless. How someone could enjoy being humiliated and degraded was beyond her imagination. She'd hated every moment of her ordeal.

Finally taking a sip of her coffee she tried to sum up her thoughts. It had been a terrifying experience, but one she had survived, albeit with a few mental scars. It had been rape, and being rape, she didn't think it meant she had broken her vows. Geoffrey didn't know and she didn't see any reason for him to know. It was a terrible secret to keep but one she must, for the sake of her marriage.

Her mind was less troubled by now and she felt able to face what she had been avoiding. What would she do next time? The possibility there would be a next time seemed irrefutable. Frank was having far too much fun to not try again. Unfortunately she had given him all the proof he needed to know she was somehow under his control. Part of her worry came from Frank's disinterest in secrecy. Bizarrely, he seemed to enjoy the fact Geoffrey might discover them at any moment.

She wasn't sure she would be any stronger next time. If Frank managed to get her alone again she might well fall into the same spell. The key would be to not allow herself to be alone with him. If Frank turned up again she would have to stick to Geoffrey's side like glue.

With that settled, she felt in sufficient control of her life to re-join the rest of the world. She promised herself she would visit Nancy and she didn't want to let Frank stop her living her life the way she wanted. Picking up the phone she dialled Nancy's new number.

'Hello?'

'Guess who!' teased Mary trying to give herself a needed boost by saying something silly to her old friend.

'Oh-my-God,' cried Nancy. 'Mary, is that you?'

'Of course it's me. How was the honeymoon?'

'Simply wonderful: we had such a good time.'

'I'd love to hear all about it.'

'How long have you got?' said Nancy with a laugh.

'Today, I'm a bit busy,' she lied, not yet ready to venture out. 'But that's why I rang; I'm free tomorrow if you'd like a visitor?'

'That would be wonderful,' cried Nancy. 'Have you got the address?'

'You gave it to me at the Hens night,' she confirmed. 'Are you sure it's OK? I know you two must be busy getting organised.'

'Don't even give it a second thought; we'd never be too busy for you!'

Mary felt a tear come to her eye. She knew her friend hadn't meant it to be a criticism of her own actions, once she'd married Geoffrey, but that was exactly what she'd done. She'd ignored all her old friends.

Sensing the tension that had suddenly developed, even over the phone, Nancy slipped in, 'Why don't you come for lunch? That way it will give me time to collect all those photos we put in to be developed.'

'That sounds great. I am so looking forward to seeing you again.'

'Me too!' After a slight pause, Nancy asked, 'Is everything OK?'

'Everything's fine,' said Mary, forcing a smile into her voice.

'Sorry, but I'd better go, I've got things to organise if I'm going to be ready by tomorrow!'

This time Mary's smile was genuine. Nancy sounded so excited by the prospect of a visit. 'Don't go to any trouble just for me.'

'Are you serious? You think I am going to let you come to my new house and not do something special!'

Mary couldn't help but laugh. 'Just don't go crazy.'

'I promise nothing!'

As she hung up the phone she realised it had been the best thing for her. She couldn't let her life slip by. She had problems, but so did most people. Her problems were bad, but others had worse. Hiding wasn't going to solve anything. Getting on with her life just might.

✳ ✳ ✳

Chantelle was becoming frantic. She'd called Geoffrey three times already today and he hadn't answered a single one of them, nor had he returned any of them. It was so unlike him. She knew Geoffrey could be arrogant and uncaring with others but he had never been either of these things with her. They had a special relationship. They were both far too similar to allow the other get away with any nonsense.

With a sense of foreboding she tried his mobile again.

'Hello, Chantelle.'

While she felt relieved to hear his voice, she detected a level of strain in it. 'I have to see you!'

'It's a little tricky right now.'

She knew him well enough to understand others could hear what he was saying. 'Can you get away?' she persisted. 'I'm so hot for you, I'm ready to burst!'

'Can it wait until tomorrow?'

Anger flared in her. She wasn't used to being fobbed off like this. Feeling piqued, she told him, 'No! But if I must, I suppose I'll have too!'

'Please don't be like that. I'll explain everything tomorrow.'

She hung up without bothering to reply.

'Shit!' cursed Geoffrey into the empty phone. Why did everything have to get complicated at once?

It took some doing but he managed to organise a long lunch the following day. He rang Robert to check he was at his office at the docks. Making up an excuse he talked with his brother for a short time before heading off to meet his wife.

He knew Chantelle was angry with him the moment he saw her. As usual, she was waiting for him on the sofa in her studio; however, today was very different. Normally Chantelle would be naked; today she was dressed from neck to toe in a leather pantsuit. 'Hello,' he said brightly, trying to stave off a possible argument.

She didn't bother to look at him, as she said, 'You managed to spare me a few minutes of your precious time I see!'

'Come on, Chantelle, don't be like that. Things are happening at the bank: things I don't like the look of.'

She finally turned to half-face him. 'Whatever! Come over here and make yourself useful and open the champagne!'

Deciding arguing wasn't worth the effort, he walked over to the small table she'd positioned in front of the sofa. On it were two crystal champagne flutes and a bottle sitting in an ice bucket. As the cork popped he poured some of the flowing wine into one of the flutes before slowly filling both glasses. Picking up the sparkling glasses he stepped closer. Chantelle still wasn't smiling. She was sitting with her legs crossed and her arms folded across her chest. It wasn't a welcoming look. 'Are we celebrating something?' he asked, holding out a glass to her.

Chantelle looked at him properly for the first time. Ignoring his question, she asked one of her own. 'Do you like my new suit? I had it made especially for you.'

Chantelle's cold tone had been replaced with her usual sexy purr. Intrigued now, he studied her more closely. The matching baby pink leather jacket and pants had been tailored to a skin-tight fit. On most women it would have looked ridiculously cutesy but, with her blonde hair and pale skin, it looked just right. He found himself wondering how it would feel to run his hand over it, to follow her body's contours under the tight fitting leather. 'It looks very nice.'

'Very nice? Is that all you can say after all the trouble I went to!'

He noticed her tone belied her angry words. Her tone was still her sexy purr. Before he had the chance to reply, she unfolded her arms and placed them across the top of the sofa. Her jacket fell open. She smiled for the first time as his eyes fixed on her exposed breasts, her nipples standing out as stiff as little flagpoles. With a look of amusement on her beautiful face she uncrossed her legs, pushing her knees wide apart. With her voice thick with lust, she asked, 'Now what do you think?'

With her leg uncrossed he could see the pants were crutchless. Her tiny patch of neatly trimmed pubic hair stared back at him, inviting him closer. With the appearance of casualness he sat on the lounge next to her. She wasn't fooled and a look of gloating spread slowly across her face. 'You are the most beautiful woman I have ever seen,' he said, in appreciation of her efforts. Her arms were still draped across the top of the sofa so Geoffrey placed a glass to her lips. Chantelle took a minuscule sip.

'We are celebrating something!' she said, answering his earlier question.

'And what are we celebrating?'

With a satisfied smile, she told him, 'My painting sold!'

'Did it?' cried Geoffrey, genuinely excited for her. 'I knew it was good, but that is exceptionally quick.'

She suddenly threw her arms around his neck causing some of the champagne to spill over her. While smothering him in kisses, she managed to say, 'It sold on the second day, can you believe it, the second day!'

It was with some difficulty that Geoffrey managed to place the glasses on the table. She was holding on tight and he didn't want to spill any more champagne on her. Once his hands were free he wrapped them around her waist and hugged her. 'I think that is marvellous!' That was as far as he got before Chantelle covered his mouth with hers. As they kissed he peeled the tight fitting jacket from her, leaving her naked from the waist up. Geoffrey found her breasts and squeezed them as they kissed. Chantelle took one of his hands and placed it between her spread legs, groaning as Geoffrey stroked her with his fingers.

'I have been so excited,' she moaned. 'I've been bursting to tell someone.'

As she unbuttoned his shirt, he told her, 'I'm so sorry; if I'd have known I would have come straight over.'

'But how could I tell you, I wanted it to be a surprise! You are the first to know.'

'Doesn't Robert know?'

'Why would I tell him? He doesn't even understand my paintings. You are the only one I wanted to share this moment with.'

Over the years Geoffrey had become accustomed to discussing his brother's relationship with his wife as he and Chantelle made love. At first it had been a little disconcerting; now it was second nature. Chantelle often made comparisons between the two brothers, comparisons that were never complimentary to her husband.

'I need you! I need you now!' she said with an urgent, lustful voice. With cat like grace she climbed over him. Planting her knees on the sofa she bent over the padded arm. She was facing the glass wall and she gazed out over the harbour leaving Geoffrey with full access to her body.

He knew she was ready but he took his time. His view was as tantalising as hers. Besides being crutchless the leather pants were cut away to expose Chantelle's firm, rounded buttocks. He teased her by exploring her with his fingers.

'Please don't do this to me,' she pleaded, as she slowly gyrated her hips to entice him. 'You know what I want. Please, my darling, please take me now!'

Giving her bare buttocks a firm slap he removed the rest of his clothes. Only when he was finally ready, did he climb up behind her.

'Do whatever you want with me, my darling,' she urged him throatily. She arched her back, thrusting her buttocks back at him. 'You can take me anyway you desire!'

He smiled. At times she could be so transparent. She was pretending it was his choice but, with Chantelle positioned like that, he knew exactly what she wanted. At first she screamed with the pain of it. Later she begged for more.

They were lying on the sofa, both sated. Geoffrey sighed with the knowledge he was about to spoil the perfect mood she had created for them. 'I have a very bad feeling that everything is all starting to unravel.'

'Mmm,' she said dreamily.

'I only hope I can walk away with my job intact.'

Chantelle raised her head to look at him. 'What are you saying?

His anger flared. 'Have you heard a word I've said?'

'Don't you start with me!' she said, her own eyes flaring. 'If you're only going to talk nonsense, why should I listen?'

'I'm afraid it isn't nonsense. They are investigating me and it is only a matter of time before they discover something.'

She slapped his bare shoulder. 'And this is how you react? You lie down and cry like a baby?'

'What do you suggest?'

'I know Robert would roll over but I expect better from you. I expect you to fight; that is why I love you so much!'

Geoffrey felt his anger slipping away. He sat a little straighter on the sofa.

'Who knows more about your work than you?' she demanded of him. 'Does old Roberts?'

'Don't make me laugh! That fool only serves to vindicate my theory about middle-level managers. Upper management appoint the ones who know the least, leaving the ones who do know what they're doing to get on with the work!'

'So what are you worried about?' she asked triumphantly.

'I think this is bigger than Roberts.'

'Good. This way those fools at the bank might realise who is the clever one. It's about time you got the credit you deserve.'

Geoffrey could feel his spirits rising. He knew Chantelle's logic didn't really make sense but her positive attitude was infectious. 'There really shouldn't be any problems unless they find out about the money.'

'Exactly and they are not likely to discover that. You're far too clever for them!'

Geoffrey didn't know about that. Banks weren't usually known for their inability to understand money transactions, but he didn't argue. There was no point. They would either discover what he'd done with the money or they wouldn't. The trick would be to make sure they didn't look. 'I need to throw them off the scent.' Talking more to himself than to Chantelle, he said, 'How can I stop them from looking?' Chantelle continued to stroke his naked body as he put his mind to his question.

'What have you done so far?' she asked. 'Other than wait for them to collect their evidence and come for you.'

Her tone told him her question was rhetorical; however he answered it anyway. 'What else can I do?'

'Go on the offensive! Ask for a meeting with someone high up and go to them with what you've done and demand they give you more freedom.'

Geoffrey's mind began to whirl. Chantelle could be right. If he went to them, he wouldn't look so guilty. It would look as though he honestly believed he was justified in what he'd done. They still wouldn't like it but at least it would look as though he was trying to be honest with them. If he could convince them he had the bank's best interest at heart, they might stop the investigation and, if they stopped the investigation, they wouldn't find the money! Throwing his arms around Chantelle, he kissed her passionately. 'You're a genius!' he shouted. 'That might just work!'

Chantelle threw one of her long, leather clad legs over him. Straddling him, she purred, 'Show me how much you like my idea.'

∗ ∗ ∗

Geoffrey left some time ago but Chantelle still lay on the sofa dressed only in her erotic leather suit. She felt very contented. No-one else ever made her feel this way. She was imagining what it would be like to have Geoffrey all to herself. She hadn't decided whether to get rid of Robert or not, but Mary would have to go. Mary was stopping her from getting what she wanted and no-one ever stood in her way for long.

She never understood why Geoffrey married her in the first place. She'd begged him not too. If he wanted someone to look after his house, why didn't he just hire a maid? Surely it would have been easier then marrying that ugly pig.

What really angered her was the fact that Mary was his wife. And wives had privileges maids didn't. When she challenged him, Geoffrey laughed at her. 'Of course I'm sleeping with her. She's my wife for God's sake!'

She had her own stable of lovers and she didn't expect Geoffrey to remain faithful to her. Theirs wasn't that sort of relationship. But Mary! She wasn't even pretty...not really. She told herself she might have understood if Geoffrey married a truly beautiful woman, someone more befitting of him. Mary was an insult! A wicked smile curled her lips as she remembered how she'd done her best to make the bitch's life hell. She knew all about the little trips to the hospital and how the stupid bitch suffered. But none of it was enough for her. Mary should suffer and suffer again and again.

Geoffrey tried to console her by saying Mary meant nothing to him. She knew he had Mary twisted around his little finger but that only angered her even more, knowing he wasn't taking full advantage of his control over the bitch. Mary was a timid little mouse who did as she was told, when she was told. So why hadn't Geoffrey told Mary how much he really loved her. That way they could be together whenever they wanted. Surely Mary wouldn't object? And if she did, well, she'd have more little trips to the hospital until she learnt her place.

Geoffrey must have enough money by now to keep her. As soon as he sorted out this little problem out with the bank she would tell Robert about them. He was so weak she was convinced he wouldn't even speak out. He'd curl up like a whipped dog and do exactly what she told him to do, like he'd always done. She stretched like a contented cat as she fantasised about making Robert stand at the end of the bed and watch her and Geoffrey. He'd probably cry like a baby but he'd do it. He'd do other things too. Her mind whirled with the possibilities. It would be a fitting punishment for all he'd put her through!

Then new possibilities came to her. Just maybe she'd allow Mary to stay. After all, they'd need someone to wash and clean. And it would be so delicious to make the stupid bitch watch her and Mary's precious Geoffrey together. She pictured Mary down on her hands and knees, scrubbing the kitchen floor, while she waited for Geoffrey to be finished in the bedroom, all the time knowing what he was doing and who he was doing it with. Yes, that would be so much better than sending her away!

If they kept Robert and Mary to cook and clean for them it would leave Geoffrey and her so much more time to do whatever they wanted, especially with each other.

Chantelle giggled at the thought. It was intoxicating. All Geoffrey had to do was fix this business at the bank and all her fantasies would come true!

A B Given

CHAPTER 11

On Friday morning Mary did something she normally hated doing; she went to her recipe jar and took out some of her precious money. She counted out a hundred and fifty dollars then, with a shrug, she took out another fifty. Her friend was worth it.

Not wanting to waste any of her money she walked down to the shops. There was a nice little gift shop and she headed inside. Checking her watch she worried she was going to be late. Her problem wasn't a lack of suitable things to buy; rather there were too many lovely choices. That and Mary had lost touch with Nancy's tastes. She had no idea what sort of décor her friend had chosen for her home. She hated to rush her decision, but she had to go. The wedding gift had been easier. She had picked out a lovely crystal vase and a set of crystal wineglasses. This gift she wanted to be special. She wanted this to be something personal.

Making one last circuit of the store she finally settled on a pair of ceramic giraffes. She had no idea why. The taller one stood about three feet high and the other slightly lower, as though it might be a mother and child. They seemed such a preposterous gift, yet she had been continually drawn to them. To her relief the lady behind the counter offered to gift-wrap them. With her gift finally organised, she headed back outside and made her way to the taxi stand. Fortunately there was a taxi sitting waiting.

Her nerves began to tingle as she approached her destination. Nancy had given her a good reception on her hens night and at the wedding, and Nancy sounded excited on the phone; however, Mary couldn't forget how she had cut herself off from her friends after her own marriage. She wouldn't blame Nancy if she were a little cool on her arrival.

She needn't have concerned herself. The moment the taxi pulled up the front door was flung open and an excited Nancy rushed out. A bemused taxi driver was forced to wait through a teary greeting between the two young women before they began to argue over who would pay his bill. While they argued, in a good-natured way, he slipped out and took the woman's strange parcels out of the boot and placed them on the footpath. In the end Nancy wrapped one of her arms firmly around Mary and tossed a handful of notes through the open window of the taxi. Giggling so hard she could hardly make herself understood, she said, 'Is that enough?'

Mary was laughing too as she tried to free herself. 'Don't be silly, it's my taxi!'

The driver retrieved the notes and quickly counted them. There was more than enough and he decided to accept the remainder as a tip. 'That's fine, lady.'

With that settled to her satisfaction, Nancy dragged a still struggling Mary away from the taxi and towards the house. Only as the taxi pulled away did she let her friend go.

'You idiot,' said Mary, still laughing. 'My things are still on the footpath!'

'What things?'

Mary was laughing and it felt so good. It was as if someone had drawn back a curtain on her life and let the light back in. 'I bought you and Ricky a house-warming present.'

Turning around Nancy spotted the two loosely wrapped parcels sitting on the edge of the footpath. 'Bloody hell, what did you buy?'

Mary's laughing finally dried up. Feeling more serious, she said, 'I know you will probably say I shouldn't have, but I wanted to.'

'What a load of bullshit, of course you had to buy me something!' giggled Nancy, giving Mary a friendly push to show she was only joking.

Mary took hold of the larger parcel and Nancy picked up the slightly smaller one. 'Christ, what did you buy?'

Ricky was standing at the door waiting patiently for the two women to finally enter the house. 'Come on you pair!' he chided them with a smile. 'I can't stand here all day waiting for you!'

'God, we're in trouble now,' said Nancy. 'His Lord and Master has spoken.'

Mary didn't hear the joke in her friend's words and she thought Ricky might really be upset. Geoffrey would have been. Her laughter dried up. In a serious, respectful tone, she said, 'I am very sorry, Ricky, it was all my fault.'

Ricky didn't how to take Mary's declaration. One minute she was laughing and carrying on like a silly schoolgirl, while the next she seemed frightened, frightened of him. He looked to his wife for inspiration and she didn't let him down. Freeing one hand she gave him a playful slap. 'Get out of the way, you idiot, I've got presents to unwrap.'

Stepping aside, he allowed the two women to enter the house before following them. He didn't understand why or how but the atmosphere had suddenly become frosty. All the laughing and joking died, leaving him feeling uncomfortable, as though somehow he was to blame.

'I don't know why I bought these really,' babbled Mary, her nervousness showing. 'If you don't like them you can exchange them for something else.'

Nancy was too busy ripping paper away to listen. Looking up at her friend with an incredulous expression on her face, she cried, 'They're giraffes!'

'Yes,' was all Mary could think of to say, while she waited for her friend's verdict. When Nancy continued to stare at the two ceramic animals, Mary tentatively asked, 'Do you like them?' She was unprepared for Nancy's reaction. Nancy threw herself over her. Hugging her tightly, she cried out, 'I love them, I love them, I love them!' Jumping to her feet, she pulled Mary up with her. 'Where shall I put them?'

The pair carried the two figures into various rooms until finally deciding to place them in a corner of the entranceway. 'What do you think?'

'I like them there,' said Mary, as she had said every time they placed them.

'So do I! This way everyone who comes will see them and I can tell them, my friend Mary gave them to me!'

'Do you like them, Ricky?' asked Mary, timidly.

Ricky had been standing back, allowing the two women to find just the right spot without him getting into trouble by offering a suggestion. 'I think they're lovely,' he said, as he stepped forward. Placing his hand on Mary's arm he lent forward to give her a thank you peck on the cheek. His lips never touched her face. Instinctively Mary shied away as his hand settled on her arm. 'I'm sorry, I…' he trailed off lamely, unsure what he was sorry for.

'Come on you pair, I'm starving,' said Nancy to break the tension that had suddenly built up again. Nancy was no cook so she'd enlisted the help of the local bakery. In the oven she had a delicious looking quiche and an assortment of savoury pastries.

They were settling themselves in the tiny dining room when Nancy handed Ricky a bottle of wine. 'Here, make yourself useful.'

Mary watched as Ricky smiled and gave Nancy a kiss as he took the bottle from her and headed to the kitchen. 'He's useful for some things,' said Nancy with a laugh.

Mary knew she was spoiling things and the heavy atmosphere that now existed was due to her. She knew what the mistake was. She was looking at Nancy and Ricky's relationship through the prism of her own marriage. She tried to remember back to when she and Geoffrey had just returned from their honeymoon. Back to when her marriage had seemed blissful. That was how she should be viewing Nancy and Ricky. Determined to try and lighten things up, she took a deep breath and asked with a wink, 'Is he good for anything else?'

Nancy pretended to look shocked before turning as if to see if Ricky was coming back. Then in a mock whisper, that was loud enough for him to hear, she confided, 'He isn't much good in bed yet but I'm working with him!'

'I heard that!' he called out, before adding, 'I can't find the bottle opener.'
Nancy rolled her eyes theatrically. 'Try the second drawer under the sink.'
After a slight pause, he called, 'Got it!'
'Wonders will never cease!'

Mary could feel Nancy's eyes on her but when she looked up Nancy's eyes darted away. Instinctively she knew her friend had been looking at the scar in her right eyebrow. Nancy would know it hadn't been there before her marriage and Mary felt uncomfortable again. She'd placed all the blame for her not seeing her friends on Geoffrey. In that moment she realised she was partly to blame. When she noticed the stilted quality of the conversation between her and her friends, as though they were uncomfortable in her presence, she begun to withdraw. Harder still were the questions about her recent string of *accidents*. She knew Geoffrey wanted her to stay at home and it was easier for her to comply; she didn't have to lie to her friends that way. She burnt a lot of bridges and a number of them might never be rebuilt but she hoped and prayed it wasn't too late with Nancy. Earlier it felt as though nothing had changed. They laughed and Nancy was her usual silly self. Now the air felt heavy and tense and she knew she was the cause. But that was OK because, if she was the cause, she could also be the cure. She did something she hadn't done in a long time; she decided to take charge. If she was the problem, then she was also the answer. The power to change things was with her! The thought sent a shiver running along her spine. She hadn't thought of herself as having the power to do or change anything in a long time. Yet it was true; it had to be true! If it was her actions that caused this meeting with her friend and her new husband to become filled with uncomfortable silences, then only she could change that. Only a change in her behaviour could rescue the situation. It was up to her. Although she didn't know exactly what she was going to say, she was determined to do something. When Ricky returned he was carrying a tray loaded with three crystal wineglasses and an opened bottle of wine. With great pomp and ceremony he approached her and extended the tray. 'Would Madam like a glass of wine?' he asked, in a poor attempt at an English accent.

'Why thank you, kind sir,' she said, doing a better job of the accent. She sipped her drink before adding in the same voice, 'A cheeky little wine, full of oak and fruit flavours.'

Nancy laughed. 'You're so full of it!'

Mary felt relieved but there was more work to be done. Looking at the glass in her hand, she said to Ricky, 'This is very nice.'

He gave her a sheepish grin. 'They're our nicest set.'

It was the set she'd given them as a wedding gift and she felt chuffed they had bothered to use them today.

Nancy leant forward and clinked her glass against Mary's. Mary and Ricky followed suit. 'What are we toasting?' asked Ricky, looking a little bemused.

'What about, to old friends and happy times,' suggested Nancy.

She knew Nancy had spoken with feeling and it was a nice toast but Mary knew she still had a lot of work to do if she was going to pull this situation out of the fire. Taking the bull by the horns, she countered with, 'That sounds a little maudlin. What about–To Ricky, may he improve with practice!'

Nancy nearly choked, though Ricky took it in the spirit it was intended. With a wink, he said, 'It might take a lot of practice but I'm prepared for the sacrifice.'

With the mood a little brighter Nancy suggested they start lunch.

They chatted happily though the meal and the mood continued to brighten and Mary no longer jumped each time Ricky spoke. Afterwards Nancy gathered all the photos they had taken on the honeymoon. The three sat on the lounge and Mary viewed the parade of fantastic and the not so fantastic views of New Zealand. The not so fantastic photos appeared to be more as a result of poor photography than the subject material. She felt truly jealous as the happy couple re-lived the two weeks overseas. 'It all looks so lovely.'

'Oh it is!' said Nancy with feeling. 'We would still be there if we had the money.'

'You liked it that much?'

'I don't know that I'd actually move there but two weeks certainly was not enough.'

'And what about the people?' asked Mary, surprising herself with her interest.

Ricky laughed. 'Apart from the funny accents, they are great: really friendly and welcoming.'

Lunch was done, the photos were done and Ricky sensed it now time for him to leave the two women alone. 'If you two lovely ladies will excuse me, there are some things I need to be doing outside.'

Once he departed Mary turned to Nancy, 'Should you be helping? I can go if you have things to do?'

Nancy waved a hand in her friend's direction, 'Don't worry about it. All he'll be doing is having a beer and listening to the cricket on the radio.'

'Oh...' was all she said as she caught Nancy staring at the ugly scar in her eyebrow again. Nancy's eyes darted away and she felt it was time to explain. Without it, their relationship might never be the same. 'He does love me!' she said quietly but firmly.

'I'm sure he does.'

'He is handsome, witty and charming and I love him. Sometimes he gets angry but he is always sorry afterwards.'

'He treats you like a doormat!' Nancy looked flushed as though she regretted being so forthright. 'I am so sorry,' she said, suddenly teary. 'I shouldn't have said that to you!'

Mary was looking down at her lap as she spoke. 'It's OK, I probably deserved it.'

'No, you don't.' said Nancy. 'Don't you see, that's the whole point! You don't deserve any of this. It's not your fault; you haven't done anything wrong!'

Mary had tears of her own flowing now. 'My mother said I had to look after him better.'

Nancy was shouting now, as she said, 'Fuck your mother! You have done nothing wrong!'

Mary's mind was in a whirl. She liked Nancy, only how could she be right and Geoffrey and her mother both be wrong. Nothing was making sense. 'I think I should go.'

'No, I'm sorry. Please don't go, I shouldn't have said those things.' Then Nancy's jaw firmed. She stared straight at Mary as she told her, 'No, I was right! I'm sorry if it hurts but you have to hear the truth. Geoffrey has been abusing you and making you feel as though it's your fault. If your mother couldn't see that, then I am sorry for that too, but it doesn't change the facts. You need to do something about your marriage before he goes too far!'

'What do you mean, too far?'

'Look at your face,' said Nancy, through her tears. 'Look at the scars. You didn't have any of them three years ago. What if he hurts you permanently? What if he kills you?'

'He would never do that!'

'He might not do it deliberately but it could happen. What if you hit your head the wrong way? It happens all the time.' Nancy took a hold of her by the shoulders and shook her. Slowly and carefully, as though she was speaking to a child, she said, 'You can't let him hit you anymore! Do you hear me? You can't let him hit you anymore! You just can't.' Nancy drew Mary to her and they cried on each other's shoulder. 'Promise me!' Nancy whispered into her ear.

Mary had no reply; what could she say? Even if she said yes, what would it mean? She had no control over Geoffrey and now there was Frank as well. He hadn't hurt her physically, but surely it as only a matter of time! How did her life end up in such a mess? 'I really have to go,' was all she could bring herself to say.

Looking emotionally drained Nancy released her and followed listlessly to the front door. Here she brightened a little as she saw her new giraffes. Sniffing loudly, she said, 'They look perfect there, don't they?'

'I am glad you like them.' After a pause, she said, 'I'll call you.' It sounded ominously like a last farewell.

Nancy took her by the shoulders, before telling her, 'I'll give you one week.' Nancy's smile softened her words. 'If I haven't heard from you by then, I'll come looking for you!'

Mary turned to go before she hesitated. Turning back she gave her friend a kiss on the cheek. 'Thank you. I mean that, thank you for everything!'

Tears flowed steadily as Nancy watched Mary slowly walk away.

'Hey, Honey, what's the matter?' cried Ricky, concerned as she approached him.

'I'm just worried about Mary?' she said through her tears.

'I know what you mean, she's terrified of something.'

'That something is her husband!' spat Nancy with feeling. 'The prick beats her.'

Ricky felt his hands clench and unclench. 'Do you want me to go over and have a talk with him?'

Nancy knew it wasn't an idle threat. Her husband would do it if she said yes and she knew he didn't mean to *talk* with Geoffrey. He would beat the crap out of him. 'No, I don't think it would help.'

With his face turning red with anger, he said, 'Let me know if you change your mind.' He liked Mary and now that he understood her problem, he was feeling as angry as he possibly could. As a child he watched helplessly as his father beat his mother. When he got old enough and big enough, he put a stop to it, but by then it was too late. His mother's willingness to live was already broken. She was old before her time. She died soon after and Ricky still refused to speak to his father.

✲✲✲

By the time Geoffrey made it back to the bank it was already after three and he didn't think it was the right time to set up the meeting Chantelle had suggested. He was feeling exhausted after an afternoon with her and he wasn't in the mood to get caught up in a lengthy meeting. He'd have to be on his toes when he challenged the bank to find fault with what he'd done.

It was murder waiting for a new day but it had to be done. Mary helped by keeping out of his way. The last thing he needed tonight was to be worried about her. She served him his meal and they ate in silence. He poured himself a wine, while Mary drank water. He hadn't offered her any of the wine but after a time it annoyed him to watch her sipping her water. Didn't she have a tongue in her head? Couldn't she ask for a glass of wine without waiting for him to serve her like some sort of fucking waiter! God she could be so useless! 'What?' he suddenly demanded, making her jump.

'What is it, Dear?'

'If you're too stupid to know, I'm not going to fucking waste my time explaining it to you!' He stood up and took the rest of the bottle to his games room. Once he'd calmed down he realised none of it had been Mary's fault but he didn't go to her and apologise. He didn't want to look weak in front of her. They went to bed without speaking.

She had his breakfast ready in the morning and he complimented her on it even though it was only average. It was his way of apologising. Mary vindicated his thoughts by the way she preened at his compliment. Good, there was nothing else to be said.

Sitting at his desk he sipped coffee while he waited for what he judged would be the right time. It was Friday so he couldn't waste too much time, yet he didn't want to put them offside by hitting them with this too early. He wanted to give them the opportunity to take care of any urgent business that may have arisen overnight before dropping his bombshell.

Excitement coursed through his body. He'd lain awake most of the night thinking this over. As his ideas began to click together he began to wonder at the possibilities. He didn't bother too much with negative thoughts; he was far too much of an egotist for that. In his mind he saw them swallowing everything he told them.

Chantelle was right; the key was to turn defence into attack. Instead of waiting for them, he would hit them with his version of the facts. Once they thought they knew everything, there would be no reason for them to continue investigating and he would be free and clear with the money he'd stolen.

Ten o'clock ticked over and his hand reached for the phone. Ignoring his own manager, Geoffrey called Roberts's manager.

'Good morning, Mr. Christian's office, how may I help you?' came the polished tone of his secretary.

'Good morning, Deborah, it's Geoffrey Parker. Is Peter available to see me some time this morning?'

'Well hello, Geoffrey,' said Deborah replacing her polished tone with a friendlier one. Like many of the women who worked at the bank she'd had her eye on him for years. 'Let me see what I can do.' After a pause she asked casually, 'Is it important? His schedule is quite full today.'

'I don't like to be a bother but it is rather important. I think he will want to hear what I have to say.'

Deborah's eyebrows rose in surprise. She hadn't expected that reply. 'Give me a minute.' She pressed the hold button leaving Geoffrey listening to Elton John.

Poking her head into her boss's office she reverted to her polished voice as she said, 'I have Geoffrey Parker on the phone. He is asking to speak with you, says it is urgent. Do you want me to make room for him?'

Peter Christian looked up surprised. 'Parker, did you say?'

'Yes, Geoffrey Parker, from Futures.'

As was his custom, Peter held up one finger to indicate he was thinking and she was to wait. This was very interesting indeed! Peter knew all about the investigation and he knew someone would have to go as a result. So he was doing his best to distance himself from Roberts, trying to ensure it was the lower-level manager who took all the blame. Checking his watch he made a decision. 'Give me until ten-thirty, I'll see him then. And clear all my other appointments for this morning!'

'Yes, Sir.'

When the annoying music was suddenly replaced with Deborah's voice, Geoffrey felt his jaw muscles tighten. 'He'll see you at ten-thirty,' she told him in her official voice. Then dropping to a confidential whisper, she asked, 'Is everything OK? Is there anything I can help you with?'

Despite the grimness of the situation he smiled to himself as he remembered Deborah throwing herself at him one Christmas party. The older woman was still very attractive, with a full curvy figure. He made sure no-one was watching as he guided her out of the room. He spent a very pleasant night at her flat. She turned out to be a lot kinkier than he'd expected but he hadn't been interested enough to return. For her part, Deborah made sure he knew there was always an open invitation for him, any time he felt inclined. 'Everything is fine.'

'I'll see you at ten-thirty then.'

'Thank you, Deborah,' he said as he rang off, not wanting to waste any more time talking to her.

A B Given

CHAPTER 12

Peter Christian spent a few minutes deep in thought before he made his own phone call.

'Blake!' came the gruff rely.

'Hello, Mr. Blake, Peter Christian. My secretary just received a call from Geoffrey Parker asking to meet with me?'

'Did she just,' came the thoughtful rely. 'What did he say he wanted to talk to you about?'

'He didn't and I didn't want to put him off by pressing him,' lied Peter, kicking himself because he hadn't thought to ask.

'No matter. What have you done?'

'I told him to come up at ten-thirty.'

'Mmm! That gives me just under half an hour,' Blake said, in a tone that suggested Peter should have done better.

'Do you want me to change the time for a later on,' he offered, eager to be seen to be of assistance.

'As you say, we don't want to spook him now. I'll call you!'

Peter was about to reply when he realised the Security Manager had hung up on him. He sat there waiting for the phone to ring. It didn't. Instead, Deborah knocked softly on his door ten minutes later and introduced a stranger to him. 'Mr. Harvey to see you. Apparently you are expecting him,' she said in an uncertain tone.

'Did Wilson Blake send you?' asked Peter, from behind his large mahogany desk.

'That's right,' confirmed the young man before giving a meaningful glance in Deborah's direction. She had stayed slightly between the young stranger and her boss as though as a human shield, ready to protect him from any and all unwanted visitors.

'Thank you, Deborah, that will be all for now,' he said, dismissing her. Once the door was closed he asked in a dry tone, 'And you are?' He might have to suck up to

Wilson Blake and the top management but he didn't think this person warranted such special consideration.

Stepping forward the young man held out his hand. With an easy smile, he said, 'I'm Jonathan Castle and I have been reviewing the computer records for your department.'

'It's Roberts's department actually,' said Peter, in reflex.

'Either way, Mr. Blake thought I should come down and share with you what I've found so far. That way you can compare it with whatever Parker tells you.'

'I see,' said Peter, not sure if he did.

'Obviously we need to know if he is telling the truth or at least how much of it is true. If you know something about what he's been up to, Mr. Blake feels you should be able to make a determination,' said the young man, still smiling.

Peter nearly smiled himself. He was convinced Blake wouldn't give him this task if the bank blamed him for whatever is was Parker had been up to. He felt confident he'd managed to place all the blame onto Roberts. Poor Roberts, he didn't even know an investigation was taking place. 'Take a seat,' he said, feeling more congenially towards the young man.

Jonathan steeled himself in a chair opposite Peter. Placing his briefcase on the desk he opened it. Taking out several thickly stuffed manila folders he proceeded to work methodically through them. 'As you can see,' said the young man, as he repacked his briefcase, 'on the one hand we have quite a lot, whereas, on the other hand, we don't really know anything much at all.'

Despite the young man's poor choice of phraseology, Peter was forced to agree with him. Despite weeks of analysing old records they knew something was definitely wrong but they had yet to put their finger on it. They were hoping Parker had come to confess. It would make their job a lot easier if they knew what they were looking for.

Jonathan barely managed to depart before Geoffrey arrived, punctual as ever. He gave Deborah a wink she returned.

'I'll show you through,' she said. Smiling, she leant forward as she stood up, letting Geoffrey have a good look down her ample cleavage. She felt his eyes on her and she had to work hard to suppress her satisfied grin.

Geoffrey was trying equally hard to quiet his nerves and flirting with Deborah took his mind off what he was about to do. Besides, it was so easy with these older ones, all you had to do was look at them and they went weak at the knees. Despite the situation, he found himself wondering how far he could push her. What would she be willing to do? What could he make her do?

'Take a seat, Geoffrey, and tell me what's on your mind.'

Peter's voice broke through Geoffrey's thoughts, bringing him back to reality. Taking the same seat recently vacated by Jonathan, he placed his briefcase in almost the exact same place the other man had, before opening it and taking out number of manila folders.

Peter had to shake his head to clear it, so strong was the sense of déjà vu.

Geoffrey looked up with an expression he hoped portrayed honesty. 'Let me begin by stating I have always acted with the best interest of the bank in mind.'

'That sounds a little ominous.'

'I hope you will not be thinking that way when I've finished,' Geoffrey said as he began his tale, explaining it in a way that would hopefully leave the bank viewing his activities in the best possible light. He'd planned this methodically. He gave Peter just enough information to prove some of what he had been up to, while hoping it would be enough to satisfy them. 'As you can see,' he said, full of brash confidence, 'I'm more than capable of safely Trading outside the constrictive guidelines set down by Roberts.'

Peter looked a little stunned as he asked, 'So, what exactly are you suggesting?'

In a tone that suggested it should have been self-evident, Geoffrey said, 'That you get rid of Roberts and put me in charge of the Department.'

'You say you have been working alone on this?' asked Peter, steering the conversation down a different track.

'Absolutely. I wouldn't trust anyone else at this stage. Only once they have received tuition from me would I consider letting others follow my lead.'

'And this is everything you have done?' asked Peter, placing his hand on the pile of manila folders and sliding them closer to himself.

Geoffrey noticed the action but didn't bat an eyelid. Those files had been doctored to such an extent even he would have trouble sorting out the truth from the lies. They could have them and have their experts go over them as much as they liked, they wouldn't find much.

After a long pause Peter shook his head, saying, 'I honestly don't quite know what to say. Obviously you have given me a lot to think about. Leave these here with me and I'll have a look at them over the weekend and we can discuss this further on Monday.'

Feeling very pleased with his performance, Geoffrey stood up and shook Peter's hand. 'Thank you for listening to me and I appreciate the time you have given me.'

A feeling of euphoria came over him as he stepped into the outer office. He felt invincible: on top of the world. He truly believed he had pulled it off. He was sure he'd convinced Peter he'd done nothing wrong and soon his talents would be rewarded by being promoted to the Head of the Department. He saw Deborah looking at him and he made sure to close the door behind him. With a smug expression he moved to her side. She smiled as he leaned forward to look down her gaping blouse. He was convinced it was more tightly buttoned when he arrived. *The bitch is panting for it!*

As she stroked his thigh, she asked, 'Are you sure there isn't anything I can do for you?'

Normally he wouldn't have considered flirting with another woman like this but his head was spinning so fast he was having trouble focusing his thoughts. For three years he had been content with just Chantelle and his wife; now seemed the perfect time to extend his range of enjoyment. Bending low he licked her ear before whispering throatily, 'That depends...are you prepared to do as you're told?'

Deborah's chest felt so tight she was having difficulty breathing. She knew she shouldn't be allowing this to happen here. What if someone walked in and saw Geoffrey licking her ear? How could she explain it? Peter had made the occasional half-hearted pass at her but she'd spurned his attempts to provoke her. If he saw her now he might even have her replaced. She should tell him to stop! Instead she turned her mouth to his and they kissed. Geoffrey found one of her nipples and twisted it painfully. In response Deborah slid her tongue into his mouth, groaning in pleasure at the pain.

'If things work out the way I want, I'll need to celebrate and I might enjoy having some fun with you,' he told her, in his high-handed way. 'Do you have any plans for next week?'

'Some.'

'Cancel them. I may need you at short notice.'

Deborah could feel the power in him and she wilted. Looking like a starry-eyed schoolgirl, she said, 'I'll be waiting for you.'

To further exert his power over her, he told her, 'When I arrive, I expect you to be completely naked.'

'I'll be ready!' she assured him breathlessly.

As Geoffrey walked to the door an image of Deborah tied to her bed as he whipped her came into his head. He turned and asked her, 'Do you own a leather riding crop?'

The suddenness of the question, with all the connotations it threw up, sent Deborah's body shaking uncontrollably. 'No,' she said, her voice no more than a squeak.

'Buy one!' He turned and left.

Deborah knew it was madness. He wasn't that good she should allow herself to be used like this. Only he was–he was! With a shaking hand she reached for the Yellow Pages and looked up equestrian suppliers.

***

Peter sat for a long time thinking about his meeting with Geoffrey. It was this that saved his secretary's reputation. By the time he picked up Geoffrey's manila folders and walked into the outer office, Deborah was talking to someone on the phone, the Yellow Pages spread out in front of her. 'I am going up to see Wilson Blake. Hold all my calls until I get back.'

Deborah didn't even hear him. She was too engrossed in her conversation with a young man with a nice sounding voice at the equestrian store.

Peter caught the lift to the seventeenth floor and knocked respectfully on Wilson Blake's door before entering. Blake didn't bother to acknowledge Peter's greeting, instead he stood up and walked through the door Peter had just entered. 'Come on, we're going up stairs,' he called back over his shoulder.

Startled, Peter followed lamely behind as Blake bounded up a private set of stairs linking the seventeenth floor with the eighteenth. Peter's heart was pounding but not from the exertion of trying to keep up with Blake, who despite his age was racing up the stairs two at a time. The eighteenth floor was a mysterious place few ever visited: even managers of his level. The eighteenth floor only had three occupants. Strictly speaking it held a lot more than that, but the others were only there to serve the important three. Sir Godfrey Winstanley was the bank's Chairman and he shared his domain with Michael O'leary and Patrick Mason-Grey.

Peter had been here before but not under these circumstances. He'd been invited on three occasions to make personal reports and once he'd even reported directly to the Board. Now he was fighting to save his job and he knew it.

Peter's own office was large compared to friends of his but it was nothing compared to the opulent use of space this floor represented in a crowed city. The Boardroom, with its accompanying rooms, took up fully one-third of the entire floor.

The other two thirds were divided unevenly between the three other occupants. Michael O'Leary and Patrick Mason-Grey had office suits of roughly the same size, where they and their assistants worked. Sir Winstanley's suite reflected his position within the Bank. It was into this cavernous space, with its imposing and intimidating dark timber panelling and its massive timber desk, cleared of any obstructions, including a computer, making it look twice its actual size, that Peter entered.

One wall was made of glass with a view over most of the City and its beautiful harbor, but Peter saw none of it. His eyes were glued to the tall, aged man with the aristocratic bearing sitting behind the desk. It was only when Blake did the introductions that Peter even noticed the other two men sitting off to one side.

Michael O'Leary assisted Sir Winstanley in looking after the Australian operations, while Patrick Mason-Grey was responsible for the overseas operations, reporting directly to Sir Winstanley, of course. Between them and the substantial Board they controlled every aspect of the bank, and they were not happy.

Peter swallowed convulsively as he mumbled his greetings and took the indicated chair. He noted Blake move away leaving him singled out, feeling small and alone while confronted with the three most powerful men at the bank. He sat quietly, looking like a naughty schoolboy in the Headmasters Office, while Blake gave Sir Winstanley an update.

'Then, to our surprise, Parker contacted Peter this morning asking for a meeting. I had him updated on the latest information we had so he could compare it with what Parker had to say,' said Blake, finishing his report.

All eyes then turned to Peter and he could feel himself shrivel under their combined stare.

'So, what did our Mr. Parker have to say for himself?' asked Sir Winstanley, in his usual brisk tone.

Peter was glad he had taken those few minutes back in his office to think before coming up to see Blake. He hadn't been expecting any of this and he would have looked a complete fool if he didn't have some kind of a response ready. Speaking in a clear voice, with a confidence he didn't feel, he began to recite Geoffrey's claims. He didn't bother to open the files. These men were not interested in such details. That would be for their underlings. It would be their job to pour through the files, checking, comparing and analysing every word and every figure they contained with other known and assumed facts, looking for points of confirmation and areas of discrepancy.

As Peter wound up, Sir Winstanley demanded, 'And your assessment of the situation?'

'I have no doubt he has done it. In fact, he is very proud of what he has done. The man is a complete megalomaniac. He fully believes we are going to get rid of Roberts and promote him to his position.'

'He is right about one thing,' confirmed Sir Winstanley, 'Roberts is gone. However, we do not reward wilful disobedience, nor do we reward incompetence.'

Peter was starting to feel slightly less intimidated until he heard the last statement. He took it as a warning that his position at the bank was tenuous at best.

'What do you think of his claim that he was working alone?' shot out Sir Winstanley.

Peter almost jumped. 'I think it is credible, Sir,' he said without really thinking about it.

'Why?' demanded Sir Winstanley.

Peter could feel sweat running down his back and he wiped his brow before he answered. 'I believe him when he said he didn't trust anyone else to do what he was doing. As I've said, the man is a complete megalomaniac. He thinks he is indestructible, infallible if you will. I just don't see him trusting others with his precious plan.'

Sir Winstanley nodded absently as he thought over Peter's words. 'Thank you, we will be in touch.'

'Thank you, Sir,' said Peter as he stood up to leave. He desperately wanted to say something that would elevate himself in their eyes before he left but nothing came to him. He felt their eyes on him as he walked out on his own.

'What do you think?' asked Sir Winstanley after Peter had departed.

'It is difficult to know for sure before we go through those files and see what he has put together for us. It might just be that he is telling the truth,' replied Blake.

'But you don't believe it?' commented Michael, speaking for the first time.

'Let's just say, I like to keep an open mind.'

Michael nodded thoughtfully, before asking, 'So you think there are others involved?'

'I have a man planted in there and he is convinced of it.'

'Any names so far?' asked Sir Winstanley.

'I can supply you with a complete report if you like,' offered Blake. 'But it seems likely they are taking orders from Parker. He is the brains behind it all. I'm not too worried about them at this stage. When we have a better idea of what they've been up to, it will pay to get them in for a little chat. They're more likely to break than Parker.'

'Do you think that is why he doesn't want us to know about them?' asked Michael, finding his voice again.

'Oh yes,' confirmed the Head of Security. 'I doubt very much that Parker is in any way attempting to protect them. He is more worried about what they will say to us.'

'You don't like him, do you?' slipped in Patrick Mason-Grey.

Blake turned to face him, pausing before saying, 'I have yet to meet him in person, but no, I do not like him. He is arrogant and selfish. He thinks rules are for other people, people not as clever as he.'

'Do you think those files contain what he's really up to?'

'I would seriously doubt it.'

'Well that's good enough for me,' said Sir Winstanley, wrapping up the meeting. 'Get your people to go through these and we'll see what we have.' Then almost as an afterthought, he asked, 'When do you think you should be able to meet with him.'

'My men have the rest of today and the weekend. Monday morning they should be able to tie up any loose ends. I can book a meeting with him for Monday.'

Sir Winstanley waited until Wilson Blake had left before turning to his two main advisers. Some things couldn't even be said in front of a trusted employee like Blake. 'What do you think?'

'It is difficult to say right now but I think we should start making contingency plans. We don't want this to get out of hand,' said Michael O'Leary. 'I think this is much more than just a case of an employee disobeying bank protocols. A situation like this could have far reaching implications. With the state of the economy, such as it is, the last thing the bank needs is to be seen as unsteady. We have always been known as rock-solid, but I have seen how rumours can take hold. All it would take was for someone to add two and two and get three. This could be seen by some that we were taking unnecessary risks, which would make them wonder why. The next thing there would be rumours that we were in trouble and trying desperate measures to save ourselves. This Parker may have unwittingly placed our reputation as a reliable institution in great jeopardy. The flow on implications could be disastrous.'

Sir Winstanley nodded in agreement before turning to his adviser on international matters. 'What do you say, Patrick?'

'I agree with everything Michael has said. I can only add that internationally the effect could be even worse. To many overseas we are still an unknown. We don't have the long-standing reputation we enjoy here in Australia, and first impressions can be lasting. If the first thing others hear about us is we have a rogue trader working for us, sanctioned or not, it could take a very long time to repair the damage. If the news gets out, no matter what we do or say, many will believe Parker acted with our blessing and we hung him out to dry when things turned sour.

Sir Winstanley sat deep in thought for a time. This Parker had created a great deal of potential trouble for the bank and it was his responsibility to ensure none if it came to fruition. 'I see three things,' said Sir Winstanley suddenly. 'One, Parker has to go, no matter what. We have to make an example of him so others won't be tempted to disobey bank guidelines in the future.

Two, we need to keep this as quiet as possible, which does make the first point more difficult, yet I believe our reputation is paramount.' He paused for a moment while his two advisers nodded in agreement.

'Three, we must discover the full extent of what he has been up to.'

'I completely agree,' said Michael. 'I suggest we hit him as hard as possible and try to break him. We need to know exactly what he's done. No fairy-tales this time; we need the truth so we can guard against it. The last thing we need is for little surprises to keep popping up. If we don't, sooner or later one of them will bite us.'

With an agreement reached they set about planning how to accomplish their aims.

CHAPTER 13

When Peter Christian returned to his office he found it unattended. There was a note on his desk from his secretary.
Peter,
I am sorry but I had to duck out for a short time. Hope it doesn't cause you too much inconvenience.
Deborah.

'Too much inconvenience?' he shouted to no-one. 'Of course it's a bloody inconvenience, you stupid woman! I need you here.'

Slumping to his desk he held his head in his hands while he wondered what he would do if the bank let him go.

While Peter sat with his head in his hands, wallowing in despair, Deborah was having the time of her life with the young man with the nice voice. Nathan turned out to be a cheeky lad who easily guessed at her intentions and was having some fun at her expense. Picking out a crop from the display case he ran his hand along the shaft as he smiled at her. 'This one feels very nice on the skin.'

Deborah was so excited by Geoffrey's sudden change in his attentions towards her that her natural inhibitions deserted her. Giggling like a schoolgirl, she cooed, 'Money is no object. I'm more interested in one that will do the job...properly.'

The kid eyed her over, making sure she saw him. 'I would willingly help you find out which works the best, if it's any help?'

'I bet you would!' giggled Deborah. 'But I think that one will do,' she said, indicating to the one he was holding.

Nathan was passed just having some idle fun. This woman was having an effect on him, one he had never experienced before. In a serious tone, he asked, almost begged, 'Are you sure I can't be of service?' He hoped he hadn't gone too far. The last thing he wanted was for the woman to make a complaint, yet, for a reason he couldn't explain, he needed her to know how he felt.

Smiling at the boy, Deborah placed one of her perfectly manicured hands on his shoulder, as she softly said, 'I appreciate the offer but I am old enough to be your mother.' With a wink, she advised him, 'I think it would be more fun if you found someone closer to your own age.' All the same, she made a show of taking a business card with his name on it.

Nathan took her money and let her go, unsure how to make her realise the feelings she had aroused in him.

* * *

Geoffrey was sitting at his desk preparing to finish for the day. He'd talked with Chantelle and managed to get a message to Brett whom he hoped had passed it onto the others. It was a simple message. 'I've taken all the blame so they shouldn't even know you are involved. Just hold tight and don't do anything silly and everything will be alright.'

He smiled to himself when he remembered how relieved Brett looked when he told him he had accepted full responsibility, denying anyone else was involved. Brett thanked him so many times it was pathetic. Brett actually thought he did it for their sakes. He couldn't see he had done it because he didn't trust them. Besides, if everything worked out as he hoped, he would be left to claim all the glory for himself.

Yes, things were working out just fine!

Now the first wave of euphoria was wearing off, he started to have second thoughts about Deborah. He was soon to become a Manager; should he be having that sort of a relationship with a mere secretary? She did promise to be an interesting evening, so maybe just one wouldn't hurt. If he enjoyed it there were plenty of low-level female managers to choose from. He felt confident he could find one willing to play any sort of game with him.

The phone interrupted his mental plans. Picking it up he found Peter Christian on the other end.

'Just want to give you some advance notice. A meeting has been organised for Monday afternoon where you can put your case directly to Sir Winstanley.'

Geoffrey knew most people at the bank would be quivering with fear at the suggestion but he was bigger than them. He relished an opportunity to tackle the great man. 'That's wonderful. Thank so much, Peter, for organising this so quickly.'

'No trouble at all, Geoffrey. Now you have a good weekend and I'll see you Monday.'

Peter disconnected from Parker and looked at his phone. 'Stupid prat!' Normally he didn't finish on Friday until late, and even though he was now well behind on his work, he packed his briefcase and headed home. On the way out he noticed Deborah was yet to return. He thought about leaving her a note, then left without doing so. If she wasn't there to know what was happening it was her fault, not his.

Geoffrey understood it wasn't really Peter who had made this happen so quickly. There were people at the bank who at least suspected what he was up to. What surprised him was the fact Sir Winstanley himself was involved. Surely this proved his plan had worked. Sir Winstanley wouldn't be involved if they were simply going to dismiss him. Maybe, just maybe, they were so impressed with what he had shown Christian they were going to promote him even higher than Roberts's position. He tried in vain to get a grip on his imagination. 'Don't get ahead of yourself, boy,' he told himself over and over again.

Just before he left for the day he called Deborah.

'Oh, hello,' she purred into the phone.

'Deborah I need to know what Peter thinks of what I showed him earlier. Did he say anything to you?'

'He was very impressed,' she said trying her best to please him. 'I know he looked at it for a while before taking it upstairs.'

Geoffrey could hardly believe it; it was true. In his mind Deborah's comments confirmed it all. Everything was working out exactly as he'd hoped. 'You're sure he liked what he saw?' he demanded again, seeking further assurance.

'I can have a look through his private files for you, if you like?'

Geoffrey was horrified. He didn't know Peter had left for the day and the last thing he needed now was some sex mad old bitch getting caught looking through his private files and messing everything up. 'No, I am sure everything is fine. Don't do anything,' he told her firmly.

'Guess where I've just been?' she asked without realising she was talking to a dial tone. Shaking the handpiece as though it would reconnect her, she sighed angrily. Geoffrey could be so inconsiderate at times. He was lucky he was so good looking or she would never let him do what he promised to do to her.

Geoffrey was walking away towards the lift when Frank approached him. 'Ready for a few drinks?'

'Actually, no, not tonight.'

Frank's jaw dropped in surprise. 'Surely you can come for a couple?'

Geoffrey still didn't know what role Frank was playing but he didn't want to get friendly with the man, especially not now. Now wasn't the time to let something slip. 'I have something planned,' he said, turning his back on the other man.

Frank grabbed him by the shoulder and pulled him around. 'Come on, just a couple of drinks.'

Geoffrey looked down his nose at him as though he was something a dog had just deposited on the floor. 'I have already told you, no! If getting drunk is so important to you, I am sure there are many like you in any hotel. Have a drink with any of them,' he said, loud enough for anyone close to hear. He heard a satisfying titter of laughter coming from somewhere to his left. Frank obviously heard it too because he turned bright red.

Looking angry now, Frank said in a low tone, 'There are things you need to know!'

The lift door opened and Geoffrey stepped inside. Facing Frank, he said in his most supercilious voice, 'It is too late, Frank, I already know everything.'

When Geoffrey arrived he found Mary sitting patiently waiting at the dining room table. Her make-up was fixed, she was wearing a nice dress and their meals were in the oven. The fact he hadn't been home on Friday night for dinner in weeks didn't matter to him. He expected Mary to be prepared and she was; everything was as it should be.

'Hello!' cried Mary excitedly as she ran to him. 'You're home early tonight,' she said, without a hint of reproach in her voice for the nights when he wasn't.

'I've had the most wonderful day and I want to share tonight with my wife!' he announced grandly as though he was doing her a great favour.

'The dinner is ready. Do you want me to open a bottle of wine?' she asked, beginning to share his in sense of excitement.

'No, we are going out!'

'Where?'

'Does it matter?' he said in his usual way of answering her questions with one of his own.

'Only so that I can decide what to wear,' she explained.

Geoffrey eyed her over. He grinned. 'You look beautiful exactly as you are!'

Mary blushed, not used to such compliments. Giggling like a schoolgirl she allowed Geoffrey to guide her to the car. As they drove down the street, neither of them recognised Frank's car parked a little down the street.

***

The lift door closed and Geoffrey disappeared from view. Frank was frantic. He had to have Mary. He had to have her tonight! Knowing how stupidly he was acting he caught the next lift and followed Geoffrey home. Frank knew he was playing a dangerous game and the stakes were high. But Mary was like a drug to him. He needed her; he needed to control her.

He followed Geoffrey home and parked where he could watch the house and yet not be easily seen. He was working out his plan of action when the garage door began to roll up again. To his dismay Geoffrey drove off with Mary sitting alongside him.

Frank couldn't believe it. Geoffrey did have something planned for tonight! But what about his plans, he'd been working on them all week. He'd even gone to the trouble to source out someone who could sell him a small vial of a clear odourless liquid. The drug was used in date rapes. It could be easily introduced into someone's drink and within half an hour they would be out for the night. He planned to slip some into Geoffrey's drink once they were back here. That would give him the whole night alone with Mary. They wouldn't have to stay hidden away tonight. He would have the freedom to do what he wanted, where he wanted. He was the one who had plans!

He was a shattered man as he watched Geoffrey's car disappear around the next corner. All the planning he'd done for tonight just went up in smoke. For a few wild moments he thought about breaking into the house and waiting for them to come home. Those thoughts didn't last long. He was a trained professional and he knew there was little chance he could do anything tonight that wouldn't get him sacked or arrested.

In frustration he took out the small glass vial out of his pocket and threw it out of the car window. He watched with satisfaction as it smashed on the road. The momentary elation he felt was quickly replaced by the realisation he might still have found a use for it another time.

* * *

Mary was having a wonderful evening. Geoffrey was his most charming self, showering her with compliments. Mindful to keep the facts vague he told her how Sir Winstanley himself had asked for a meeting with him on Monday. 'I think they are very impressed with the work I have been doing lately.' Tapping the side of his nose with his forefinger, he added, 'I wouldn't be surprised if they offer me a Manager's position Monday.'

'Oh that would be wonderful!' she cried. 'It's about time they recognised how important you are to them.'

'This certainly has been a big week. Chantelle's painting sold and I am to finally get my promotion.' The mention of her sister-in-law's name dimmed a little of the excitement she was feeling. Then he nearly ruined her night completely. 'Did I mention we are going over to Robert's again tomorrow night?'

'No, you didn't.'

When Geoffrey saw her face, he said sternly, 'Now don't sulk. I don't want you spoiling my night with your silliness.'

'I'm sorry, Dear,' she said, forcing herself to smile.

While the rest of the evening was perfect, Mary had to struggle to regain her former good mood. Two Saturday nights in a row with Chantelle was not what she needed right now.

To force herself to be cheerful, for Geoffrey's sake, she looked on the positive side. Frank was nowhere to be seen and his name hadn't been mentioned all night. Just maybe he was on the outer for some reason. She knew her husband could be fickle with his friends. One day they couldn't do a thing wrong and then for some unexplained reason they were never mentioned again. Mary hoped Frank had said or done something to upset her husband and he had taken him off his list of friends.

When Geoffrey escorted her to the small dance floor her remaining worries drifted away, at least for the time being. Geoffrey couldn't have been more attentive and she revelled in it. Later, she felt so grateful she willing dressed in the ridiculous cowgirl outfit and showed him how much she appreciated the wonderful evening.

* * *

'Come on, wake up!'

Hearing her husband's voice Mary struggled to rouse herself from the deep sleep she was in. She felt groggy and wondered how much she had drunk the night before. 'I'm sorry, Dear, I'll have your breakfast ready in no time.'

'Open your eyes.'

It was his tone more than the words that caught Mary's attention. Even in her dazed state the tender benevolence in his voice surprised her. When she finally looked up at him, she found Geoffrey was standing next to the bed with a tray loaded with breakfast things.

Smiling happily, he told her, 'I have already made breakfast!'

At first she didn't know what to do. Geoffrey had never made her breakfast before, let alone served it to her in bed. Not even when she came first back from the hospital. Working her way into a sitting position she propped herself up with a couple of pillows. Geoffrey waited patiently for her and placed the tray in her lap. Slipping around the bed he climbed in next to her.

Mary stared at the tray in disbelief. There were two cups of coffee, a plate of gently browned toast, a tub of margarine and two jars: one jar of marmalade and one of strawberry jam. All her devotion and all her trust in him now seemed justified by this one simple act. Turning to Geoffrey, she kissed him. 'Thank you so much,' she said, feeling a little teary.

'Well come on, butter the toast before it goes cold.'

Buttering a slice of toast she loaded it heavily with marmalade, just the way Geoffrey liked it. Handing it to him she buttered a second for herself. This she gave a light covering of the strawberry jam. Munching on her toast she couldn't remember ever being so happy. She had re-established her friendship with Nancy and Geoffrey was acting as she had always hoped he would. Last night had been so wonderful and this morning he'd gone one step further. Even the shadow of Frank seemed to have been lifted.

Geoffrey noticed the smile on her lips and asked light-heartedly, 'What are you grinning at?'

'I am just feeling rather pleased with myself today,' she answered with a giggle. She couldn't remember when she had giggled and laughed so much. She seemed to have been doing it a lot since Thursday. 'What shall we do today?' she suddenly asked. 'I don't feel like sitting at home today, do you?'

Geoffrey thought about her suggestion for a moment, 'We could go to the pictures this afternoon. There is one on at the moment I wouldn't mind seeing.'

Mary didn't even both to ask what the film was; she didn't care. Geoffrey wanted to see it and she wanted to go out; what else did she need to know. 'That sounds wonderful.'

Geoffrey finished his first piece of toast and Mary buttered him another. It was risky but Mary felt buoyed enough to ask, 'What was Frank going to do last night?'

'Him!' snorted Geoffrey. 'All the man can think about is drinking. I think he has a real problem there.'

Geoffrey's tone told Mary all she needed to know. Frank was definitely on the outer. She didn't have to worry about him ever turning up at the house again. A sense of contentment washed over her. *Life doesn't get any better than this!*

* * *

Mary had such a lovely day that even the prospect of going to Robert and Chantelle's for dinner didn't dampen her spirits. Looking through her wardrobe she decided not to bother worrying about what Chantelle would say. After all, it didn't matter anyway. Chantelle would belittle her no matter what she wore. Slipping into the first nice dress she came across she applied a light layer of makeup and was ready.

'Do you know if there will be anyone else there tonight?' she asked, trying to sound as casual as possible. What she really wanted to know was if the artistic Nadia and the unemployable Rupert would be there but she didn't dare be so obvious.

'I'm not sure,' he answered absent-mindedly as he concentrated on his driving. Geoffrey didn't like to talk when he was driving. He said no-one else seemed to understand the road rules as well as he did so he had to continually be on his guard. According to him all other drivers were idiots who should be banned from the roads.

Parking on the precarious parking bay Geoffrey took her by the hand as they walked to the house. Even after everything else that had happened in the last twenty-four hours, she was taken aback. Geoffrey usually seemed so preoccupied when he was at his brother's house. She knew he was secretly jealous of Robert's success. Geoffrey was doing well at the bank but his brother owned his own business and one that was very successful. She attributed Geoffrey's distant mood towards her, whenever they were here, to his jealousy of his brother.

Geoffrey had barely pressed the bell when Robert answered it. 'Come in, come in,' he said happily.

'Hello, Robert,' said Geoffrey, stiffly.

Robert gave Mary a quick, almost shy kiss on the cheek before leading them down the stairs to where Chantelle awaited them.

Chantelle waited for Geoffrey to come to her before throwing her arms around him and kissing him. 'Hello, Geoffrey.'

As Geoffrey extricated himself from her grasp Chantelle glanced passed him and a look of surprise came over her face as she saw Mary waiting patiently at the base of the stairs. 'Hello,' she said in an amused tone.

She was so used to Chantelle's antics now she was becoming immune to her. In a flat, even voice, she said, 'Hello, Chantelle.' To Mary's delight Chantelle seemed piqued when she didn't get flustered the way she usually did.

Quickly turning away from her, Chantelle glared at Robert. 'Where is the champagne?'

'Coming right up,' he said as he turned and sped to the kitchen.

She wished for once Robert would tell Chantelle to get it herself, though she doubted it would ever happen. Poor Robert, he was completely under her thumb.

In no time at all Robert returned carrying a tray with four sparkling glasses. He handed them around before taking the last for himself.

'So?' asked Geoffrey. 'What are we celebrating?'

'Don't ask me,' said Robert with a laugh. 'Even I don't know. Chantelle is being very mysterious about the whole thing.'

Chantelle took the opportunity to move to one side where she would be the focus of attention, then paused for effect before she spoke. 'My painting sold!' she finally blurted out.

'That is wonderful!' cried Robert.

'When did all this happen?' asked Geoffrey, as he gave her another kiss. 'I told you it was good, didn't I!'

The two men babbled on about how wonderful she was and how marvellous it was that her painting sold. No-one took any notice of Mary as she stood to one side with a puzzled expression. Robert obviously didn't know Chantelle's painting had sold and Geoffrey seemed as surprised as his brother when Chantelle made her announcement, yet she was positive Geoffrey had mentioned it last night. It didn't make any sense. How could Geoffrey have known and Robert not? And if he knew, why did he pretend just now he didn't? Maybe she had only imagined it? Surely that must be it! She was having such a wonderful time last night, when Geoffrey mentioned they were coming here tonight, and her mind must have made the connection. That had to be it! She did her best to convince herself it was true but in the back of her head a lingering doubt persisted.

She remained quiet through the meal but that wasn't anything unusual. Geoffrey and Chantelle always dominated the conversation. She and Robert seemed to be there only to make up the numbers...and to serve, of course.

As the meal drew to an end Chantelle was telling Geoffrey about her newest project. 'Would you like a sneak preview?'

'I'd love one,' he said, sounding pleased to be asked. The pair traipsed off seemingly oblivious to the fact they were leaving Robert and Mary to clean up after them.

Robert gave Mary an apologetic shrug as he started to gather some of the plates together. 'It seems we aren't invited,' he said, trying to make it sound like a joke.

She could tell he was hurt by not being asked to join Chantelle and his brother in the studio on the lower floor. 'I don't like her paintings anyway,' she whispered, in a mock confidential manner, trying her best to make Robert feel better.

In turn, he smiled back. 'Neither do I, really. I don't understand what others see in them!'

'Come on,' she suggested. 'Let's clean these up and then we can make some coffee.'

Mary and Robert didn't talk very much as they worked, yet they both sensed a feeling of shared camaraderie. It was as if they were so comfortable in each other's presence they didn't need to talk to communicate. Besides, there were many things they both wanted to leave unsaid. They were related by marriage. There was no point exploring their mutual desires or their common aspirations. They felt dominated by their partners, yet loved them to the point of exclusion of other possibilities. In another time and place they might have been more than friends and in-laws but that now could never be, so why torture themselves. The only physical contact they permitted themselves was a chaste kiss on the cheek as they met.

A B Given

CHAPTER 14

Chantelle stopped halfway down the stars to turn and face Geoffrey. Slipping her arms around him she kissed him passionately. The thought that Robert and Mary were only metres away excited her. She longed to tell them; confident in the fact their partners were too weak to do anything about it. In her mind she pictured Robert and Mary waiting patiently while she took Geoffrey off to bed. She had no doubt the pair were mousy enough to do as they were told. When their spirits had been completely broken, Chantelle would make them watch. Her body tingled with excitement as she mentally pictured her husband and the dishrag sitting on the lounge while Geoffrey and she made love on the rug in front of them. She would beg Geoffrey to do all the things she had denied her husband, just to show him how little she really thought of him.

She felt Geoffrey responding as her tongue explored his mouth. 'I need you!' she breathed into his ear.

Geoffrey slid a hand under her top and fondled her breast. 'We haven't enough time.'

She lifted her top over her head and caste it aside. Not wearing a bra she pulled his mouth to her breast. As he sucked on her nipple, she implored him, 'Please, Geoffrey, take me here...now!'

Chantelle was standing topless only just out of sight of someone on the next level. She knew if Robert or Mary were to come to the top of the stairs for any reason they would see them and the thought was making her incredibly horny. She had planned to go to her studio and have sex on her sofa as they normally did; now she changed her plans. Dropping to her knees she smiled up at Geoffrey as she opened his trousers.

'Not here!' But his protests ceased the moment her mouth closed around him. She had him in her grip and she wasn't likely to let him go, not until she was ready. Held in her grasp he ran his fingers though her hair as her head bobbed up and down. 'Shh,' he cautioned her when the sounds of her sucking became unnecessarily loud.

She once made the mistake of telling him of her plans for Robert and Geoffrey had been shocked. He refused outright to take part in her scheme. To her it was only an inconvenience. Geoffrey would come around in time. She was hoping someone, if not both of them, would discover them in this compromising position. The excessive sucking sounds she was making were serving her ends.

To her chagrin, Geoffrey reached his orgasm without them being discovered. She wasn't finished yet though. Taking a hold of his arm she half-dragged him down the stairs. Quickly slipping out of the rest of her clothes she helped Geoffrey to remove his. Then just as expertly she brought Geoffrey to another erection. Satisfied, she let him take over. Geoffrey pulled her back by her hair, forcing her to bend backwards over the padded arm of the leather lounge. As she called out encouragements, he took her. When her cries of ecstasy began to get too loud, he held a hand over her mouth to quiet her. Chantelle's eyes shone with merriment, knowing she was unsettling him with her calls. She bit his finger but he only twisted his hand around so they were clear of her teeth while keeping her mouth clamped shut.

They were still dressing when Robert called from the top of the stairs, 'Come on you two, coffee's ready!'

'Coming,' replied Geoffrey. Chantelle was still topless. 'Come on, you can't go up like that!' he said, sounding a little irritated now with her antics.

'I can't find my top.'

'Oh-my-God,' said Geoffrey as he raced to the stairs. Looking up he saw Chantelle's top lying across the bannister in plain view of anyone at the top. 'Do you think Robert saw it?'

With a smile on her lips, she asked, 'Does it matter if he did?'

'Please tell me you didn't leave it there on purpose?'

His attitude was starting to annoy her again. What she did in her own house was up to her, not him! 'What if I did?' she said, challenging him.

Shaking his head in silent disapproval he crept up the stairs until he could reach her top. He tossed it back to her, whispering, 'Put this on and please behave yourself.'

Chantelle merely giggled as she struggled into it. Tossing her hair from side to side she challenged him, 'Make me!'

'For God's sake, Chantelle, please be serious!'

'I am!' She smiled, enjoying the feeling of power she felt over him at this moment.

'I am warning you,' he said, as he turned and climbed to the next level.

Robert was sitting at the head of the table with Mary to his left. Geoffrey sat next to Robert on his right side, keeping Chantelle at least one seat away from her husband. Desperate not to give Chantelle an opportunity, he asked Robert about his pet project. 'How is the three-quarter boat going?'

Robert gave a sheepish grin, assuming his brother was going to rib him about the unsuccessful venture again. Geoffrey seemed to take delight whenever one of Robert's ideas didn't work out as well as he'd hoped. The three-quarter boat, as Robert affectionately called it, had been a spectacular failure to date. 'I'm slowly ironing out some of the bugs.'

'What have you been trying?'

Robert was preparing to be evasive but his brother's tone caught him unprepared. Geoffrey genuinely sounded interested. There was none of the usual sarcasm in his voice. 'We changed the angle of the propeller arm and that seems to have helped,' he found himself saying.

'Has that let it plane?'

The biggest problem with Robert's new design was that the boat wouldn't plane: that is, it wouldn't ride smoothly over the top of the water at full throttle. 'No, not yet,' admitted Robert, pleased and surprised at Geoffrey's level of interest. 'We also tried different V configurations for the hull and we're having some success there. A wider V at the stern seems to be helping but we have also discovered we can go too wide, which suggests it isn't the only problem.'

The two brothers continued to discuss the difficulties with Robert's project. Now they had started, Geoffrey found himself fascinated by the problem and was putting his mind to finding a solution. With nothing in common to talk about Mary and Chantelle were left looking at each other across the table.

Mary noticed Chantelle no longer wearing any lipstick. She was positive her sister-in-law had been wearing a bright shade of red earlier. She wasn't overly interested in the mystery, it was more that she had nothing else to do at the moment. Without realising it she found herself staring at Chantelle's face.

Chantelle became aware of Mary's attentions and of the puzzled frown. *If only you knew!* she thought to herself. Then another thought come to her. *Why shouldn't you know?* The more Chantelle thought about it the more she liked the idea. Geoffrey had been quite firm about her telling Robert but he hadn't said anything about Mary. She knew she was splitting hairs because she hadn't suggested telling Mary. Still...? If the dishrag figured it out all by herself, Geoffrey could hardly blame her, could he? Of course the dishrag was far too stupid to actually figure it out on her own, so she'd have to give her a push in the right direction. This way Geoffrey couldn't be angry with her and, if he was, she could deny she had done it deliberately. After all, surely a dishrag like her couldn't believe a man like Geoffrey would be satisfied with just her.

Within seconds she'd come up with a plan.

She placed a hand on Geoffrey's shoulder and began to gently stroke it. While neither Geoffrey nor Robert took any notice, she saw Mary's eyes move to watch her hand. She allowed her fingers to run over a patch of red on his collar. It was the remnants of her lipstick. Patiently she waited for Mary to look back at her face. When Mary did, she pulled back slightly so she was hidden from Robert's view. Staring straight into Mary's eyes she ran her tongue over her lips. When Mary's puzzled frown deepened, Chantelle shaped her lips into a round circle while making a silent sucking action with her cheeks. As a look of horror came over Mary's face, Chantelle leant against Geoffrey's back, stroking him possessively. Looking back at Mary, she mouthed, *He's mine!*

The penny finally dropped and Mary couldn't believe she hadn't seen it earlier. It all made sense now: Geoffrey's attitude towards her whenever Chantelle was around, and the fact he'd known her painting had sold before even Robert knew. They were having an affair. With her mind running at a fever pitch, she wondered how long it had been going on. Geoffrey was engrossed in his discussion with Robert but surely he must know it was Chantelle who was leaning on him and caressing him that way. It looked an action born out of long association and familiarity. It had become so familiar it wasn't even registering on his conscious mind.

She felt like screaming but her voice wouldn't come. She wanted to run but her muscles deserted her, leaving her with no option but to stare into the face of evil. Chantelle stared back with a gloating expression. Mary now knew why Chantelle wasn't wearing any lipstick and it felt as though her heart might stop. She had been cleaning this bitch's dirty dishes while Chantelle was down in her studio sucking Geoffrey's dick!

She tried to calm herself. What if she was letting her imagination run away with her? After all, it wouldn't be the first time Chantelle had tried to mess with her mind. The bitch hated her and had made it her life's work to make her suffer. Oh-my-God! Even that made sense now. She'd never understood Chantelle's animosity towards her, but this would explain that too. A rage slowly built from somewhere deep down inside her as she remembered all the humiliation and the pain she'd been put through and all the abuse she'd taken, all because of her love for Geoffrey and her unquestioning belief in the sanctity of their marriage. Geoffrey even invited that terrible man, Frank, into their house and Frank had raped her. Feeling guilty over the rape, she beat herself up questioning whether being raped constituted a violation of their vows. And all the time Geoffrey was fucking this over-dressed bitch!

She looked over at the two men. They both seemed oblivious to what had just happened. They were still talking happily about hull shapes and other things she didn't understand. She wondered if Robert suspected.

She looked back at Chantelle, who was smirking now. A satisfied smile curled Chantelle's lips. Chantelle seemed to be challenging her to speak. It was as if

Chantelle wanted her to make a scene, right here, right now. Her world was crumbling around her and no-one noticed, except the person who had done it to her. Everything she thought she knew now seemed to have dissolved into smoke. It wasn't fair, it just wasn't fair! She had put up with so much, confident in her husband's fidelity, confident that anything was worth his undivided love. And all the time he had been screwing this trollop, this bitch who had been making her life hell since they first met. It was no wonder he never came to her rescue; he didn't want to upset his lover...his slut. But one thing she did know, she had no intentions of doing anything Chantelle wanted.

She was visibly shaking now. Her life was in tatters and she didn't know how to deal with it. 'Geoffrey?'

'What is it?' he asked sounding concerned.

'I am sorry but can we go home.'

'You look terrible. Are you alright?'

'No, I don't feel very well. Can we go?'

Geoffrey shot Chantelle a quick glance but she had a look of total disinterest on her face. Turning back to Robert, he said, 'I am sorry but it looks as though we have to leave.'

Robert was already halfway to his feet. 'Of course you must go.' Turning to face Mary, he asked, 'Is there anything I can get you?'

A gun, so I can shoot your slut wife! was the only thing that came to mind, but she left the thought unspoken. 'No, thank you,' she said instead. 'I think I just need to go home.'

Geoffrey came around the table and helped her to her feet. His touch felt alien to her; as though his hands now belonged to someone she didn't know. Without his support though, she would have stumbled even before she reached the stairs. Geoffrey swept her into his arms.

'I hope you're feeling better soon,' called Chantelle.

For the first time it was Mary, not Chantelle, who was the centre of attention and no-one responded to her mocking call. Geoffrey carried Mary up the stairs and out to the car; Robert running ahead to open the doors for him.

'Let me know how things go,' said Robert as Geoffrey started the car.

'I will,' answered Geoffrey absently as he backed off the parking bay and onto the roadway. With a roar of the powerful engine he headed towards their home.

'What do you think is the matter?' asked Geoffrey, sounding genuinely concerned.

She felt like laughing and nearly did. Of all the times for him to be the perfect husband! 'I think it's just the late night last night catching up with me!' she said lamely.

Geoffrey didn't look as though he believed her but he let it go. 'We will be home soon,' he assured her.

With nothing else to say, she remained quiet the rest of the journey home. Her thoughts should have been in turmoil but she was too confused and too hurt. Instead her mind went gone numb from the shock. Tomorrow might be different but tonight her body was shielding her from herself.

By the time they arrived home she had recovered enough to want to walk on her own, but Geoffrey wouldn't hear of it. He rushed around to her and, picking her up, carried her into the house. He even helped her get ready for bed before helping her into it.

'Is there anything else I can do?' he asked.

'No, I am all right now,' she said, with a shaky voice that didn't reassure him.

'Well, I'll be right here if you need me,' he told her, as he turned out the light.

Mary thought she would never get to sleep, but she was wrong. The shock she felt set off her body's natural defences, shutting her mind down and within minutes she was asleep. Although it wasn't a natural sleep, it was one that spared her wondering what she should do.

***

When Robert came back down the stairs he recognized the look on his wife's face. He had seen that same gloating face each time she signed up a new customer. It was the face she put on when she thought she had done something very clever. 'What did you do?' he demanded with the certainty she was responsible for Mary's sudden illness.

'Don't take that tone with me!' she spat back. 'It wasn't anything to do with me.'

In a more reasonable tone, he asked, 'Then why did Mary look like she'd seen a ghost?'

'She's always been the nervy type. I can't be responsible for her turns.'

Robert didn't believe her but he didn't know what else to say.

'She seemed to have some sort of fit. I don't know why you'd blame me!'

Robert noticed her gloating look had returned but said nothing.

***

When Geoffrey woke he found himself lying alone. Mary was nowhere to be seen. His concern for her returned; last night she'd looked terrible. Chantelle still loomed as a possible reason but surely Mary would have said something by now? Silently he cursed Chantelle; she could be so contrary at times. He couldn't control her, which is what kept him coming back to her time and again.

Getting out of bed he found Mary sitting alone in the lounge room staring blankly at the television which wasn't on. 'Are you alright?' he asked tentatively, almost afraid of what she might say.

When Mary spoke it was in such muted tones he had to strain to catch what she said. 'No, I don't think I am. I don't think I ever will be again.'

Not sure what else to do, he asked, 'Is there anything I can get you?'

Mary slowly swivelled to face him. 'No.' She stood up and did what she always did. She made him breakfast. Unsure what to do he did nothing. Soon life fell back into its old routine as if nothing had happened. Mary didn't eat any of her food, though he didn't notice. In his mind he was going through what he'd told Peter on Friday so he wouldn't make a slip up tomorrow. Tomorrow was going to be the biggest day of his life. He was going to meet with Sir Winstanley himself.

When he looked up, Mary was doing the dishes. Her movements looked a little robotic but at least she was back on her feet. She still puzzled him but he couldn't afford the time right now; he had to prepare for tomorrow. She was back doing what she liked to do, looking after him, so he would talk to her after tomorrow.

He pushed her out of his thoughts and headed to his study and re-read copies of the files he'd given to Peter. There didn't seem to be anything in there that leapt out at him as being false. Congratulating himself on his cleverness he went to work on what he would say to Sir Winstanley. After all, Sir Winstanley wasn't like any of the others he was forced to put up with at the bank. Sir Winstanley knew his stuff. He hadn't become Chairman of the bank for nothing.

As Chairman of the bank, Sir Winstanley would be harder to convince than Peter Christian, but he was supremely confident in his own abilities. In his head he pictured himself dazzling the elderly statesman with his genius.

True, he had gone against bank policy but Geoffrey would use terms like *stretching the envelope* and *accepting the challenge* to change the focus to a more positive one. He would explain to Sir Winstanley how the policies laid out by Roberts were stifling him and how he couldn't do his job properly under those constricting conditions. Sir Winstanley would nod his head sagely, understanding Geoffrey's actions had been necessary in advancing the bank's interests. Geoffrey was convinced Sir Winstanley would be appreciative of his efforts.

Despite his conviction he could pull this off, nagging doubts persisted. There was still the matter of the money he'd kept for himself. If the bank auditors kept searching they would eventually discover the inconstancies in the records. If that happened there would be no explaining his way out. It wouldn't matter how he tried to dress it up; there was no way he could explain the missing money. Theft was such an ugly word and he never used it himself in connection with the money he collected but that would be the word the bank would use. Theft, embezzlement and corruption were only some of the words they would have to choose from. He would be turned out on his ear and he would never be able to work in this industry again. There would never be anyone willing to trust him again and that would be a waste and a shame.

He forced these unsettling thoughts from his conscious mind. He had to concentrate on making sure it didn't happen. He had to convince Sir Winstanley he was honest and trustworthy despite breaking all the rules. It would not be easy but he felt ready for the challenge.

CHAPTER 15

Mary stood at the sink without knowing why she was there. Yesterday was one of the happiest days of her married life. How could it have ended the way it did? How could *he* have allowed it to end that way? How could *he* have spent the day with her, being so attentive, so caring, only to go off with that slut the very same evening?

Mary knew she should be angry, yet strangely she didn't feel that way. What she felt was hollow, like she had been gutted. She felt like an empty shell, a shell with no emotions, no anger…just numbness.

Having cleared the breakfast things she began to clean the rest of the house. She didn't know what she was cleaning or if it needed to be cleaned but falling back into her old routine was the easiest thing to do. She washed the kitchen floor as tears ran down her face. She sobbed as she polished the timber dining room table. Despair was slowing creeping over her as the morning went on. She sat on a dining room chair with a can of Mr. Sheen in one hand and a soiled cloth in the other as tears flowed freely down her face. Geoffrey's study was on the other side of the house so he didn't hear her. She sat there for over an hour and did nothing but cry.

She had never felt so low in spirit. Geoffrey had tried to break her before, but each time there remained a tiny bit of her spirit she used to cling onto her sanity. Now there was no fight, no resolve left in her. All she could do was cry. Mary felt her sanity slip.

Why? she asked herself over and over again.

Why had this happened to her? She knew if her mother was still alive she would have blamed her. It didn't seem to matter what happened to her, everyone blamed her. 'This is not my fault!' she said through her tears.

She sniffed loudly, shaking herself out of her morose state. 'This is not my fault!' she said again, this time louder. This simple statement seemed to give her strength. Her mother blamed her for everything. She blamed her when Geoffrey split her eyebrow open, telling her to take better care of her husband. Well, she had taken care of him. She cooked, she cleaned, and she accepted the beatings. Her mother told her to make sure Geoffrey was satisfied in the bedroom and she did everything possible to do that. She never refused him anything. She was a willing participant in any game he invented. She wore the silly, sexy outfits he bought for her and she acted out his fantasies. She played the part of the promiscuous nurse, the raunchy cowgirl and the seductive maid. She belittled and demeaned herself and she did it all willingly because it brought Geoffrey pleasure. Because that was what a wife did for her husband and in return the husband was supposed to remain faithful. What a husband didn't do was off and fuck his brother's wife! Only Geoffrey had, he'd fucked that whore and Chantelle had laughed at her behind her back. In her mind she could see Chantelle laughing at dopey old Mary, sitting at home cleaning and cooking, while Geoffrey writhed on a bed with her.

'This is not my fault!'

She was beginning to like the sound of it.

'This is not my fault!' Everything had always been her fault. When Geoffrey got drunk and beat her until she ended up in hospital, somehow it always managed to be her fault and dopey old Mary had accepted it. Chantelle probably rushed over and they'd used her nice clean bed with its freshly washed sheets for their dirty sex while she lay in the hospital. Oh how Chantelle must have laughed!

'This is not my fault!'

Those five words were starting to become her personal mantra. Each time she said them, a little of her sanity returned. Each time a little of her self-respect ebbed back. Mary sat a little straighter in her chair.

'This is not my fault!' This time she said it with some conviction. Previously it had sounded as though she was trying to convince herself it was true. Now she began to believe it, to really believe it.

'This is not my fault!'

She put down the can of Mr. Sheen and the soiled cloth and wiped her face on her apron. Taking out a handkerchief she noisily blew her nose. Her eyes were red and blotchy and she still sniffed occasionally but she no longer felt like crying.

'This is not my fault!'

She'd given Geoffrey no cause to stray from their bed. If he chose to lie with that trollop, that was his decision and his decision alone. The weakness lay with Geoffrey. The fault lay with Geoffrey!

Her returning resolve slipped a little when she thought about Robert. Did he know? She hoped he didn't, after all; it would be even worse for him. His wife wasn't just having sex with someone else; she was having sex with his younger brother.

That thought caused her to wonder how long the affair had been going. Was it possible it had been going on for before her marriage to Geoffrey? Could he have stood in that church and sworn to be true to her, knowing Chantelle was sitting in the pew behind him?

How could Chantelle have gone to the church and said nothing, knowing what she knew. How could she sit there and listen to Geoffrey swear before God that he would be true to me, forsaking all others, knowing Geoffrey would be in her bed the first chance he had.

'This is not my fault!'

Mary moved back to the kitchen and made Geoffrey his lunch. Placing it on a tray she carried it into the study and placed it carefully on the end of the desk where he could easily reach it when he was ready.

'Thanks!' he said, sounding distracted. He didn't even look up. He didn't see the red blotchy eyes or the streak marks from her tears. He didn't see the haggard dishevelled look to her face and clothes. Nor did he see the firming of her mouth as she turned and walked away.

Safe in the knowledge Geoffrey was entrenched in the study for the rest of the afternoon, she returned to stare at the television that still wasn't turned on.

'This is not my fault!' *But what do I do now?*

It was one thing to decide this wasn't her fault; it was another to work out what she wanted to do about it. As she pondered this question, she thought about the day she spent with Nancy and Ricky. It started badly but she desperately wanted Ricky to feel more comfortable with her. She sensed she had the power to change herself and she seized that power and she changed things for the better.

'This is not my fault...and I have the power!'

What power she had in this instance wasn't immediately clear, yet she didn't doubt it existed. Then, in a flash, it came to her. She had the power to stay or to go. She could stay and put up with the abuse, the demands and the cheating or she could go. That was her power! She had the power to decide her future!

The money tucked away in her little recipe jar might come in useful after all. There wasn't much but it was more than Geoffrey knew she had.

'This is not my fault...and I have the power!'

Standing up she went back to the kitchen and with a shaking hand brought down her recipe jar. Taking out the carefully cut out recipes she put them to one side. Her hands shook as she counted the money hidden beneath them.

When she had her total she was, at the same time, happily surprised and disappointed. She managed to collect just under four thousand dollars since the time Geoffrey split open her eyebrow. She was happy because she had no idea she could have stashed away so much. At the same time she was disappointed to think this would be all she would have to show for her marriage. She had no other money; she didn't even have a bank account of her own. She didn't own a car so she wouldn't be able to take anything with her other what she could load into a taxi. Thinking about what she would take, she decided she didn't want anything. Everything here would only remind her of Geoffrey and she didn't want to be reminded of him after she left.

She would pack a small case of clothes and a few personal belongings and leave. Geoffrey could have the rest; she didn't want any of it. Everything else was tainted with his scent. She didn't know where she would go or what she would do but at least she would be away from here, away from Geoffrey.

'This is not my fault...and I have the power!'

She cooked dinner for them both for the last time. Hers remained on her plate uneaten. Geoffrey was still in high spirits and didn't notice. The irony of the situation wasn't lost on her. All her married life she had waited for her husband to act like this and now it didn't matter. Now it was too late! It was too little, too late! He had cheated on her and she could never forgive him for that. She had forgiven him everything else, but not this. Not with that bitch!

This is not my fault...and I have the power!

She took two aspirin into the bedroom. She swallowed them before getting in the bed. Geoffrey didn't take the hint. As she turned off the light she felt his arm wrap around her waist as he pulled her close. She wanted to tell him to piss off. She wanted to scratch his eyes out and to scream and shout. What she did was to lie very still, waiting for him to finish.

***

Geoffrey woke early. He was showered and dressed long before he needed to be. He dressed with particular care this morning. He wore his best suit. He handed his shoes to Mary who polished until they shone like a mirror. The tie had been the trickiest decision. Geoffrey liked ties and he had a large collection. At first he put on the new silk one. It was a lovely pale blue with small darker blue squares spread randomly over it.

Looking at himself in the mirror he wasn't so sure. Maybe something more conservative would be better. Sir Winstanley might prefer that. Geoffrey searched thought the racks of ties looking for just the right one. When he spotted the one with the bank emblem he knew this was the one. He was sure Sir Winstanley would like the touch.

Satisfied with his appearance he moved to the kitchen. Mary had his breakfast ready for him. As he ate he went over his notes once more. By the time he finished breakfast, he was primed. Brimming with confidence he practiced the little impromptu speech he would give when Sir Winstanley offered him a managerial position. Convinced he had thought of every possible contingency, he kissed Mary goodbye and headed for the bank.

Even the idiotic drivers he came across didn't bother him this morning. Parking his shiny new BMW in the reserved car parking space, for which he paid by the month, he collected his briefcase and strode purposefully to the bank. Soon he would have his own allocated parking space in the basement of the bank building itself. He would be able to ride up in the lift reserved for servicing the secure basement. He wouldn't be forced to mix with the general rabble who worked at the bank as he moved through the foyer and up the common use lifts, as he did this morning.

'Hello, Geoffrey.'

He turned to see Mary's friend at his shoulder. 'Good morning,' he answered coolly, hoping she didn't want to start a conversation. Then he noticed the look her husband was giving him. He was taken aback by the angry glare on Ricky's face. He wasn't sure what it meant. From memory Ricky was a Grade Five and probably always would be. Soon, the only time he would be forced to associate with someone that low would be to give them an order. Ignoring the couple he strode purposefully in the opposite direction. But his head snapped back around when he half-heard Ricky make some sort of comment to his droll wife. Geoffrey didn't catch it all but he was sure he heard the words: *makes me sick!* He didn't need any distractions this morning; however, he couldn't allow this base-level clerk, to get away with insulting him. In his most demeaning voice, he asked, 'Is there a problem?'

Ricky was about to say something when Nancy pulled him by the arm 'Don't be silly, not here!'

Geoffrey was riding the crest of a wave and his sense of personal power had never been higher. Aware of others around him watching the exchange, he looked down his nose at Ricky and advised him, 'If you want to continue working here, you'd be advised to keep a civil tongue in your head!'

Ricky stabbed a finger in his direction. 'I know what you are and don't you forget it!'

'Are you threatening me?'

Nancy was pulling frantically on her husband's arm but Ricky held firm as he spat back, 'I'm watching you, pal!'

This was getting out of hand now. He would see to it that this unruly fellow was sacked as soon as he could possibly arrange it. Not wanting to be distracted any further, he gave Ricky a disdainful glare and stepped into a waiting lift. As the lift rose he wondered what Mary had been telling this friend of hers. It occurred to him he had been far too lenient with her lately. He would have to have a stern talk with her about the type of friends she kept.

✳ ✳ ✳

'Are you mad?' demanded Nancy.

'I'm sorry, Honey. I just lost it when I saw him!'

'You can't just go around threatening him. What if he takes it out on Mary?'

'I didn't think of that,' he confessed. 'But it makes me so angry when I think about that prick hitting someone as nice as her.'

'It makes me angry too, but making things harder for Mary doesn't help!'

'I'm sorry,' he said again, this time sounding as though he meant it.

She stroked his muscular arm as she told him, 'I know you meant well, but next time you see him, please just ignore him, for Mary's sake!'

Her words were meant to placate him only Ricky wasn't ready yet. Looking into her eyes, he told her, 'If he ever touches her again, I want you to tell me!' When she hesitated, he persisted. In a tone that said he wasn't going to take no as an answer, he said, 'I mean it; I want you to tell me!'

'What are you going to do?' she asked, already knowing the answer.

'I am going to have a little talk with the prat: only next time, somewhere more private.'

'I don't think it would do any good!'

Ricky mashed one of his large fists against the palm of his other hand. 'Once he realises the consequences of his actions, I'm sure he'll think twice before hitting Mary again.'

Nancy was feeling seriously worried now. 'Won't you get into trouble?'

Ricky shrugged. 'Would you rather I did nothing?'

'Maybe it won't come to that?'

'It's up to him. If he doesn't hit her, then we won't have to talk, will we?'

'No, that's right,' she said, looking unconvinced. 'Do you think it's likely he'll stop?'

His face became a stony mask. 'You just let me know.'

※ ※ ※

Shaking the incident with Ricky off him like a duck shaking water from its back, Geoffrey sat at his desk trying his best to maintain a relaxed air. He pretended to carry on as usual, while he waited for the call to come. Fortunately he wasn't kept waiting too long. A confused looking Roberts came over and gained his attention by clearing his throat. When he looked up at him expectantly, Roberts muttered in a tone that said he wasn't sure if it was good news or bad news, 'Peter Christian wants to see you up in his office.'

Trying not to give anything away, Geoffrey used his best poker face as he asked, 'Does he want to see me straight away?'

'Yes. He said something about you having a meeting with Sir Winstanley this morning, but he would like to see you first.'

By this tone, Roberts's made it clear he wasn't happy he didn't know anything about it. Geoffrey had no intention of explaining. Standing, he gave Roberts a supercilious smirk as he informed him, 'I am afraid I don't have time for a chat right now; however, if I am at liberty to speak later, I'll fill you in.'

Roberts was left fuming as he watched his pompous employee walk away from him. He kept hoping Parker would fall on his arse one day. He was half-hoping this sudden call would mean just that but Parker's obvious joy wiped out any chance of it happening today. One thing was for sure; Parker wasn't surprised by the request.

Roberts was tempted to call him back and demand some answers. As the head of the department he should know why one of his employees was speaking with the Chairman. Feeling slighted, he rushed back to his own office. With only a couple of minutes to spare, before Parker would reach Peter Christian's office, he dived for his phone. Without any preamble, he said, 'I demand to know what is going on?'

'If it's decided you need to know, I'm sure you will be told!'

Roberts felt his heart sink low in his chest. This didn't sound good at all. With his feeling of ire deflated, he began again in a more respectful tone, 'Can't you tell me anything? I'm completely in the dark here!'

The change in tone had an equally calming effect on Peter. In a low, confidential voice, he said 'It doesn't look good. Some discrepancies have been found and heads are going to roll.'

Roberts swallowed noisily. 'Which heads?' The extended pause told him all he needed to know. Not waiting for Peter to confirm what he now knew, he asked, 'Was Parker the one?'

Peter considered his reply for a moment or two. Then deciding it wouldn't matter now, he confirmed, 'Yes, and probably a couple of others.'

'My God!' was all Roberts could say. Then, as thoughts rushed through his head, he asked, 'What did they do?'

'I am afraid I can't say.' Peter's tone was kindly, as he added, 'I'll talk with you as soon as I am able to.'

'Thanks,' mumbled Roberts as he dropped the phone heavily into the cradle. Pushing his chair back he took a long look out the window. He loved this view and it was one of the things he would miss the most.

***

After a troubled night Mary woke even earlier than her husband and had his breakfast ready when he appeared, looking his resplendent best. Even in the depth of her despair she noticed how nice he looked this morning. The fact he picked this morning to look his best only served to make her decision harder. In her heart she still loved him. She would probably always love him, but what he had done was unforgivable.

He chatted happily, not noticing her quietness. With a conspiratorial wink he kissed her cheek. 'I'll see you tonight!'

She was vaguely aware he was due for some sort of a promotion today and he would be expecting to celebrate tonight. Forcing herself to smile, she said, 'I'll be waiting.' Only she wouldn't be waiting. She was done with waiting for him to come home. The next time Geoffrey returned it would be to an empty house. His faithful wife would have finally woken up to herself and left.

He gave her backside a playful slap and whistling he strode away from her for the last time.

Out of reflex she cleaned the breakfast dishes before taking out the broom and sweeping the kitchen floor. It was only as she reached for the mop she managed to force herself to stop. This was no longer her life! It was time to leave.

Moving slowly she showered. She dressed even more slowly. She knew she was stalling, not wanting to believe she was actually leaving. Taking out a small suitcase she filled it with a selection of her clothes. Looking about her at the various knick-knacks she pondered what, if any, she should take.

Picking up a small framed photograph of their wedding day she hugged it to her breast. Sliding onto the bed she cradled the photograph as tears began to fall. This had always been her favourite photograph. It hadn't been taken by the expensive photographer Geoffrey hired. It was taken by a fourteen year old boy with a disposable camera. The wedding reception had been a small, although plush, affair. Each table had been supplied with a small disposable camera and the guests were invited to take candid shots in the hope a gem or two would be produced. This photograph was one such gem.

She was facing slightly away, talking with someone who didn't make it into the photograph. Geoffrey was caught looking at his new wife's profile, which in itself wasn't anything memorable. It was the look of adoration on his face she loved so much. It was this candid photograph, more than any of Geoffrey's declarations of love, that convinced her their marriage was genuine. Even though she was now planning to leave him forever, she couldn't bear to part with this photograph. Some part of her still needed to believe Geoffrey had loved her, despite his infidelity.

Pushing the chrome frame deep under her clothes she sealed the case without adding anything else. There wasn't anything more she wanted from this house. Even though she had lived here all her married life it had somehow always felt like Geoffrey's house. He lived here before they married and she had been unable to imprint herself on the character of the house.

Standing with her suitcase in hand she looked about her and felt like someone who has stepped through the wrong door. This was no longer her home. Despite everything she knew she would miss Geoffrey. In his own way he had loved her and she knew it would take a long time for her feelings for him to die, if they ever did.

It was with the deepest regret she took down the little recipe jar and up-ended its contents onto the counter. Pushing the recipes to one side, she gathered the uncovered notes towards her. Slowly she stacked them into piles of the same denomination. It wasn't really necessary. It was only another way of stalling the inevitable, but she couldn't stop herself from doing it. With the notes stacked into neat piles she began to count them again. There was three thousand, eight hundred and ninety dollars. It wasn't much to show for her life so far but Geoffrey had claimed everything else, including her mother's tiny inheritance.

A tear ran down her cheek as she wondered where she would go. The money wasn't going to get her very far. It seemed funny to her but until now she hadn't actually thought about where she should go. All she knew was that she would leave.

Rallying herself, she squared her shoulders and sat a little straighter. Looking at the clock, she decided she still had time to figure out what to do. Geoffrey wouldn't be back for hours yet. Scooping up the money, she put it back in the jar. Somehow it seemed too final to put the money in her purse.

She walked through to the laundry and out into the backyard. Taking a chair from the small setting under the patio, she carried it to her little garden. She might not miss the house but was going to miss her little garden. With the warm sun on her back she sat on the chair by her beloved garden. Just the nearness of it calmed her. Her resolve to leave was bolstered by the peacefulness washing over her. She may not know where she was going yet, but she did know she would have a little garden when she got there.

Putting her mind to the problem, she listed some options in her head. She didn't have much money so going too far was out of the question. Maybe she could catch a bus to any of the small country towns in New South Wales, or even Victoria, to try and find some work.

A sudden thought sent a shiver through her. What if Geoffrey came after her? She hadn't considered this question before. She assumed she was free to leave and begin again but Geoffrey might not see it that way. She could imagine any number of reasons Geoffrey might look for her. He might really love her and not bear the thought of losing her. A more likely reason was he might decide she was his property and he would want her back. After all, who would cook and clean when she was gone. She couldn't imagine Chantelle taking over those roles in her absence.

What if he went to the police? If they found her, would they tell him where she was? She didn't know the answer to either of those questions. She only knew that once she left, she wouldn't want to be found. She wouldn't want to be forced to return. Which meant, whatever she did and wherever she went, it had be somewhere she couldn't be traced.

She would have to change her name. That meant she couldn't claim unemployment benefits or any other form of government assistance. If she did, the police would find her in no time at all. Suddenly, Victoria felt like a better option. She didn't know if it would make it harder to find her if she went to a different state but it couldn't hurt. She would go to the bus station and buy a ticket to Melbourne. From there she could back-track to any town she decided on: one that wasn't so small that a stranger would attract attention. Ballarat came to mind as a possible option.

With her action plan decided her mind returned to her surroundings. This garden had given her so much pleasure. She hated to leave it behind but there wasn't any other choice. Geoffrey's infidelity had made a joke of her marriage and she could no longer stay. Slowly rising to her feet she took one last walk though her garden.

She lovingly touched the leaves of her dwarf beans as she passed. She noticed the tomatoes were setting. Soon the first of the succulent red fruit would begin to form. The capsicums didn't look as good this year and she wondered why. She had composted as usual, digging in horse manure and extra pea straw before planting the tiny seedlings. Squatting, she studied a couple of the plants. Although they looked healthy they were not as tall or as bushy as they had been last year. With a shrug she realised it didn't matter; she wouldn't be here to tend for them. After she'd gone, they would wither and die from neglect. Just one more casualty of Geoffrey's infidelity!

CHAPTER 16

In a low voice said Geoffrey, 'Hello, Gorgeous,' as he stepped into Deborah's office. He was delighted to see her face light up when she realised who had spoken.

'Good morning,' she said primly as she looked around her. 'I have one!' she uttered cryptically.

Despite the circumstances he felt a rush of excitement. Stopping at her desk, he whispered, 'Remember, you must answer the door naked!'

'I'll be waiting for you!' she confirmed as she stepped over to her boss's door. 'Mr. Parker to see you, Sir.'

'Send him in.'

Deborah made sure she stood half-blocking Geoffrey's path, forcing him to brush passed her as he entered the room. The furtive contact sending shivers of excitement through both of them.

Geoffrey didn't know why Christian wanted to see him. He only hoped Peter didn't waste too much of his time. He had convinced himself his meeting with Sir Winstanley was to promote him up into the ranks of management, where he truly belonged. Any time spent with someone like Peter Christian was only time wasted so he wasn't disappointed when Peter stood up and stepped around his desk. 'Come on, we had better not keep them waiting.'

Geoffrey couldn't keep the pleased smirk off his face as they stepped into the lift. It was only when the lift stopped and he realised that they weren't at the eighteenth floor that he turned to Peter. 'Why are we here?' he demanded, not bothering to hide his displeasure.

'We're picking up someone on the way.'

The answer calmed him but he still disliked the delay. Silently he followed Peter out of the lift and into a large office. A short bald man sat behind the desk with a file opened in front of him. It wasn't the short bald man who caught Geoffrey's attention though. Frank stood at one side of the desk and the sight of him sent an ominous shiver down Geoffrey's spine. For the first time he had an inkling this morning might not be going to go the way he had planned. When Peter closed the door behind him, his suspicions were somewhat confirmed.

'Geoffrey Parker!' said the short bald man, forcing Geoffrey to look at him. 'My name is Wilson Blake and I am the Head of Security for the bank. There are a few things I would like to discuss with you. Please, take a seat.'

Geoffrey wanted to tell him where to go but he was caught completely by surprise. His knees felt too weak to hold him and he slithered into the only other chair in the room.

Blake turned away, looking back at the file in front of him. Without looking up, he said, 'You have been causing us a great deal of concern for some time now.' Whipping up his head so he stared directly into Geoffrey's eyes, he added, 'I have read this crap you gave Christian. Now I want the truth. What have you been up to?'

Geoffrey was desperately trying to gather his wits. Attempting to look indignant, he spat back, 'I have already explained this once; why should I bother telling you?'

'Because I am the only person between you and the police!'

Geoffrey tried to see what Blake was looking at without making it obvious. He didn't succeed. Not knowing what information Blake had at his disposal, he would have to try and bluff. 'As I explained to Peter, the guidelines laid out by my department head, Roberts, are far too restrictive. Someone with my abilities is able to work quite safely far beyond these limited fields. I thought the bank should know what I am able to achieve for them if I was allowed. Over the past twelve months I have been setting my own goals.' With his confidence returning, he looked smugly at Blake as he finished. 'I have achieved all of them.'

Blake only said one word in reply. 'Crap!'

Geoffrey was recovering from the shock and Blake's attitude was now annoying him. 'Does Sir Winstanley know I'm wasting time here? I have a meeting scheduled with him this morning!'

Blake sat back more comfortably in his chair. Looking pleased, he told Geoffrey, 'I am afraid that meeting has been cancelled.'

'On whose authority?'

'On my authority. Now, why don't you simply tell me the truth and stop wasting everyone's time?'

Geoffrey gave a furtive glance in Frank's direction as he told the head of security, 'I don't know what you mean.'

Blake sighed resignedly. 'Let me help you. Over the last twelve months you have blatantly ignored the bank's guidelines and traded in areas that are forbidden. Why?' As Geoffrey opened his mouth to speak, Blake slipped in, 'And don't tell me about restrictive guidelines stifling your natural talents and abilities; I don't care. I want to know what you did. I want dates and I want names. I want everything and I want it now!'

'I have nothing to say to you!'

Blake nodded as he said, 'Fair enough, you don't have to talk to me.'

Looking very uncomfortable Peter Christian stepped forward and blurted out, 'Geoffrey Parker, your employment with this Bank is terminated forthwith. It is the opinion of the bank that your actions are of a criminal nature and the police will be contacted and proceedings will be enacted against you.' With his set piece said Peter again stepped back out of the way.

Geoffrey was astute enough to realise this was designed to rattle him. He sensed something else was coming from the head of Security. To show it hadn't worked, he looked at Blake and smiled. 'Or?'

Blake returned the smile, conceding the point. 'Or,' he began slowly. 'you can return tomorrow and begin to unravel what you've done. Make no mistake, your services have been terminated and your assistance will in no way atone for what you have done.'

'Then why would I bother?'

'If you don't return tomorrow, ready to provide any and all assistance that may be required of you, the police will be contacted and proceedings will be taken against you!' Blake leant forward and gave Geoffrey a piercing stare. 'Don't try and run; I will find you wherever you go!'

Geoffrey was proud of the way he managed to stand and walk from the room without his legs giving way. He took the lift alone to the ground floor and walked from the building for the last time as an employee.

Slowly his emotions changed from fear to anger. Leaving the building he picked up his car and headed for home. If they thought they could scare him they didn't know him very well. He still had the money he'd stolen. 'Let Blake try and find me!' he shouted at an old man crossing the road. The old man scurried on as Geoffrey roared through the intersection.

Blake might think he had frightened him with threats of the police but he hadn't. Now he'd had time to think it over, he took it as a challenge. They obviously didn't know about the money: yet. If they did they wouldn't have let him just walk away. With the resources that kind of money offered, they would never find him. He would pack some of his things and get back over to the bank. He reasoned they wouldn't be expecting him to return so quickly. He would collect the money before destroying as many of his files as he could lay his hands on. If he got the opportunity he might even be able to delete some of the computer files. That should slow the bastards up.

Pulling out his mobile phone, he dialled Chantelle. 'I don't have long to talk. The shit's hit the fan at the bank and I have to take off. I have to leave straight away. Do you want to come with me?'

Without any other qualification, she asked 'How long have I got?'

'I don't know exactly; I'll be by sometime this afternoon.'

'What about the money?'

Despite everything Geoffrey was smiling as he told her, 'I'll have it with me.'

'Do I have time to clean out our accounts too?'

'Don't bother,' he said, not wanting to complicate things. 'Just bring all your cards with you. We can do that from anywhere.' Before Chantelle could ask anything more, he told her, 'I've got to go; I'm nearly home. See you soon.'

As Geoffrey approached his house his anger turned to rage. By the time he pulled into the garage he was ready to explode. Slamming the door to his beloved BMW behind him, he raced inside. Throwing the keys on the kitchen bench, he was stopped in his tracks. At the end of the bench was a small suitcase. Disbelieving, he picked it up and placed it on the bench and opened it. His rage burned even deeper than before when he discovered it was full of Mary's clothes. 'The bitch!' His rage found a familiar target. His head snapped up when he heard the outside door open. His breath came in raged, hoarse gulps as he waited for his wife to appear.

'Oh, shit!' exclaimed Mary, her hands flying to her face.

'Oh shit indeed,' said Geoffrey in a low, quiet tone that was more threatening than if he'd shouted.

Looking very scared, she asked, 'Why are you home so early?'

In the same quiet tone, he said, 'Those short-sighted fools at the Bank terminated my employment.' The fear in her eyes fed his sense of righteous indignation and his voice slowly rose. 'They think they have me over a barrel. Do you know what they said to me?'

'No!'

He noticed how Mary's eyes continued to dart to the opened suitcase but he chose to ignore it. His anger burned hot but he was enjoying the feel of it now. He fanned the flames, allowing them to glow white hot, ready for when he would erupt. 'They offered me an ultimatum. They said if I don't go back tomorrow, and tell them everything, they will call the police. They expect me to go crawling back to on my belly and roll over while they sink their boots into me. Well I'm not.' He paused, enjoying the trails of sweat running down Mary's face. She looked terrified and well might she should. By the time he was finished with her she would know who was in charge here. 'I met your slut friend and her moronic husband this morning.'

Mary's eyes widened but she didn't speak.

'What is his name again?' he asked, almost politely.

'Ricky!'

'That's right, Ricky.' His face turned stony hard as he asked, 'Do you know what that ignorant prick said to me?'

Mary began to shake now. 'No.'

'He said he was going to keep his eye on me! What do you think he meant by that?'

'I don't know,' Mary said through the tears streaming down her face.

Finally giving vent to his anger, Geoffrey shouted at her, 'What lies have you been spreading about me?' When Mary didn't say anything, he roared, 'What did you say to that fucking slut friend of yours?'

'I didn't say anything,' she said, in low scared voice.

'Then what is this?' he demanded, finally looking down at the open suitcase.

Surprisingly, Mary seemed to rally herself. Standing a little taller, she said, 'I know all about you and Chantelle.'

He was too angry for the words to impact on him as they should have. 'So you thought you would just pack up and leave. Leave me!' He gave her a look of disgust. 'You are nothing and you have always been nothing. You're not leaving me, because I am leaving you!' The lack of logic in his threat didn't diminish his feeling of superiority. 'Your mother was a stupid, drunken slut and even she was better than you. Without me, you are nothing. You hear me? Nothing!' Looking around him, he spotted the silly ceramic jar where she kept old recipes. Snatching at it he raised it over his head. He didn't hear Mary's agonized scream as he hurled it at her. At this close range he couldn't miss and he didn't. The heavy base of the jar crashed into Mary's forehead, shattering the jar and sending the contents fluttering to the floor.

The sight of the money floating through the air momentarily stilled his rage. Dazed, Mary slowly sunk to the floor as he stepped over to her and began to collect the notes. Bending low he held the money in front of her face as he demanded, 'What is this?'

'It's mine!' she wailed, snatching for the money.

He pulled it back, while continuing to hold it where she could see it. Waving it back and forth to tease her, he told her, 'But you don't have any money; I made sure of that. So, if you don't have any money, this must be mine.' Straightening, he put it in his pocket.

Mary slumped into an untidy pile on the floor. She sobbed hysterically and didn't resist as he took hold of her and pulled her to her feet. Bracing her slack form against the wall with one hand he punched her unprotected stomach as hard as he could with the other. He liked the way his fist felt as it pounded into her so he punched her again and again. It was only when he couldn't hold her slack weight any longer that he allowed her to collapse back to the floor. Her desperate, rattled breath was music to his ears as he looked down at her. 'Not feeling so clever now, are you, bitch?'

He swung his foot and caught her in the middle of her sternum. The grunt Mary gave wasn't anywhere as satisfying as he would have liked so he tried again. When she let out a scream he felt better. He considered kicking her again but decided against it. There was no need to rush he still had some time. He could have some fun taking out his frustrations and his anger on her before going back for his money.

Turning away he walked to the games room and went to the bar. Stepping behind it he took out the bottle of Johnny Walker Black Label. Looking at the bottle he was disappointed to find it was already half empty. Still, that might not be a bad thing. He shouldn't really drink too much. He still had a lot to accomplish today. First he would take care of his wife, teaching her a lesson for the wrongs she had committed against him; then he would go to the bank. Half filling his favourite whisky glass he downed it in one noisy swallow.

Sighing with satisfaction, he waited as the fiery liquid burnt a path to his stomach. Pouring out another good measure of the whisky, he swallowed it, again in a single gulp. He was quickly feeling more like his old self. When he topped up the glass a third time he sipped it more slowly, savouring the feel and the taste of it.

***

Mary's breath was slowly coming back to her. With her breathing becoming easier, her head began to clear. The dizziness receded only to be replaced by an agonising pain in her stomach and her chest. Even so she knew the pain would soon be worse. She looked about her and was surprised when she didn't see Geoffrey. She knew with certainty this wasn't over. If she didn't take this opportunity and get out of the house now, she mightn't be alive to do it later. Groaning with the pain that gripped her chest, she reached out with her hands. Taking hold of the door frame she pulled herself towards it. Another wave of dizziness threatened to overcome her as she used the door handle to pull herself to her knees. She was forced to waste several precious seconds as she waited for the room to stop spinning. With spots dancing before her eyes she gave one last effort and hauled herself to her feet. Swaying uncertainly she looked down to make sure she was really on her feet and not just imagining it. She couldn't feel the lower half of her body so it was with an awkward lurching step she staggered towards the outer door.

Just as the first glimmer of hope shone through the pain a hand closed around her hair. 'Where in the fuck do you think you're going?'

Reaching out for anything she would use to stop Geoffrey dragging her back into the kitchen, her hand found the iron. In her panic her fingers wrapped around the handle, grasping it so tightly her knuckles went white. Geoffrey was using her hair to pull her backwards. As terrified as she was, she detected the scent of whisky in the air. Oh how she hated the scent of whiskey! Geoffrey was always at his worst when whiskey was involved. With a scream of terror she swung wildly with the iron. She felt it hit something. Geoffrey's grip on her hair slackened. Her vision was blurred with a mixture of tears and swirling spots wavering in front of her eyes. She threatened to black out and she fought it with all the strength she could muster. It wasn't much but it was enough. The spots settled a little and she looked across at her husband. He was lying on his side, facing away from her. She was on her knees so she tentatively nudged him with her free hand. When he didn't move she pushed him a little harder. Geoffrey didn't move or make a sound. Mary was too scared to feel any relief. Her previous thoughts of trying to escape now felt too hard. Too drained to do anything, she sat on the floor while her senses slowly returned to her. Her breathing was still ragged and her chest and stomach were hurting like hell, but she was alive.

'I have the power!'

Any confidence she'd gained soon evaporated when she realised she was still in danger. She was sure Geoffrey was only stunned. What she needed to do was get out before he came around. If he regained his senses before then, she knew it would come down to him or her. Despite her fear and her longing to keep on living she doubted she be able to overpower him again.

Remembering Geoffrey putting her money in his pocket, she crawled a little closer. Very carefully she reached out with a shaking hand and slipped it into his pocket. It was empty. To reach his other pocket she would have to lean over him. Not able to look at him, her hand searched blindly through his clothing. As she her fingers found the opening a hand clasped firmly around her wrist. Surprised, she screamed. Finding she still had hold of the iron, she swung it as hard as she could. She kept on screaming and she kept on swinging the iron against Geoffrey's head until her arm could no longer lift it. Exhausted, she slumped to the floor and a welcome blackness came over her.

* * *

Blake was relatively happy with how the Parker business was going but he knew this wasn't the time to become complacent. What Parker had done was against all the rules but it was only borderline criminal. Besides, Parker was a bright boy. Parker would know he was mostly bluffing. The bank wouldn't like the publicity court action would bring. But Parker would also know he would save himself a lot of grief by cooperating. 'How much do we know and how much is still guess work?'

Graham shuffled his feet. Swallowing noisily, he began. 'I believe we have a pretty good handle on what your friend has been up to. He was using encrypted files which held us up until we broke the code. Breaking it down was still only the first step. Parker's really good at hiding what he did. We have two of the bank's best auditors wading through the files trying to work out exactly what he was up to. It was slow going for a time but as they became used to the way he worked, it became easier and now they're making good progress.'

Blake nodded, deep in thought. He was convinced Parker would show in the morning and he wanted to be ready for him. Finally looking up at the computer whiz, he said, 'Thank you for all your efforts with this. You and your department have done an exceptional job.'

Graham looked surprised by the praise. 'It has been our pleasure.'

Allowing himself a rare smile, Blake admitted, 'Parker has been a challenge.' His business-like manner returning, he said, 'I'm expecting Parker tomorrow and I need to be able to compare what he tells us against what we already know so I can gauge how much truth he is willing to provide and how much pressure I need to apply to get the rest. So I'll need everything you have by morning. I want everything, even if it's only wild speculation. Just make sure it is labelled accordingly. I want it separated into known facts and guesses.'

'I'll take care of it personally.' With a self-conscious smile, he added, 'It is funny though.'

Blake's head snapped up. It was his experience the best leads came from the little things that puzzled people. He'd learnt the hard way to not ignore an opportunity no matter how it presented itself. 'What's funny?'

'It just seems funny to me that this Parker has gone to all this trouble to show how clever he is and yet he didn't make a difference.'

Blake was the one who was puzzled now. 'I am afraid I don't understand what you mean!'

Graham paused as he searched for the right words to express his thoughts. 'The auditors have given the accounts a good going over and he's only brought in the usual level of return. I thought the point was to show how he could make more money?'

A tingling sensation was spreading up Blake's spine. Forcing himself to stay calm, he asked, 'Explain to me the bit about the Parker only making the usual amount of money.'

'I don't really understand it completely; it's the auditor's field really. I only supplied them the information.'

To put the other man at ease, Blake forced a smile as he said, 'I don't need a detailed explanation; I just want to see things the way you see them.'

Graham paused again as he took a couple of breaths. Beginning hesitantly, he said, 'Parker is some kind of financial wheeler-dealer and his effectiveness is gauged by the level of profit he makes. While each transaction can be evaluated and assessed, there are also trends over time which are important. And apparently, Parker's level of income has been flat-lined for some time.'

Speaking slowly and carefully, Blake sought confirmation of what he thought he'd just heard. 'What you are saying is that while Parker has been off speculating in high risk areas, he hasn't generated any more income for the bank?'

Shrugging his shoulders, Graham said, apologetically, 'I guess that's what I am saying.'

Blake was looking like a shattered man. *Why didn't I see this before?* He'd run a check to see if any money was missing and he was assured the balance sheet looked fine. He felt so relieved at the news he hadn't dug any deeper and that had been a mistake.

'What is it?' asked Graham looking afraid of what the answer might be.

'Parker told us himself, he's been making lots of extra money. If the bank doesn't have it, where is it?'

Graham looked alarmed now. 'I don't know.'

'Forget everything else,' said Blake, snapping back into action. 'I want you to pick any file you want. Then I want you and the auditors to go over everything Parker has touched in connection with that file. Somewhere, somehow he's been skimming off the extra profits and I want to know where they are...and I want to know by morning!'

'But that could take all night, if not days!'

'Then I suggest you get started straight away.'

'Yes, Sir.'

When Graham left, Blake jumped onto the phone. He had to get to the bottom of this before Sir Winstanley started asking his own questions. 'Frank, I need the names of anyone you think might have been helping Parker!' Scribbling fast, he wrote three names on the pad in front of him. Without saying anything further he hung up and redialled. 'This is Wilson Blake. I need something done and I need it done now!'

'What is it?' asked Janet Hamley.

'I need the complete financial records for four of our employees and I want Parker's accounts with us frozen.'

'You know you don't have authority to do that?'

'I know. I'll take full responsibility, but I want it done!'

'If it was anyone else, you know I'd ask for that in writing...but seeing as it's you...I'll see to it personally.'

Blake gave a sigh of relief. Feeling happier now, he chanced his arm. 'How many friends do you have at the other banks?'

'Some,' she answered, hesitantly.

'Can you ask them to supply us with a record of any transactions these four may have made with them over the last twelve months?'

There was a long pause before Janet said, 'This had better be important. I may have to make some pretty heavy promises in return.'

'It is important and I need it yesterday.'

'I'll see what I can do.'

'That is all I can ask.' Blake hung up the phone confident Janet would get it done. Sitting back, he reviewed what he'd done so far to see if there was anything he had missed. Only one item loomed large. He should never have let Parker out of his sight. He could only hope it wasn't too late. Dialling again, he phoned an old friend of his.

This man had never worked for the bank and never would, officially. 'I need a favour.'

'Is that you?' asked Harry, deliberately not using a name.

'Shut up and listen. There's a house I need watching. If anyone leaves, call me. If it's a man, I want you to follow him.'

'How long do you want me to watch it?'

'Only one day. I am expecting him to come to the bank tomorrow but I'm worried he'll run first.'

'No worries. Where am I going and what does he look like?'

It only took Blake a few minutes to provide enough details for the ex-cop. With that done, Blake tried to relax. All he could hope was that he'd acted quickly enough.

* * *

Chantelle was frantic. She'd rung Geoffrey's phone non-stop but she couldn't get through. Robert was due home soon and she would have to hide the suitcase she packed before then.

While she hoped Geoffrey wasn't experiencing trouble collecting the money, she hoped it was only something as simple as that. Confident he would contact her when he could she carried her case upstairs and tucked it at the back of her wardrobe.

She was torn. The last thing she wanted to do was to act too quickly. She couldn't afford to dump Robert before she knew Geoffrey could get his hands on the money. She wanted to be rid of her husband, but not if it meant being left without any money.

* * *

Deborah was feeling very excited. It was nearly time to leave. Peter was being unusually evasive about Geoffrey's meeting, which was annoying. She was hoping for good news because it would mean Geoffrey would feel like celebrating and she hoped be a part of his plans.

Her skin tingled. Geoffrey was impossibly arrogant, yet it was this trait that attracted her to him. He infuriated her as much as he excited her. She longed to be made to submit and possibly only someone as arrogant as Geoffrey Parker would have the necessary will to ensure she didn't back out. Tonight could well be a turning point in her life.

CHAPTER 17

Mary sat, half-leaning against the doorway for a long time, unable to move. Her body felt completely drained of energy and her mind shut down. In front of her Geoffrey's skull lay shattered, while a stream of blood and grey-matter formed a pool on the floor. As it dried it turned a disgusting red-brown colour. It made her feel like vomiting but she couldn't draw her eyes away. Fortunately Geoffrey's face was hidden from her so she didn't have to look into his lifeless eyes. She didn't think she could handle that.

At first she felt like praying. She wasn't sure if it should be for forgiveness or thanks for being alive. She argued with herself about the two options for some time. What would God want her to pray for? At first she thought it would have to be for forgiveness; after all she had just killed her husband. Then, as she was about to pray, she began to wonder. Had He intervened to save her life? How else could she explain the way her blind, groping hand found the iron? The very thing that saved her life! It felt conceited to think God would bother with her but how else could she explain why Geoffrey was dead while she was still alive? By the time she finished arguing with herself praying didn't seem relevant any more. Geoffrey was dead and she was alive; that was how it was and that was all that mattered. Instead of prayer, Mary resorted to her own mantra. 'This is not my fault!' she said, barely above a whisper. 'And I have the power.'

The simple phrase began to relax her frayed nerves like a soothing balm. Saying this one sentence over and over to herself the day before had helped and she hoped it would help again.

'This is not my fault!' she said, her voice firming. 'And I have the power.'

Her stomach and chest burned, making breathing difficult. Miraculously, she didn't think she had any broken ribs. With her experience she didn't need x-rays to know if she had any serious damage; she could just tell. Deciding it would still be better if she took the pressure off her ribcage she slowly dragged herself to her knees. Crawling past Geoffrey she slowly made her way to the kitchen bench, making sure to avoid contact with the drying pool of blood and brains. She didn't think she could cope with that. Reaching up with both hands she took hold of the lip of the bench top and pulled herself up. The pain was intense as she hoisted herself up but once she was standing, if a little uncertainly, the pain quickly subsided to its previous level. She still hurt, but she was right; her breathing was a little easier now.

Stepping around her husband's body, she staggered to her bedroom. She would have to call the Police but she didn't think she could cope with all the questions that would follow until she had cleaned herself up a little. She felt disgusting. Her skin seemed to be alive with unseen bugs.

After stripping off her dress, which proved more difficult than she hoped, she gingerly reached into the shower alcove and adjusted the taps until a steady stream of hot water flowed. Very carefully she slipped over the step and stood under the jet of water. She stood like that for a long time, not bothering with the soap, just letting the hot water sluice away her fears. Even her sore chest and stomach started to feel a little better. Her bruised and tight muscles began to relax, allowing the blood to flow more readily. She didn't know how long she stayed like that before finally lathering her hands and washing herself completely.

Mary dressed in clean clothes before bracing herself to look at her forehead. The cut made by her recipe jar didn't look as bad with the blood washed away. It should have been stitched but she knew butterfly plasters would work. The area around the cut was bruised and tender so she gingerly applied three butterfly clips before covering the whole thing with a padded bandage held in place with two strips of plaster.

With a deep breath she went back to the kitchen. Geoffrey was exactly as she had left him, which didn't surprise her, considering. She was standing there, looking down at him, when his mobile phone rang. Her nerves were on edge and the sudden, shrill sound startled her. She screamed as she jumped back. She didn't want to go any closer but she couldn't put up with that sound. Creeping up on her husband's body she reached into his suit pocket and took out his phone. Looking at the display she immediately recognised Robert's home phone number. Deep inside she knew it wasn't Robert trying to reach him, but Chantelle. Mary let it ring out to the message bank before removing the battery. 'Get him now, bitch!'

The sound of her voice scared her a little. It sounded close to hysterical. Taking a number of deep breaths, she forced herself to calm. She would never get through the police interviews like this. She couldn't afford to become hysterical with them: it would look too bad.

Maybe she should wait a little longer before calling?

She started to wonder when would be the best time. 'What about next year!' she said to try and help defuse her anxiety. She even forced out a small giggle at her wit. Then she wondered: why not? Why did she have to ring the Police so soon? In fact, why did she have to ring them at all? Deep down she knew she should. She should own up to what she had done and accept the consequences.

'This is not my fault! And I have the power!'

It wasn't her fault but would she be able to convince the police of that? What if they arrested her for murder? How could she convince them she was the real victim? There were all those little trips to the hospital but she had always lied for him. She always insisted she had fallen or some other stupid excuse, so how would it look now if she tried to change her story?

What was it Geoffrey had said? She wracked her tired brain, forcing it to think back. She was convinced he told her he'd been sacked from the bank, which explained why he had come home so early. If he had been sacked, they wouldn't be expecting him back, would they? If he never went back or contacted anyone there, would they think anything of it?

She was sure he'd said something about leaving her. Probably he was going to go off with that bitch, which was why she was ringing. Chantelle would be wondering where he was. Well, Chantelle could hardly say anything, could she? She was married to Robert, after all.

So if Geoffrey simply disappeared, who would ask questions? Robert would, but she could tell him about the bank and say Geoffrey was so embarrassed he'd taken himself off to Queensland. It would hold him for a while at least.

But would it work?

She thought it might. But what could she do with the body? There was only one thing she could think of; she would have to bury him. Stepping around the body she went thought the laundry and into the rear yard. Assessing the distance she would have to drag Geoffrey's body, she wasn't sure she could do it.

'This is not my fault! And I have the power!' she told herself, before adding, 'It might not be your fault but you are going to have to clean up the mess.'

Standing in the brilliant sunshine she thought back to her visit with Nancy. Things were not going well until she decided she was the only one who had the power to change what needed to be changed. The circumstances may have been different but the outcome was the same. Only she had the power to do what had to be done.

'I have the power!'

'I *have* the power!'

Walking over to the garage she took out her little spade and went to her garden. She knew she wouldn't have the strength to drag her husband's body far. If she was going to do this, it would have to be in the first section. Scratching out a rectangle in the soil, she carefully removed all the plants. She tucked them aside planning to replant them later.

At first the digging was simple, but painful. The top layer of soil had already been turned over to plant her garden.; however, once she went below this level the soil became harder. She was forced to rest often. Her stomach and her chest were soon hurting her more than before she took the shower. Her breathing became ragged and blisters formed on the palms of her hands. Flopping on the ground she began to cry. She cried for herself and then for Geoffrey because, despite everything, she knew she still loved him. It was ridiculous but it was true. She had married him for better and for worse and now she'd killed him. She almost went back into the house and called the police. The only thing stopping her was that she was too tired to move.

By the time she'd recovered enough, she didn't head to the house. She went to the garage instead and took out her pick and a pair of heavy work gloves. She hadn't used the pick much before and in the confined space of the grave she found it difficult to swing without endangering herself. She was convinced she would put it through her foot at any swing. While her body burned with exhaustion and pain her mind went numb. She ignored her discomfort and trudged on. When darkness came she ran a portable floodlight into the yard and switched it on. It gave out so much light she panicked. The last thing she needed was some nosey neighbour sticking their head over the fence to see what was going on. A grave would be difficult to explain. So she covered the light with the chair to deaden its glow.

She dug and dug in a mind-numbing rhythm, only her fear driving her on. Desperate for yet another break she found she didn't have the energy to climb out. Tossing the shovel aside, she curled up in one corner of the hole. After a time, she rose and began again. Each shovel full of dirt was an effort to throw out. Her progress had been painfully slow but with perseverance she was succeeding.

'I have the power!'

It was only when she couldn't possibly go on any more that she put thought to how she was going to get out. Taking hold of the edge she tried to haul herself up. Her arms refused to lift her. Panic set in and she scrambled at the side wall, only succeeding in collapsing the edge back onto herself. Collapsing in a huddled heap she tried to calm her shattered nerves. There had to be a way out of this!

'I have the power!' she chanted over and over again until an idea came to her. When it did she laughed, it was so simple. With the pick she dug a series of small steps into the side wall of the hole. She used these steps to climb up towards the stars. But she didn't go all the way out. Now she was confident the system would work she went back and retrieved her pick and shovel. Hurling them over the top of the grave she climbed out herself. She didn't know what the time was and she didn't care; she was too exhausted to be worried about it. What worried her was the fact she was too exhausted to do anything more tonight. She had dug most of the day and half the night and she would need to rest before she dragged Geoffrey to his resting-place and covered him over.

She looked longingly at the bed before forcing herself to undress. She could have easily fallen on top of it and slept. Instead she took another shower. The hot water felt good on her tired muscles but hurt her blistered hands. Quickly drying herself off, she did one last job before climbing into bed. Taking a sheet out from the linen closet, she tossed it over Geoffrey, covering him. That done she slipped between the sheets of her bed without even bothering to put on her nightie.

***

Out in his car Harry poured himself another cup of coffee from the large thermos and settled back. The strange light in the backyard had bothered him earlier. He'd finally decided to go and investigate it when it was suddenly turned off. Various lights were turned on inside the house soon afterwards but they too were all off now. It looked like they were finally settling in for the night. It would be a long wait but he was used to long waits.

***

Wilson Blake didn't enjoy his lunch. He was starting to sweat. Sir Winstanley wouldn't be happy if he screwed this up by letting Parker walk away. He called Harry for the eighth time that morning. 'Any sign?'

'No, not yet,' came his standard reply.

Blake was getting desperate 'You couldn't have missed him, could you?'

Feeling tired and irritable and now slighted, Harry spat back, 'I didn't miss him but he might still be inside or he might never have been there at all!'

'I'm sorry, I am under a lot of pressure on this one.'

'You want me to find out if he is in there?'

If it had been anyone else Blake would have warned them not to get caught but because it was Harry and because he had already insulted him once, he didn't. 'Call me when you know one way or the other.'

'Sure thing.'

Harry had been sitting in his car for a long time and his legs were stiff when he climbed out. Shaking them loose he strode in the direction of Parker's house. Harry had a clipboard in his hand as he walked along the fence line to the edge of the house. Peeking through the open window he studied the interior. Nothing was moving. Slowly and carefully he worked his way to the other side of the house, peering in each of the windows in turn. None of the curtains were pulled which made it seem as though they weren't trying to hide anything. Finally he went and rang the front doorbell. When he didn't get an answer he moved to the side fence. On this side of the house was a gate leading to the rear yard. Opening the gate as silently as he could he slipped through it and snuck along the side of the house. Peeking into the yard he didn't see anyone although he heard sounds coming from behind the garage. In a loud confident voice, he called out, 'Hello, is there anyone there?'

The sounds stopped but he didn't receive a reply. Harry was experienced enough not to read too much into it. Lots of people didn't like to be interrupted in this way and would simply go quiet until whoever had called out left. It didn't necessarily mean they were up to no good; however, Harry had no intentions of leaving so easily. 'I am sorry if I frightened you,' he called out in an easy voice. 'I'm from the Council and we are conducting a survey on building extensions. Did you get our letter?'

'Hello?'

It was a woman's voice and she sounded scared. The last thing he needed was a panicked woman screaming for help. Staying where he was, he called out in his friendliest voice, 'I can see you're busy so I won't take up too much of your time.' The woman peeked around the corner of the garage. She looked dishevelled but he tried not to read too much into it. So did most people working in their back yards.

'That's Ok, I was just doing a little gardening. I could do with a break. What can I help you with?'

The first thing he noticed was she didn't move any closer. The next was the fresh white bandage on her forehead. He gave her one of his friendliest smiles as he began his cover story. 'My name is Brian Harrow and I'm with the Local Council. We are conducting a survey on home extensions and improvements in the area but I don't want to hold you up if you're busy. I could talk with your husband if he is at home?'

'No, he isn't I am afraid.'

Her voice was thin and shaky. He wasn't sure if it was from nervousness or fear. He tried to broaden his smile as he took a few steps closer. 'I suppose it was a silly question really; he would be at work at this time of the day.'

'Actually he isn't at work today. He had to go to Queensland last night.'

'Half his luck.' Taking another step closer, he asked, 'Is it for work or pleasure?'

'A bit of both really. We may be moving up there and he has gone to check out some likely places.'

'I wish I was moving to Queensland. Where are you thinking of going?'

'We really don't know yet.'

'Fair enough,' said Harry not wanting to push too hard. 'As I said, we are doing this survey and I was wondering if there were any improvements or extensions you might have made in the last twelve months?'

'No, not that recently.' She paused as she thought for a moment or two. 'My husband added a room onto the back of the house but that was before we were married.'

Harry made as if he marked something on his clipboard. Smiling again, he told her, 'Thank you for your cooperation and have a nice day.'

'I will.'

Harry looked around him as he walked back through the gate. Everything looked right but his instincts told him something wasn't. But Blake wouldn't have sent him over to watch this house if there wasn't. At the car he called Blake. 'He's done a runner. He left last night for Queensland.'

'Shit! Are you sure?'

'I am not sure your man's in Queensland but I'm pretty sure his wife thinks that's where he is.'

'How certain are you?'

'As I say, he could be anywhere but I'd put money on you not seeing him at the bank today. All the curtains were open and the wife was out the back doing some gardening when I went in. She seemed nervous but I think she's just the nervous type. I told her I was from the Council and asked to see her husband. She said he had gone to Queensland last night, and get this: she said they might be moving there soon and he was checking out somewhere for them to live.'

'Shit!' said Blake again.

Harry didn't take any pleasure in Blake's discomfort. He'd been in similar situations himself too many times before. 'Your man, does he get physical with his wife?'

'There has been a rumour to that effect.'

'That would explain the fresh bandage on her head this morning. I'd say he came home in a bad mood, took out his frustrations on her and split.' When there wasn't a reply from Blake, he asked, 'You want me to hang around and see if he comes back?'

'I don't think so; I have a feeling he won't be back.'

'Sorry I couldn't be any more help.'

'It wasn't your fault. I sent you over too late, but thanks for all you've done. Send your account to the usual place and I'll see it is taken care of.'

'Yeah, no worries; call me anytime.'

Only as he hung up did he remember the strange light in the yard the night before. If the husband had already gone, what was the wife doing out there? It was a puzzle, but did it have anything to do with Blake's business? With a shrug he started his car. The husband was gone and his job was done. He was tired and he still had his own work to do. The mystery of the light would have to stay a mystery.

***

Blake rang Janet Hamley. 'How are you going with those accounts?'

'For bright boys these guys are pretty stupid,' came her dry reply.

'Why do you say that?' asked Blake, straightening in his chair again.

'The first thing they all did was pay off their mortgages.'

'That might have been stupid but we didn't pick it up until now,' he pointed out. 'How does a group of men working in a department like that suddenly pay off their mortgages and an alarm bell not ring somewhere?' he asked, speaking his thought out loud. The silence on the other end of the phone told him Janet's thoughts. He was the Head of the Security Department. It was his job to notice things like that, not anyone else. *I must be getting old!* 'Anything else?'

'Some of them have healthy accounts but nothing special.'

'Not even Parker?'

'That's the really odd thing. Like the others he paid out his mortgage but other than that he doesn't have much money in any bank, and I mean any bank. I've checked them all plus the Building Societies and Credit Unions. The only place he has an account is right here and there is only a few thousand in it.'

'Has he accessed any of it in the last twenty-four hours?'

'No, definitely not!'

'Well, he has to have money stashed somewhere. He's bolted to parts unknown, possibly Queensland, and he needed money to do that!'

'I know Parker; he's a prat but he's also a very bright boy. Maybe he managed to have an account somewhere under a different name.'

'As you say, he's a bright boy. I don't suppose it would be too hard for him to accomplish. He's been planning this for over twelve months.'

'There is one other thing. Parker has a safety deposit box with us. I checked; he hasn't visited it in the last fortnight.'

'Can I access it?'

'Not with my help! Freezing an account is one thing; opening a secure safety deposit box is something entirely different!'

For half a second he thought about trying to intimidate her into helping him. That was all it took for him to realise it wouldn't work: not with her. Janet had her own direct line to Sir Winstanley and she wouldn't hesitate to use it if she thought he was going too far. 'It was just a thought.'

'Sorry I couldn't be more help.'

Blake shook his head. He was starting to get used to hearing that statement lately. He had sadly underestimated Mr. Geoffrey Parker. 'No, you did just fine. Can you send me up a copy of everything you have?'

'It is already on its way up.'

Blake ran his hand over his bald head. Feeling disillusioned with his performance so far, he made a commitment to get on top of things and quickly. He knew Sir Winstanley didn't like adverse publicity. That was why Sir Winstanley paid him so much money: to make sure there wasn't any. But he needed outside help if he was going to find Parker. Because of his old contacts within the Force he felt sure he could convince the Police to work quietly. The story he'd give was that Parker was a missing person and that the bank was worried about him. Nothing need be mentioned about missing money or shady deals. Hopefully he could redeem himself by finding Parker and keep Sir Winstanley happy.

Deciding it was time, he moved from behind his desk. Walking to the lift he went down to the sixth floor to the Computing Department. He knew it wasn't really called the Computing Department. It had a very fancy name as all the departments had these days but it was the department that looked after the computers so that is what he called it in his head. Knocking on a door, he walked in without waiting for a response. 'How are things going?'

Graham looked up from the printout he was studying, and said, 'They aren't so far!'

'What's the problem?' asked Blake, holding back his frustration only with difficulty.

Graham put down the printout and looked directly at the Head of Security. 'The problem is we know he has done something; we just don't know exactly what.' When Blake looked as though he was about to speak, Graham held up his hand to stop him. 'I know what you're going to say, and yes, we will figure it out; I just can't tell you when. I have been working on this all night and I'm close but I'm not there yet. And no, I don't know how much longer it will take!'

The computer expert's voice had been rising the longer he spoke and Blake sensed his frustration. He knew Graham had been working on this all night and this morning without a break as a personal favour for him. With a smile, he asked, 'Do you read tea leaves as well?' When Graham only looked at him with a puzzled expression, he clarified, 'You did a pretty good job of reading my mind. You answered all my questions without me needing to ask them.'

Graham smiled too now. 'You want a coffee?'

'I'd love one. Come on, let's go somewhere where they make a decent one: my treat.'

Graham picked up his worn jacket and followed him to the lifts. Neither of them spoke about Parker again until they were seated in a little coffee lounge around the corner and had a cup of steaming coffee in front of them.

'You can't beat a really good coffee,' said Graham, with feeling as he put his cup back on the saucer.

'No you can't!' agreed Blake, even though he hadn't bothered to touch his.

Graham smiled. 'Now you've calmed me down; what is it you want?'

Blake decided Graham's forthrightness deserved a full explanation. 'I've made a huge mistake and my job might be on the line. You're possibly the only one who can save me.'

'What can I do?'

'Parker has done a runner. We think he might have gone to Queensland; at least that's what his wife appears to think. I missed the fact he'd been collecting money on the side and I let him walk out of the bank. Now I don't know where he is. I don't even know what he did and you are the only person who can unlock the key. Soon

I'm going to have to take this to Sir Winstanley and I would like to be able to tell him more than, I think Parker stole a heap of money, but I don't know how, or how much and now I don't know where he is.' He slumped in his chair. 'I'd look like a complete idiot.'

'I'd better finish my coffee and head back to work then.'

Blake felt relieved when Graham didn't try to wangle some sort of concession or favour out of him. Blake rarely caved in, but this was different. As it was, he already felt inclined to do something for the man when he could. 'Is there anything I can do to help you?'

'Is there someone from Parker's department you could trust to keep their mouth shut?'

'I don't have a name off the top of my head but I am sure there must be. Why?'

Graham shrugged apologetically. 'This will only give you a guestimate but if we show the files we have to him, he might be able to have a good guess at how much money Parker might have made. If we deduct the amount he gave to the Bank we'll have some sort of an idea of how much money he might have stolen.'

'That's brilliant!'

'At best, it will only be a good guess,' said Graham, looking embarrassed by Blake's excitement.

'But at least I will have something when I go to Sir Winstanley and I'll have to do that by the end of the day.'

'Well, you never know, I might have cracked it wide open by then and you can have the real figures.'

Blake nodded in thanks but he didn't feel hopeful.

As soon as he got back to the bank he went to see Peter Christian. 'Who in Parker's department do you trust implicitly? Preferably, not someone friendly with Parker.'

Peter looked taken aback but he blurted out, 'Constansis, Carlo Constansis. He is a bank man through and through and he's had a couple of run-ins with Parker over the years. There is no love lost there.'

'Is he clever?' persisted Blake.

'Probably the only person there who is Parker's equal; that was why they fought. Parker liked being the best.'

'Send him up to my office straight away.'

'Of course, Mr. Blake.

CHAPTER 18

Mary waited and watched until the man from the Council went back through the gate. She breathed more easily when she heard his shoes clanking on the concrete path. Only when she was sure he'd gone did she slide down to the ground. She was shaking all over now. The man hadn't been suspicious but he wasn't looking for a missing man. Robert or the police might not be so easily put off.

She couldn't remember a letter from the Council but Geoffrey handled all the mail so that wasn't anything unusual. Shrugging off the man's unexpected visit, she walked back to the rear of the garage. She had almost finished. In another hour or so the grave would be filled in. Once she spread the remaining dirt around the garden, so it didn't stand out, the job would be done. Her arms felt like lead but this wasn't the time to stop. This was one job that had to be done right!

The sun had come out and the day was warm and the sky was a beautiful shade of blue. It seemed such a strange thing to do on such a lovely day but she took up her spade and returned to filling in the grave at the back of the garage.

Looking critically at the area in front of her, Mary tried to convince herself it didn't look suspicious but her conscience prevented her from being overly confident. It would be best if whoever came looking for Geoffrey didn't come back here.

After yet another shower she checked the bandage on her forehead. Her official assessment was that it would scar. Mary was good these days at judging what would leave a scar and what wouldn't. Still, it couldn't be helped. Replacing the butterfly bandages, she covered the whole area with a new padded bandage.

She made a late lunch for herself and slowly ate it. After she washed and put away the couple of dishes she had used she went into the back yard. Knowing no-one could see her, she strolled around the yard as she looked at her handiwork from all angles. To her conscience riddled mind, the yard screamed out, *There's a freshly dug grave here!*

She went back into the house and started worrying all over again. The freshly turned over garden mightn't look suspicious to a man from the Council but, if people didn't believe her story about Geoffrey going to Queensland, her handiwork might take on a more sinister connotation.

But what could she do?

Instead of falling into despair she tried to be positive. She had done a terrible thing; she had killed her husband but she had also survived when she was convinced she was going to die. She had refused to give in and she had won out. She had been terrified but she still hadn't given in. Geoffrey was stronger, both physically and mentally. He had dominated her as her mother had before him. Now they were both dead and she was still alive, so who was the stronger now? This thought gave her a new sense of confidence, one she had never experienced before. Maybe she was stronger than she thought?

If she wanted something to change, maybe she was the best person to ensure it happened? This reasoning had worked a couple of times now; just maybe it could continue to work for her. 'I have the power!' she recited to herself.

But did she really? Did she have the power to take her life back? What was stopping her? Her mother and Geoffrey were both dead. Who had any say now in what she did besides herself? The answer was no-one had control over her any more. She was free! She giggled before saying, 'I have the power!'

Only she had the power to change her life and make something of it. If she wanted something to happen, she had to make it happen! 'I have the power!' she shouted to the empty room.

Her new mantra gave her inspiration. Gardening wasn't the only helpful show on the radio. She'd listened to people giving advice on how to improve your yard. Paving was always high on the list to give a yard a lift. She had retrieved the money from Geoffrey's pocket before dragging him to his final resting spot. She'd thrown in his mobile phone, with the battery removed, but she'd held onto the money.

Going back outside, she searched the garage until she found a tape measure and measured the area behind the garage. Not wasting any time, she went back inside and took up the money Geoffrey had tried to take from her. She always considered this money her emergency money and now she couldn't think of a greater emergency.

As she lifted the phone from its cradle to call a taxi she spotted the keys for Geoffrey's BMW on the kitchen counter. Geoffrey must have tossed them there when he arrived home yesterday. She was relieved to think they weren't still in his pocket.

Picking up the keys she went into the garage and for the first time sat behind the wheel and started the shiny new BMW. With a press of the button, the door behind her rolled open and she slipped quietly out.

There wasn't a gardening centre close to where she lived and the further she drove the more her doubts returned to haunt her. She'd been feeling quite confident when she left home but by the time she parked she was shaking again. Forcing herself out of the car she roamed around the Centre, allowing the warm sun to soothe her rattled nerves. Spotting an area set up as a paving display she wandered over.

'Can I help you, Love?' came a cheerful voice from behind her.

Startled, she turned around, saying, 'I want to buy some pavers if I can?'

'That's what we are here for!' said the man, in his overly cheerful voice.

Despite his apparent cheerfulness, she took a dislike to him. His manner might be cheerful but she found him condescending.

Stepping closer, he asked, 'What sort of paver are you thinking of. We have plain concrete, colored concrete, regular shaped, patterned and clay!'

The list of choices overwhelmed her and she stuttered out, 'I'm not sure yet.'

'Where do you want to put them? Are they for a path, patio or a driveway?'

'I just want to tidy up an area at the end of the garage,' she mumbled, apologetically.

'OK then,' he said, taking her by the arm and leading her along. 'These shaped concrete ones would look great and are easy to lay. They are a little dearer but they will look nice.'

She didn't like the feel of his hand on her arm or the way he was talking to her. He was making her feel like a small child to whom everything had to be explained in simple terms. Normally she would have put up with it; today she felt differently. Pulling her arm away, she asked, 'Can I see the cheaper ones? I might like them.'

The expression on the man's face didn't change but she thought he didn't sound quite so cheerful as he pointed to her left. 'That is them there. There certainly isn't anything wrong with them; we wouldn't be selling them if there were,' he assured her. 'I just think these look nicer.'

Unfortunately she had to agree. The small interlocking pavers in front of her did have a pleasing look to them. Feeling a little deflated, she told him, 'I like these too.'

The spark returned to the man and he demanded in his usual manner, 'How big is the area?'

Meekly she handed him the piece of paper with the dimensions on it.

Taking it from her, he glanced at it before asking, 'Does your husband want to do this himself or do you want me to recommend someone?'

'My husband is in Queensland; I was going to do it myself.'

The man smirked as he gave her a look that said, *Now I've heard everything.* 'Have you done much paving before?'

'No.'

'I tell you what; why don't I give you the name of someone I can personally recommend? A small job like this will only cost you a couple of hundred and they will have it done in an afternoon!'

Mary could feel herself beginning to tremble again. She couldn't possibly let anyone near her yard. Her fear gave her the impetus to stand up to him. Bracing herself, she said as firmly as she could, 'But I want to do it myself!'

'Hey, I know just how you feel, but some jobs are best done by the experts. After all, it will only cost you more when they have to come and undo what you've done, so they can start again.'

She didn't care what this man said, or how silly it sounded; she had to do the paving herself and she was going to. Giving him what she hoped was a hard stare, she told him slowly and carefully, 'Are you going to sell me the pavers or do I have to find someone else.' Although she had begun reluctantly she felt pleased with herself when she finished her little speech.

While the man looked offended he smiled his professional smile. 'No need to be like that, Love, I'm happy to sell you anything you want.'

Mary was tempted to tell him to stop calling her *Love* but she didn't want to push it. She had stood up for herself and she felt good about it. She didn't see a need to push it any further.

Once she'd set him straight about what she wanted, the man turned out to be very helpful. Together they picked out a base paver then, feeling adventurous, Mary picked out a different colour to lay around the edge as a contrast. The man assured her it wouldn't be any harder than laying all the same colour, so Mary bought a few more to make a small design in the middle. The Centre could deliver all the pavers and the dolomite she would need to lay as a base later that afternoon. She paid and left feeling very pleased with herself.

Arriving home she rang Nancy and asked if it would be all right to pop in later that evening. Being assured she was welcome anytime she went back to preparing the ground for her pavers. The people from the garden center were even more prompt than she'd hoped for. Tuesdays were quiet days and they virtually followed her home. By the time she changed and marked out where she wanted the pavers they had arrived with them. Using her small wheelbarrow she transferred the pavers and then the dolomite to the backyard. Fortunately it wasn't far and she managed to do it without incident. That was when she discovered listening to someone talking about doing a job wasn't the same as experience. It didn't seem to be going as well as she had planned but she refused to give in. She spent a lot longer than she hoped to get the dolomite laid and spread so it looked flat. She wasn't completely happy but it didn't look too bad once she watered it down the way the man told her to.

Now it was getting dark and she had to stop, not just because it was getting dark. She had pushed herself beyond all her limits and now she was physically and mentally exhausted. She'd deliberately kept busy all day so the reality of what she'd done didn't weigh her down. She didn't know if she could handle the self-recriminations that would come with the realisation she had actually killed Geoffrey.

Even though it felt like she had done nothing else lately she showered once more and dressed to go over to Nancy's. She didn't know what she was going to say to her friend but she needed to talk to someone. The drive over was a nightmare. Halfway there she wished she'd taken a taxi. She was so tired she could hardly keep her eyes open. Finally she reached the safe haven of Nancy's house and, pulling into the drive, felt herself relax. Covered in sweat she struggled from the car and headed to the front door. The front light flicked on as she approached it and the door was opened by Nancy even before she could ring the bell. 'Hello,' she said, trying to make her greeting sound bright and cheery. It didn't work.

When Nancy saw the fresh bandage on Mary's forehead she burst into tears. Throwing her arms around Mary, she hugged her as they both cried, neither speaking, yet communicating in a way only true friends can.

They managed to get themselves inside and Nancy installed Mary on the sofa. 'Let me take a look at that for you,' said Nancy through her tears.

Mary wanted to tell her friend she had more experience with treating cuts than her but she didn't have the strength left in her. Nancy tenderly peeled back the soft bandage to expose the raw cut underneath. 'I'll be back in a second or two.' Nancy went to the kitchen in search of her first aid kit.

'Is everything alright?'

'I don't know. Mary has a big cut on her forehead and I need the first aid kit.'

'I'll get it,' offered Ricky, jumping off the stool. Dashing into the laundry, he returned seconds later with the tiny white box. 'Do you need any help?'

Nancy gave him a loving look, knowing how much he wanted to help but was willing to stay out of the way if that was what she wanted. 'Give us a little time alone first, OK!'

'Yeah, sure thing.' His face was a grim mask as he told her. 'Call me if you need me.'

'I will,' promised Nancy as she went back to Mary. Sitting on the sofa she placed the small first aid kit next to her. Flipping it open she took out a tiny bottle of antiseptic and spilt a little over a piece of cotton wool. Wiping it around the edge of the cut, she felt as though she was at least doing something to help. Neither of them spoke until Nancy replaced the soft padding with one of her own. When she finished she put the first aid kit on a nearby table. With her back to Mary, she asked, 'Did he do this to you?'

'Yes,' came Mary's soft reply.

'Don't go back; stay here with us.'

Mary threw herself against Nancy as huge sobs wracked her body. She had neglected her friend for three years, yet Nancy was still willing help her this way. They sat together, just holding onto one another for a long time, while Mary fought back the rising madness that threatened to overwhelm her. Should she have called the police? Should she have let Geoffrey do what he wanted instead of fighting back? Geoffrey might not have killed her and he would still be alive!

I killed my husband!

She knew it was wrong to kill someone, no matter what. She had no right to kill him: no right! But he had no right sleeping with Chantelle either. It didn't excuse her killing him; it only made it worse somehow. You couldn't kill someone because they were adulterous. But that wasn't why she had killed him; she had killed him because he was going to kill her. You could protect yourself, couldn't you? Her thoughts went around and around making less sense to her each time. She was becoming so muddled it was becoming hard to remember what she had done and why.

Slowly her sobbing eased until she was close to being under control. 'It's Ok, he's gone,' she said in no more than a whisper.

'What did you say?'

'I said he's gone.'

'What about when he comes back?'

'He isn't coming back.'

Nancy gave her a look Mary couldn't interpret, before saying, 'You poor thing!' With a self-conscious smile, Nancy said, 'How can you be so sure?'

'I just know.'

'Did he say so?'

She assumed Nancy wasn't going to let this go without more from her. Remembering the lie she'd used with the man from the Council, she said, 'Geoffrey's gone to Queensland.'

'For good?'

'Yes. Apparently there was some trouble at the bank and he couldn't face anyone. You know how he is. He doesn't like being embarrassed so he's gone and he isn't coming back.'

Nancy looked at the white bandage on Mary's forehead. 'Was that a last going away gift?'

'Something like that, but the important thing is, he's gone.'

'And not before time.'

Strangely she felt offended to hear her friend talk this way about Geoffrey and she was tempted to defend him. But what could she say? Nancy appeared to have believed her story so why drag things out? 'Enough about me: let's talk about something else.'

The pair chatted for a time before Ricky felt confident enough to make an appearance. He came in carrying a tray loaded full of food and three glasses of wine. Mary thanked him even though she thought it was a wasted effort. She hadn't eaten since lunch but she wasn't hungry. She dug her fork into a single piece of pasta only to show her appreciation. The cheesy cream sauce and the fresh pasta melted in her mouth and she was soon wolfing it down. 'Where do you buy pasta like this?' she wanted to know.

'Ricky makes it himself!' answered Nancy, proudly.

'My mother taught me how,' he said, looking embarrassed by Mary's enthusiasm. 'She was Italian.'

'Well this is the best pasta I have ever eaten.'

She thought she'd successfully diverted the conversation away from herself when Nancy suddenly asked, 'There's a rumor going around that the bank let Geoffrey go?'

She ate in silence for a moment or two longer while she decided what to say. She decided they deserved the truth. Maybe not all the truth, after all she didn't want to make them accomplices. If it all ended up badly and the police found out what she had done, she didn't want Nancy's and Ricky's kindness to land them in trouble. 'It seems he was trading outside the bank's guidelines. I really don't know much more than that. He wasn't in a very talkative mood when he came home.'

'What happened?' persisted Nancy.

'He stormed in, started screaming how the fools at the bank were shortsighted and that his way was the best, but they couldn't see it.' She hesitated before adding, 'He hit me a few times then packed a bag saying he was going and wasn't coming back. He said he was going to Queensland but I don't really know where he is.'

'You're better off without him,' said Ricky, making his first real contribution to the conversation.

Mary looked at him and smiled. 'He told me what you said to him. I don't know why you did but thank you all the same. It's nice to know someone cares.'

Ricky didn't return her smile, as he said, 'If he ever tries to come back, you call me or you come straight over here. I mean it; you call me!'

She had only met him a couple of times yet she knew he meant what he said. 'I really don't think he will come back but I will, I promise,' she said, as she wiped away a tear from her face.

'What are you going to do?'

'I don't know,' she answered truthfully. In fact she hadn't even thought about it until now. 'I suppose I'll have to get a job.'

'Do you want me to ask at the bank?' offered Ricky.

'No, I don't think I want to go back there again.'

'I'll ask around; see if anyone knows of something somewhere else.'

She rewarded him with another sad smile. 'Thanks, Ricky, that would be nice.'

'What about the house and things?' asked Nancy. 'How will you pay the mortgage in the meantime?'

'I haven't thought about any of that. I don't even know how much the mortgage is each week.'

'I have some friends working in that department. I'll have a talk with them and find out some details for you.'

'I don't suppose there is a great rush,' she said, more in hope than with any real conviction.

Ricky and Nancy refused to let her go home alone. They made up the spare room for her. In truth she felt relieved; she didn't want to be in her house on her own either. Nancy lent her a nighty and to her disbelief, she fell asleep as soon as her head hit the pillow.

***

Blake didn't have a good night. Sir Winstanley had been too busy to see him the day before and he took it as a rebuke. That morning he contacted Sir Winstanley's secretary by phone instead of simply walking up the stairs as he would normally have done. She informed him Sir Winstanley would be able to see him at eleven. Blake was seriously worried now. Sir Winstanley had made this business with Parker a priority and now he could hardly get an appointment with him. While he was baffled at Sir Winstanley's sudden lack of interest he used the extra time to good advantage. Carlo Constansis was doing a great job and they now had an idea of what they were looking for. The figure put forward by Carlo staggered even Blake and he wanted Parker more than ever now.

Graham was making good progress too and he was confident he would soon know exactly what Parker had done. True to his word, he kept Blake informed of every piece of information as soon as he got it. The complete picture was still muddy but it was becoming clearer by the hour.

When eleven o'clock finally arrived, Blake walked up stairs and entered the outer office to Sir Winstanley's. 'Hello, Pat,' he said in a tired voice.

Sir Winstanley's secretary, Patricia Carmody, gave him an encouraging smile in return. 'He's ready for you so you can go straight in.'

'Good morning, Sir.'

The head of the bank looked up and smiled. 'You look terrible.'

'I feel even worse,' confessed Blake.

'What is the matter?' asked Sir Winstanley, sounding concerned.

'It's Parker; he has completely outsmarted me.'

'Take a seat and we can go through this.'

Blake was confused now. Sir Winstanley appeared to be genuinely concerned. 'I had the feeling you were annoyed with me?' he said, unable to be anything but blunt.

'Me? Whatever gave you that idea?'

'You couldn't see me last night,' he said, realising how lame it sounded.

'I have a life too you know,' said Sir Winstanley, smiling. 'Yesterday was my only grandson's birthday and I left early.'

Blake was truly surprised. Not by the fact that it was Sir Winstanley's grandsons birthday but because Sir Winstanley had a life outside of the bank. In all the years he had worked here he had never heard of Sir Winstanley taking time off before.

Waving away his family, Sir Winstanley got down to business. 'So tell me, where are we with this Parker business?'

'Parker is a very clever man. He corrupted the bank's computers to the extent we haven't been able to fully understand all that he did. We do, however, have enough information to have a fairly good guess.'

'I don't like guesses,' slipped in Sir Winstanley.

'Neither do I; however, at this stage that is all we have. Graham Watson is working around the clock to give me a full picture but it has been slow going.'

'Where is Parker? Has he refused to assist you?'

This was the part Blake had been dreading. 'Parker hasn't returned and I don't know where he is.'

Sir Winstanley obviously wasn't happy but he held himself in check. 'Well, you had better find him then.'

'To do that I will need to involve the Police. I have a number of friends there still and I'm sure we could have him listed as a missing person. There will be no mention of his activities: only the fact he is missing and we are worried about him.'

Sir Winstanley nodded in his sage-like manner. 'I will approve this action only if you can assure me the bank's reputation will not come under question.'

'I can.' Blake opened his briefcase and passed across a detailed report. 'I'll leave this with you while I'll get started.' He gave a sigh of relief as he stepped out of the office. It had gone a lot better than he had thought but he had to find Parker; Parker was the key.

A B Given

CHAPTER 19

Mary woke to find Ricky cooking her a full breakfast. She sat down to a bowl of cereal followed by a plate of scrambled eggs served with two rashes of crispy bacon, washed down by her choice of orange juice or coffee or both.

'You'll have to watch out, Nancy. If you eat like this all the time you're going to end up the size of a house.'

Nancy poked her rude finger up at her but she was smiling. Mary laughed. The sound of her laugher took her by surprise. Only yesterday she thought she would never laugh again. It amazed her and she marvelled at how wonderful a tonic friendship was. Friendship, it appeared, could cure just about anything.

'Don't worry; we don't eat like this all the time. Ricky is just showing off.'

She noticed her friend wasn't dressed for work. 'You had better get moving,' she warned her. 'You'll be late.'

'I was thinking I wouldn't go in today.'

Normally she would be pleased but she had to do her paving today and it might be hard to explain to Nancy. Trying not to hurt her friend's feelings, she said, 'I appreciate the offer but I am alright. Honest! Besides, I have some things I need to do.'

Nancy didn't look happy but she grudgingly agreed. 'But only if you promise to come back again tonight. Ricky is planning something really special.'

'Oh well, if Ricky is cooking, I wouldn't miss it for the world.'

She dressed in her clothes from the day before and headed home. She felt so much better than she thought she had a right to but she wasn't going to let that upset her. To keep her mind busy she threw herself into the task of paving, hardly noticing how fast the day flew by. She'd listened carefully when the people on the radio said the way to a good result was to have a good base so she spent most of the morning playing with the dolomite until she was finally happy with how it looked.

The first row of pavers was slow while she moved them this way and that trying to get them dead straight. After that, they slipped into place quicker than she could have ever imagined. Even the little design of contrasting pavers in the middle didn't delay her. By the time the sun was beginning to cool she stepped back and admired her job. Pushing the reason she had done it out of her mind, she was pleased with it. The paving didn't even look out of place so she doubted anyone would question why it was there. After tidying up her tools neatly in the garage she showered and changed to go over to Nancy's.

✳ ✳ ✳

Detectives Paul Pennin and Bruce Harrison looked at each other as they passed the Inspector as he walked out of their boss's office. 'What do you think he was doing in there?' asked Paul.

Bruce gave a shrug. 'I think we're about to find out.'

The pair stepped into the office. Captain Lewis looked up. 'I've got a new assignment for you.'

'What's that?'

'Guy's name is Geoffrey Parker,' said Lewis, sliding a thin file across his desk towards them. 'He's missing and his employers are worried about him. I want you pair to find him and fast!'

'This is crap!' said Paul, not able to control himself.

'No it isn't and you will give this your full attention. As of now, all your other cases have been reassigned.'

Paul and Bruce looked at each other. That could only mean one thing. Someone very high up had an interest in the outcome of this case. 'Is there anything else we should know?' asked Bruce, not trusting his partner to speak.

'As a matter of fact there is. I have been instructed to tell you two to be discreet. Someone doesn't want this to turn up in the media.'

That sealed it; they were in trouble. These cases never turned out well.

Back in their office they read and re-read the file they had been given. It listed a lot of information about Parker, including where someone had spoken with his wife. There was a cryptic comment about how she thought her husband was in Queensland but he could be anywhere. A check of his bank accounts wasn't going to give then any clues either. They'd been frozen but apparently he had access to another source of money. What that source was, it didn't say. Nor did it say how they knew.

'Where do you want to start?' asked Paul.

'Send his photo out to all the other States and we'll go over and see the wife.'

✳ ✳ ✳

Mary was just collecting her handbag before heading to Nancy's when the doorbell rang. Without wondering too much about it she answered the door.

'Mrs. Parker?' asked the taller of the two men standing there.

Mary didn't have to be told who they were; she knew. 'Yes,' she said, hoping her trembling didn't show.

'I am Detective Paul Pennin and this is Detective Bruce Harrison. May we come in and speak with you?'

'Certainly.' She stepped back from the doorway. Leading them into the lounge room, she sat down before she fell. Facing the two policemen, she waited for one of them to speak.

'This may sound a little strange; however, we have been notified by your husband's Employer that your husband is missing. Are you able to give us any information on his current whereabouts?'

Mary's mind raced. This didn't sound too bad. She'd been thinking they were going to ask why she had been digging big holes in the yard then paving over them. That she would have trouble explaining. Trying to keep her voice as even as possible, she told them, 'I'm afraid I don't know where my husband is.'

'I understand there was a thought he might be in Queensland and that you were planning to join him there?'

She was puzzled now. The only person she'd told that lie to was the strange man from the council. Why would the police have been talking to him? 'My husband and I have parted.'

Speaking for the first time, Bruce asked in a quiet, kindly voice, 'Did he do that to you?'

Instinctively Mary's hand went to her forehead. 'This is very hard for me to talk about,' she said, turning slightly away. Taking a deep breath, she told them, 'My husband has beaten me since our wedding three years ago. I have always covered for him because I loved him and I thought he loved me. On Monday he came home early, telling me he had been dismissed from the bank. When I refused to go with him, he hit me. He has left and I don't know where he is nor do I want to know.' Her tears were genuine.

Bruce stepped forward and handed her a handkerchief. He allowed her time to wipe her eyes before asking, 'I apologise for labouring the point but did you just say, your husband told you he'd been dismissed?'

'Yes. My husband was a futures trader for the bank. Apparently he was not following their guidelines and they were not happy about it.'

Bruce and Paul exchanged glances before Bruce continued. 'Do you know exactly what you husband did that upset the bank?'

'No, I'm afraid I don't. You'll have to ask them.'

Paul took a card out of his pocket and handed it to her. 'If your husband contacts you, or if you think of anything, please call me at any time.'

'I have no wish to ever see my husband again but, if he contacts me, I will gladly call you.'

'Thank you for your time, Mrs. Parker.'

They turned to leave. At the door Paul turned back and asked, 'If something comes up, is it alright if we speak with you again?'

'Anytime.'

'What do you make of that?' asked Paul as they drove away.

Bruce shook his head. 'I really don't know. I'd like to believe her but there was something about her that worries me.'

'What?' asked Paul, confident in his partner's instincts.

'She just looked so guilty.'

'I know what you mean: but guilty of what?'

'That's the sixty-four thousand dollar question!'

'And what is this business about him being fired from the bank?'

'Actually, I think it explains a lot. I'd say our man's mysterious source of money might not belong to him. I think it belongs to the bank and they want it back.'

'Why didn't they just list it as fraud?'

'Because they don't want to look like fools! They'd rather we looked for him as a missing person. Once we've found him then they'll worry how they get their money back.'

'I wonder how much money he took?'

'I wonder how much his wife knows?'

***

Wilson Blake wasn't one to rely on a single source for information. He summoned Frank to his office. 'I need you to do something for me!' he said, as Frank walked through the door.

Frank was used to Blake's manner and he smiled at the other man's abruptness. 'What is that, Mr. Blake?'

'You managed to become quite friendly with Parker, didn't you? You even spent a night at his house, I believe?'

'That's right.'

'What do you think of the wife?'

'Mousy little thing who does as she's told.'

'Do you think she is capable of covering for her husband?'

'I think she'd do anything he told her to do.'

Blake paused for a moment, thinking over Frank's replies, before adding, 'They say he beats her. Apparently she is sporting a bandage on her forehead, compliments of Monday. Do you still think she could be covering for him?'

'A bandage on her head wouldn't change anything. She is completely besotted with him. My guess is she knows exactly where he is and if she doesn't, she soon will.'

Blake nodded slowly. This had been exactly what he had been hoping to hear. 'I want you to go over there. Give her a sympathetic ear and see what you can get out of her.'

'I'll do my best, Sir.'

Blake was distracted with his own problems, yet the man's strange smile registered on him. As it wasn't important he tried to dismiss it, but it stayed with him like an itch that won't go away.

***

Mary was thinking her problems were nearly over. The police had come and gone and, while they might come back, if she stuck to her story she didn't know quite what they could do. She'd stuck doggedly to her story each time Geoffrey beat her and it had protected him, so why shouldn't it work for her?

She spent another enjoyable night with Nancy and Ricky where she received the most wonderful news. She didn't know how but there was no mortgage to pay. With no mortgage payments she felt sure she could manage things until she could sell the house. She didn't like the idea of living so close to her husband's body.

Returning home, she spent a disappointing morning going through her husband's papers only to find nothing of interest. She couldn't find any details on his bank accounts. She knew he had to have one and it would only be at the bank where he worked. Geoffrey had been like that; he would never have put any money with anyone else.

This was a real drawback to her plans. She knew Geoffrey must have some money but it didn't look as though she was going to be able to get her hands on it. That was when she found the key. It puzzled her for some time. She felt like she had seen one like it before but she couldn't think where. She was sure it didn't fit anything in the house. Rolling it over and over between her fingers she spotted a number imprinted on it. In a flash it came to her. It was a key to a bank safety deposit box. While the name of the bank wasn't on the key, she knew which bank it belonged to. She had seen keys like this one when she worked there.

When the doorbell sounded she hurriedly put the key back where she had found it. Expecting the police, she braced herself and opened the door. Despite the effort she had put into steadying herself, her surprise showed clearly on her face when she opened the door.

'You didn't think I would forget you, did you?' asked Frank, with a broad grin.

She tried to slam the door closed but Frank easily shouldered it aside and forced his way in. 'Now is that anyway to greet me?' he asked, still smiling.

'Geoffrey's not here!' she blurted out, hoping it was the reason he had come.

'I know that, Gorgeous; that's why I'm here. He won't be back so I have come to claim you for myself.'

She wasn't quite sure what he was talking about but it didn't sound good. When Geoffrey was alive she felt compelled to do what Frank said, for fear of what Geoffrey might do. Now Geoffrey was dead she no longer feared him. Of course Frank didn't know Geoffrey was dead but that didn't matter. She still wasn't going to do anything he wanted just because he told her to. Frank frightened her but not in the same way Geoffrey had. She didn't think Frank would actually kill her. He might hurt her but she had been hurt before. Being beaten no longer held any great fears for her. She would prefer not to be hurt of course, but she wouldn't let fear of pain force her into doing something she didn't want to do. Silently she said to herself: *I have the power.* She wasn't sure what she had the power to do in this instance but saying the mantra helped to steady her frayed nerves. 'I don't understand.'

Frank's smile only broadened. 'I'll make it clear for you, Gorgeous. Your husband is gone and I am going to be your new master.'

'You're insane!' she said without thinking.

Frank's hand swung so quickly she didn't see it coming. All she knew was she'd been knocked to the floor. The right side of her face hurt like hell and spots swam before her eyes. Before she could recover she felt him take hold of her hair and pull her roughly to her feet. 'Don't you ever talk to me like that, Bitch. You will treat me with the proper respect.'

She could taste blood, which didn't surprise her much. She ran her tongue over her teeth and found them all still where they should be. She shook her head to try and clear it, knowing she had to stay strong. If she let this man dominate her now she might well end up his slave.

'Take off your clothes!'

She knew it was going to cost her but, in as clear a voice as she could manage, she said, 'No!'

Frank's fist slammed into her unprotected stomach. She was still doubled over when he punched her in the side of the head knocking her to the ground a second time. She was only semi-conscious as he pulled her to her feet. Her stomach hadn't recovered from the beating Geoffrey had given her on Monday and it now hurt worse than before. Her head felt like it was packed with cotton-wool. Her thoughts wouldn't flow properly. The only thing that went around and around in her head was, *I have the power.* She hurt and she knew she was going to hurt a lot worse by the time this was finished but she now knew what she had the power to do. She had the power to say *No!* Frank may do things to her and she may not be able to stop him but he would have to do them without her help.

Using her hair, Frank slammed her back against the wall. Only his grip on her hair held her upright. 'I said, take off your clothes, you fucking bitch!'

Even through the fog surrounding her brain she could feel his spittle on her face. Frank was in a rage and she knew he was going to do things she didn't want. 'No.'

This time she spoke so softly Frank hardly heard her. He couldn't understand what was happening. He had fantasised about this for days now and it wasn't supposed to go like this. She had been willing before, so why wasn't she now? Now Geoffrey was gone, she should belong to him, she should be doing what she was told. Holding her up with one hand, he used the other to rip her dress free. Next came her pretty underwear. Even in his rage he took time to look her naked body over, taking pleasure in her pain and her humiliation.

He forced her down to her knees. Unfastening his pants he let them fall to his ankles. 'You know what to do, Bitch.'

Mary raised her face and looked at him. She knew it would be easy to do what he wanted. She'd done this many times for Geoffrey. She'd also suffered three years of humiliation in her marriage and all for nothing. She didn't want any more. She'd been set free and she didn't want to go back to that way of life. Knowing this was the only way to freedom, she whispered through her split lips, 'No.'

He reached down and pinched her breasts until she screamed in pain. 'Do it!'

'No,' she managed to squeeze out between her screams.

He lost all control and punched her so hard she blacked out.

Feeling frustrated and confused he removed the rest of his clothes and carried her prone body into the bedroom and threw her on the bed. This wasn't supposed to be happening this way. The bitch was supposed to be begging him to do things to her, not fighting him like this. He had so many plans for her but they wouldn't come true unless she submitted to him as she had before. He climbed onto the bed with her. If she wasn't going to cooperate then he would just have to make her. Spreading her legs wide apart he raped her while she was still unconscious. It released some of his frustrations but only added to others. He didn't like it like this; he wanted her to know what he was doing to her. He wanted her to know he could do anything he wanted and there wasn't anything she could do about it. If she understood that, then maybe she would behave as she was supposed to. He turned her over onto the stomach before ransacking her drawers. Using the stockings he found there he tied her to the bed and waited for her to regain consciousness.

Mary felt like she was floating. There was a dull pain she couldn't quite locate. It didn't matter; she was only dreaming. It felt like she was lying on her stomach, only she couldn't move. She shook her head, and then wished she hadn't. Pain flared inside her head, making it throb. From behind her, Frank said, 'Are you ready to behave?'

In a flash it all came back to her. *I have the power*, raced through her mind, taking over her fear. 'No!'

Crack! She groaned loudly as a burning hot line of pain spread across her exposed buttocks.

With his belt swinging easily in his hand, Frank asked again, 'Are you ready to behave?'

'No!'

Crack!

He kept this routine up even after she was no longer capable of saying no. He took her silence to his repeated question as a refusal and whipped her again and again. Only when his arm became tired did he stop. By now her back, buttocks and legs were covered with bright red welts. 'You will learn,' he told her as he climbed up behind her. He sodomised her making sure to hurt her. When he finished with her, he loosened her bonds. Rolling her over he looked down on her 'I will be back and next time I will not be so gentle. You think about that, Bitch!'

She was beyond caring when he spat in her face and he left.

She didn't know how long she lay on the bed unable to move. The phone rang a couple of times but she didn't have the energy to reach for it. When it rang the third time she was determined to try. Excruciating pain raced across her back and shoulders but she refused to give in to it. Fearful the person on the other end would hang-up before she reached it, Mary made one final lunge. Her hand came close to knocking it out of reach before she managed to wrap her fingers around the hand-piece. As she slowly dragged it towards her, she heard a voice. She didn't care about the voice or the words they were saying, she had her own message. 'Help me!' she croaked. The voice on the other end stopped momentarily. Then she thought she heard someone ask, 'Mary, is that you?'

'Help me!' she repeated as the phone slipped from her grasp, clattering onto the floor. She collapsed on the bed and thankfully slipped into oblivion.

When she woke, Nancy was sitting on the bed next to her, washing her back with an antiseptic mix. Nancy didn't know if it was helping but it was the only thing she could think of and she had to do something. 'Oh, Mary, what happened? Did Geoffrey come home after all?'

'No, not Geoffrey,' was all she had the strength to say. The burning pain had eased somewhat but she still felt terrible. She hurt almost everywhere. Her head felt like it was about to split in two and she couldn't see out of her right eye.

Nancy helped her to turn over and to get into a sitting position. Then with Nancy's help she managed to swallow a couple of tablets. 'These should help,' said Nancy, confidently. 'Ricky went to the Chemist and demanded the strongest pain killers they had.'

She didn't feel as if she could talk yet so she allowed Nancy to lower her back onto the bed again. When Nancy had washed away the dried blood from her face she found she could open her right eye a little. It was a relief to know the lid had simply been stuck with dry blood and that she didn't have any permanent damage.

She lay back and let Nancy administer what assistance she could while she waited for the painkillers to kick in. When she felt the sharp edge of her pain begin to recede she pointed to the small cupboard in the corner of the room. Through her split lips, she managed to murmur, 'Key!'

'What do you want?' asked Nancy, anxious to do anything her friend wanted.

It hurt her but she pointed again, repeating her cryptic demand. 'Key!'

Nancy slipped off the bed and went to the cupboard. Pointing to the top drawer, she asked, 'Is it in here?'

Mary shook her head and wished she hadn't. Spots floated in front of her eyes and a sharp pain raced across her forehead.

Pointing to the middle drawer, Nancy asked, 'Here?'

'Yes,' she murmured, not willing to risk nodding.

Nancy rummaged through the drawer until she found a small key. Holding it up, she asked, 'This it?' The relief in Mary's eyes told her all she needed to know. Carrying it back she placed the key in Mary's hand. Nancy didn't know what the key was for but it obviously meant a lot to Mary so she was glad she'd been able to find it.

Mary finally slept again. This time it was a more restful sleep, the strong tablets masking the pain so her mind could rest. When she woke for the second time she was surprised to find she was able to move without too much trouble. She was still very stiff and very sore but she managed to struggle off the bed. Slipping her robe over her shoulders she limped heavily to the bathroom.

Empting her bladder she felt even better. Using the furniture for support she limped out of the bedroom. That was as far as she got before she felt a strong arm wrap gently around her waist. 'Where are you going?' She recognised Ricky's concerned voice and allowed herself to slump against him for support. 'I don't know?' she answered truthfully.

'Did you want to sit up for a while?'

She wasn't sure but it sounded like a good idea. 'Yes please.'

Ricky half-carried, half-dragged her into the lounge room before gently placing her onto the sofa. 'Wait here and I'll be back.'

If she didn't know how much it would hurt her, she would have laughed. Where was she going to go?

Seconds later Nancy came running into the room. 'My God, Mary, what are you doing up?'

'I don't know,' she answered, with her best attempt at a smile.

A cut on her lip split and Nancy rushed to her and wiped away a spot of blood. 'Why did you let her get out of bed?' Nancy demanded harshly of her husband.

'She was already up when I found her!' he said, pleading his innocence.

Nancy gave him a look that said she had expected better of him before turning back to her friend. 'Is there anything I can get you?'

'Is there any more of those tablets?'

Ricky was already racing from the room before Nancy could ask him to fetch them. Once Mary had swallowed a couple, Nancy sat next to her, and asked, 'Can you talk about it?'

'Yes,' she said, knowing she wouldn't be able to tell her friend the whole truth. How could she admit something like that! How could she tell Nancy she had allowed this man to treat her the way he had? She had submitted to him, denying him nothing and this was her punishment. Only this time she felt free from guilt. This time she hadn't done anything he wanted. He had taken what he wanted by force and she felt better knowing she hadn't submitted to him.

'You said earlier that it wasn't Geoffrey?'

'No, it wasn't Geoffrey.'

'Do you know who it was?'

'A man called Frank Dobson.'

'Do you know why he did this to you?'

'He worked with Geoffrey. He wanted to know where Geoffrey was but I didn't know!'

Mary's story was plausible enough and both Nancy and Ricky believed her. 'This guy works at the bank?' asked Ricky, sounding incredulous.

Before Mary could respond, Nancy said, 'We have to call the police!'

'No police!'

The fear in Mary's eyes forced Nancy to look away. She suspected why Mary didn't want to involve the police, only she didn't want to admit it even to herself. 'Ok then. But you will come and stay with us and no arguments this time!'

The second lot of tablets were starting to take effect and she felt drowsy again. Ricky very carefully picked her up and carried her back to bed. They closed the door and went back to the lounge room. 'Why did you say we wouldn't call the cops?' demanded Ricky.

Nancy knew he wouldn't accept anything less than the truth. 'What else could I say?'

Ricky lowered his eyes, as he said, 'Because of the way she was raped?'

'Mostly, but...'

Ricky looked up. 'And what else?'

Nancy began hesitantly. 'You know when she said Geoffrey wasn't coming back?'

'Yes,' answered Ricky, wondering what Geoffrey had to do with this.

'I think there is a good reason why she knows he isn't coming back!'

Ricky stared at her with a puzzled expression until the import of her words registered with him. 'What are you saying?'

'I don't know anything for sure, but I think that's why she doesn't want to involve the police.'

'You don't think she's the reason no-one can find him, do you?'

'No!' she said, hurriedly. 'But I'm sure she knows more than she's telling us; that's why she doesn't want to talk to the police.'

'If she was the reason no-one can find him, I wouldn't blame her.'

'Neither would I, but let's leave her with her secrets, for now.'

Ricky nodded in agreement. 'Come on, we should try and get some sleep too while she is out to it.'

Nancy let him guide her to the spare room where they had set themselves up. Despite her vow to stay awake, in case Mary needed her, they were both soon fast asleep.

A B Given

CHAPTER 20

Graham finally broke the last of Geoffrey's codes and was busy deciphering all he had done. Blake was waiting anxiously for the next report. While it wouldn't be definitive, it would expose the bulk of what Parker and his friends had been up to and, more importantly, it would give them an accurate figure on how much money was missing. Blake couldn't wait.

* * *

'Hello,' said Robert uncertainly, when greeted by two well-dressed strangers at his front door.

'Good morning, Mr. Parker, I am Detective Paul Pennin and this is Detective Bruce Harrison. May we come in?'

'Yes, of course,' said Robert, making way for them. 'Follow me,' he said, leading them down the stairs to the main lounge room. Chantelle gave him a questioning look and Robert explained, 'These two gentlemen are detectives.'

'I am Detective Paul Pennin and this is Detective Bruce Harrison,' Paul repeated for Chantelle's benefit.

'What can I do for you?' asked Robert, looking decidedly nervous.

Paul smiled, hoping to put the man at ease before starting. 'Your brother's employers are concerned about him. Apparently he has been missing for a couple of days and they have asked us to try and locate him.'

Before Robert could respond, Chantelle stepped forward and took control. 'You mean the bank doesn't know where he is?'

'No, Mrs. Parker.'

'But that is ridiculous; he works there.'

'Apparently he walked out one day and they haven't seen him since,' stated Paul, blandly.

To Chantelle everything was obvious. Geoffrey had managed to get the money and now the bank was looking for him. She didn't believe this story the bank was putting out...but if he had the money, why hadn't he contacted her? The answer came to her in a flash! 'It's that bitch wife of his. She's done something to him!'

Over the years the two detectives had worked out a routine for questioning people: a routine they now followed unconsciously. Paul would introduce them and state why they were there and then Bruce would take over, so it was he who responded to Chantelle's accusation. 'Why do you say that?'

'It's the only thing that makes any sense. Geoffrey wouldn't just run off and not say anything to me!'

'Why do you believe Mr. Parker would feel compelled to contact you?'

Chantelle realised she'd made a mistake. 'Because he just wouldn't! Not without letting Robert know where he was.'

'I see,' said Bruce, before adding, 'His wife claims her husband has gone to Queensland and is looking for a new place for them to live.'

'That's a lie!'

'Can you tell me how you know that, Mrs. Parker?'

'Because he told me he was leaving her. If he is missing it's because she did something to him.'

Robert had been standing back listening to the conversation. The two detectives might be confused but he wasn't. He understood exactly what was going on. His wife knew Geoffrey was leaving Mary because they were lovers. He worked it out long ago but he didn't know how to broach the subject with either of them. Geoffrey's sudden disappearance explained Chantelle's mood over the last couple of days. She'd been waiting to hear from him, probably so she could join him. Robert liked Mary and he didn't want to see her good name ruined by his wife's malicious tongue. 'Geoffrey isn't missing,' he said, stepping forward. 'I spoke with him yesterday. He is in Cairns.'

'Why didn't you mention this earlier?' asked Bruce.

Giving Chantelle a glare, he said, 'I would have but I couldn't get a word in.'

'Did he say where exactly in Cairns he was?'

'No, I'm afraid he didn't. As Mary said, he is moving around looking for somewhere for them to live.'

'That is a lie!' shouted Chantelle. 'He's lying!'

'And why would your husband lie to us?'

When Chantelle didn't speak up, Robert did. 'Because my wife is under the mistaken impression Geoffrey was going to take her with him.' Giving the two detectives an apologetic shrug, he told them, 'I am afraid my wife has always been infatuated with my younger brother and he was moving to get away from her. That is why he spoke with me and not my wife.'

'Liar!' screamed Chantelle throwing herself at him. 'He loves me, he loves me!'

It took both the detectives to restrain her. Even while they held her she continued to rant and rave at her husband, cursing him and shouting out the foulest obscenities they'd heard. 'Mrs. Parker, get hold of yourself!' shouted Bruce, trying to make himself heard over her screams. When Chantelle appeared to relax they released their hold on her. Chantelle took the opportunity to attack Robert again, raking his face with her long nails.

This time they handcuffed her. Bruce told her sternly, 'Mrs. Parker, I am arresting you for the assault of your husband.'

Paul went to Robert's aid, placing a handkerchief to his bleeding face. 'Are you alright, Sir,' he asked, feeling more shaken than he would have admitted. The venom of the woman's attack had surprised even him. 'We're taking your wife down to the Station while we try and calm her down. I suggest you go to the hospital and have someone look at your face and then come down to the station where we can try and sort this out.'

Chantelle fell into a fit of uncontrolled sobbing so Paul and Bruce had to half-carry her up the stairs and out to the car.

✸ ✸ ✸

Mary woke feeling a little better. She was incredibly stiff and sore but the majority of the sharp pains had gone. Her head still throbbed but she hoped two more of Ricky's tablets would help. She had a job that had to be done.

She slipped gingerly out of bed and made her way to the shower. The warm water felt good on her bruises but stung her many welts. Drying herself, she hobbled back to the bedroom to find Nancy sitting on the bed.

'And what are you doing?'

'I have to go to the bank.'

'No you don't: not today. You get back in that bed, right now!'

'Nancy, I love you dearly and I owe you a lot, but I have to do this, so you can either help me or get out of my way!'

Nancy's shock showed on her face. 'Are you sure?' she answered meekly.

Mary gave her a smile that hurt her lip but one that said she was sorry for speaking to her that way. 'I know you're only thinking of me but I do have to do this. Can you help me?'

'Of course I'll help you if it means that much to you.'

Nancy assisted Mary into her clothes: not that she ended up wearing much. Her breasts hurt when she tried to put on her bra so they left it off. Dressed only in a brief pair of knickers and a loose cotton dress she allowed Nancy to help her out to the waiting BMW.

'Where is Ricky?' asked Mary, realising she hadn't seen him.

'He apologises for leaving but he had something he needed to do today at the bank.'

She didn't give Ricky another thought as Nancy sat herself behind the wheel. 'I hope I don't crash. I've never driven anything this expensive before!' Nancy drove safely, although nervously, to the bank without incident. She was forced to drive around the block four times until she found a park close enough for Mary to walk. Mary was conscious of the stares she received from everyone they passed. 'I must look a sight,' she whispered to Nancy.

'Ignore them.' With a wink, Nancy added, 'They're all looking at me anyway.'

'You always were conceited,' said Mary, her spirits receiving a needed lift.

'Me? Conceited?' said Nancy, in mock indignation. 'You were always the conceited one!'

The pair continued their banter, which took Mary's mind off her problems until they reached the bank. Once inside, Nancy deposited Mary on a chair and went to find someone who could help them. When Nancy asked for permission for her friend to enter the safety deposit box vault, the man told her to wait.

A few minutes later a tall willowy woman dressed very fashionably in a matching skirt and jacket approached her. Holding out her hand, she asked Nancy, 'Are you Mrs. Parker?'

Nancy accepted the hand and replied, 'No, Ms. Hamley, I am her friend.'

Janet didn't bother asking how the woman knew who she was. Instead, she said, 'Can you take me to her, please?' She followed her to a battered and bruised woman sitting alone on a chair. 'Mrs. Parker?' Janet asked again, tentatively holding out her hand.

'That's right,' said Mary, her speech slightly slurred because she couldn't open her mouth properly without hurting her lip.

Coming straight to the point, Janet told her, 'I am afraid I cannot grant you access to the vault at this time.'

'Why not? I have the key.'

'The bank has frozen your husband's assets until a certain matter has been clarified.'

'Can you do that?' asked Nancy.

Mary decided arguing wouldn't get them anywhere. In as clear a voice as she could muster, she said, 'I would like to speak with Sir Winstanley.'

'I am afraid Sir Winstanley is a very busy man. If you would like I can make you an appointment?'

Mary sat as straight as her battered body would allow. Looking straight at the imposing women, she told her, 'No, I don't want an appointment. What I want is for you to call Sir Winstanley and tell him, Mrs. Geoffrey Parker has some information for him.'

Janet didn't like it but she did as Mary asked. Returning moments later she took Mary by the arm and led her towards the lifts.

'Do you mind waiting here?' Mary asked Nancy, not wanting to get her any more involved.

'No, but I'll be right here when you get back,' said Nancy, giving Janet Hamley a look that said she would hold her accountable if anything happened to her friend.

When the lift opened Janet escorted Mary through the outer office directly into Sir Winstanley's. Sir Winstanley wasn't quick enough to hide his surprise at Mary's condition and she caught a grimace on his face before he smiled and greeted her. 'Good morning, Mrs. Parker,' he said, placing a chair for her on the other side of his desk.

'You can call me, Mary,' she said pleasantly, as he helped her settle into the chair.

Dismissing Janet with a look, he went back around his desk and sat down. Getting straight to the point, he asked, 'You said you had something to tell me?'

Mary gave him the best smile she could under the circumstances and said, 'I lied.'

For the second time Sir Winstanley's surprise showed his face. 'I don't understand.'

'I wanted to see you and it was the only way I could get up here.'

Not looking as friendly as he had only moments ago, he asked, 'Now that you are here, what do you want?'

'I was paid a visit by one of your staff.'

When she stopped he shrugged and said, 'So?'

Pointing to her face, she told him, 'He did this to me.'

'Why would one of my staff do such a thing?'

'He wanted to know where my husband is. I don't know so I couldn't tell him.'

'How can you be sure he works for the bank?'

'Because I have met him before. His name is Frank Dobson, but that is not why I came.'

'Then why did you come?'

Mary stood awkwardly, using the desk for support. Before Sir Winstanley realised what she was doing she released the catches at her shoulders and her dress slipped down her to the floor. Left standing in only a pair of brief knickers her bruised and battered body was fully exposed. 'He did this to me too!' She let the elderly man take a good look at the bruises on her breasts, where Frank had pinched them and at the bruises where he had punched her. Then she turned around. She smiled a satisfied smile when she heard him gasp as he saw the damage to her back.

It was a different Sir Winstanley who raced around his desk and helped her back into her dress. All the pomposity had gone out of him now and he looked visibly shaken. In truth, he helped her back into her dress mainly because the sight of her battered and bruised body was making him feel nauseous. He couldn't begin to imagine what sort of pain the woman was suffering. 'I don't know what to say; words fail me,' he said, conscious of not accepting blame. He had lived for too long protecting the bank's image for the habit to slip so readily.

'But that is not why I came,' she repeated.

This time Sir Winstanley was too afraid to ask why she had come. He made his way back to his chair and slumped into it as he waited for Mary to continue in her own time.

'He raped me!' she finally blurted out. 'More than once!'

Sir Winstanley was completely lost for words. He had no idea how to comfort the woman sitting on the other side of his desk. This kind of thing didn't happen in his world and he had no point of reference. He sat there with his mouth hanging open looking like a man on the verge of collapse. But she hadn't finished with him yet. She had been playing him like a fish on a line and now she was ready to reel him in. Very slowly, she said, 'But that is not why I came.'

'My god, there is more?' asked sir Winstanley, looking as shattered as she felt.

'I came to see you because he said he would come back.'

Sir Winstanley's shattered nerves meshed into action. Finally there was something he could act on. Picking up the phone he bellowed into it, 'Blake, get in here, now!' before slamming it back down. Noticing how Mary jumped at the sudden noise he apologised, saying, 'I am very sorry, Mrs. Parker, the last thing I want to do is cause you any further discomfort.'

'It's alright,' she said, wishing she had some more of Ricky's pills.

When Wilson Blake entered the room seconds later, only Mary's presence in the room saved him from Sir Winstanley's wrath. 'Do you know Mrs. Parker?'

Blake took in the way Sir Winstanley was shaking and the bruises on the woman's face and his bowels threatened to loosen. 'Not personally, Sir.'

'Apparently she knows one of your staff. Someone called Frank Dobson.'

Blake's eyes went wide. 'Frank did this?'

'And much worse!' said Sir Winstanley, not going into details. Beginning to shake with the anger he felt, he added, 'I have never heard of such a cowardly act in all my life!' He paused only to glare at Blake as though challenging Blake to contradict him. 'To make matters even worse, he threatened to return. Now I want to make it perfectly clear, I would like this poor woman to be able to rest easy in the knowledge there is no, I repeat, no possible likelihood of this man or any other man paying her another visit. Do I have your assurance on this?'

'Certainly, Sir.'

'Now get out of my sight,' said Sir Winstanley with all the disgust he felt coming through his voice.

Once Blake had hurried from the room Sir Winstanley turned back to Mary. When he spoke his voice held a softness it hadn't in years. 'I am terribly sorry for what you have been through. I know there isn't any way I can make it up to you but I want you to know I am truly sorry.' Turning slightly more businesslike, he offered, 'I know you have our assurance you will be left alone; however, I couldn't blame you if you doubted me. If it would make you feel safer, I would be happy to have a security guard stationed at your house: at our expense, of course.'

'Thank you, but it won't be necessary. I am staying with friends who are taking good care of me. There is something you can do for me though.'

'Just name it!'

'I was refused access to my husband's safety deposit box. I would like to clear it out. I also would like my husband's account closed and the money handed to me.'

Sir Winstanley had seen Graham's latest report and knew how much money was missing. He knew Parker had hidden it somewhere and it didn't take a genius to figure out it was probably held in the safety deposit box. With his mind working at full speed he quickly calculated the damage to the bank if this woman's story got out to the media. Besides, this money was extra money. Although it legally belonged to the bank, the bank wasn't going to be left short if it wasn't retrieved. 'I know I don't have the right to ask, but...' he gave an apologetic shrug. 'I would like a favour in return.'

'And that is?'

'That this whole sordid affair remains between us.'

'You don't have to worry, Sir Winstanley, I have no desire to tell anyone my story.'

'Again, I apologise for asking anything of you, but would you be willing to sign a confidentiality agreement to that effect?'

'All I want is to be left alone so I'll sign anything you want.'

Sir Winstanley picked up the phone again and spoke with Janet Hamley. With the arrangements made he personally escorted Mary to the vault.

When she opened the box it was full of papers she didn't recognise. She hadn't known what to expect but she had been hoping to find cash. Putting everything into her bag, she put the box back and hobbled out. Sir Winstanley was waiting for her and he handed her a small parcel. 'This is the contents of your husband's account.' Taking her arm, he walked her to the door. When Nancy came over Mary introduced them. 'Sir Winstanley, this is my friend, Nancy Forbes. She is the one who is looking after me.'

Sir Winstanley gave Nancy a polite bow, before telling her, 'You must be a very good friend and I don't want to insult you; however, I would take it as a personal favour if you sent me an account for any expenses you incur while looking after this dear lady.'

Sir Winstanley was legendary for his gruffness and Nancy was taken completely by surprise. In reply, she could only mumble, 'I will.'

Deciding to push her luck, Mary said, 'Actually, Nancy works here: at the bank. Would it be asking too much for her to be given some leave?'

Sir Winstanley clicked his fingers and Janet rushed forward. 'Please see to it Mrs. Forbes is granted whatever leave she requires, paid of course, while she nurses Mrs. Parker back to health.'

He watched the two women for a time before turning to walk back to the lifts. As he rose to his floor his anger grew inside him until it threatened to boil over.

※ ※ ※

Blake tapped his foot on the floor as he waited for Frank to arrive. It was an old habit and anyone who knew him well, would know to stay out of his way. As Frank stepped through the door, Blake demanded, 'What happened when you saw Mrs. Parker?'

'Nothing. We talked but she didn't know anything.'

'Nothing else you want to add?'

'Like what?' asked Frank, looking nervous.

'You know, like torturing and raping her?'

'You have to understand, it wasn't like that. This woman is different; she likes it.'

Blake's foot suddenly stopped tapping which was an even worse sign. 'The only thing I have to understand is she has spoken to Sir Winstanley...personally, and the only reason I don't kill you here and now is because I don't have the time. Sir Winstanley is expecting me back in his office to explain.' Picking up an envelope he threw it in Frank's face. 'That is an airline ticket for Darwin; be on it. Oh, and by the way: you're fired!'

Frank stooped to pick up the fallen envelope. For a moment it looked as though he might say something. Evidently thinking better of it, he turned to leave. When he reached the door, Blake called out to him, 'I don't have to tell you to stay away from her, do I?' Frank didn't bother to answer. He didn't have to. He wanted Mary more than anything, but she wasn't worth dying for.

CHAPTER 21

Geoffrey had dismissed Ricky as only a Grade Five Clerk but Ricky was well liked at the bank and when he arrived at work that morning he started to call in some favours.

The phone rang on Ricky's desk and he snatched for it.

'He's leaving now via the underground carpark.'

Ricky didn't need to speak; he knew all he needed to know. Slamming the phone down, he raced for the stairs. Down in the basement he waited. As a man approached him, he demanded, 'Frank Dobson?'

'Who wants to know?'

Ricky's first punch was parried but the second caught enough of Frank's jaw to stun him. The third landed solidly against the side of Frank's head, knocking him to the ground. Bending over him, Ricky said, 'I want to know!' He kicked Frank hard in the face, breaking his nose. Frank shook his head, sending a spray of blood over himself.

He lifted Frank up so he could look into his face. 'I'm a friend of Mary Parker, a good friend, and I have a message for you. She doesn't ever want to see you again.'

Ricky spent the next fifteen minutes explaining in clear terms how he felt when he saw Mary. Leaving Frank lying unconscious on the concrete floor, in a pool of his own blood, Ricky went back to work where any number of people would vouch he had never left.

Picking up the phone he said only two words before hanging up. 'I'm back.'

In the Security Control Room the mysterious problem that had cut out the cameras in the basement carpark fixed itself. The image on their screens returned to show a man lying prone on the concrete floor. While they finished their coffee they argued over who should ring Wilson Blake. Just as they were about to make the call, the figure began to stir. A guard gave a sigh of relief as he put the phone down. They went back to watching as the figure staggered to a car and drove away.

∗ ∗ ∗

'I am more disappointed than I can express,' said Sir Winstanley heavily.

Blake had no reply; he felt the same way.

'The Parker woman has given me her word, and I accept it, that she will not speak to anyone about this. I no longer care about anything Parker did. What I want is for any record he ever worked here expunged.' With a withering glare, he added, 'Do you think you can handle that?'

'Yes, Sir Winstanley,' said Blake, accepting the rebuke meekly.

***

Three of Geoffrey's colleagues were marched into Blake's office later that afternoon. There was a piece of paper lying in the desk in front of each of them. 'Sign these!' said Blake gruffly without any other greeting.

'What is it?' asked Brett, the spokesperson for the group in the absence of Geoffrey.

'Your resignations,' said Blake, his face a blank mask.

'I don't understand!' said Brett, unconvincingly.

'You three really are stupid. The first thing you all did was pay off your mortgages.'

'It wasn't us,' whined Kevin, 'It was Geoffrey Parker, he...'

'Shut up, Kevin,' interrupted Brett.

'It doesn't matter; we already know everything,' confirmed Blake. 'If you sign those now, we will let you keep your houses. If you choose not to...' he finished leaving his threat hanging.

The three looked at each other. Realising they had no other choice they picked up the pens supplied and signed the papers in front of them. Blake collected them and put them neatly in a folder. He then produced three other pieces of paper and laid one out in front of each of them.

When he didn't speak, Brett asked, 'And what are these?'

'This is your lucky day. For reasons that don't concern you, Sir Winstanley is more interested in your silence than getting rid of you. Those are confidentiality agreements. So long as you agree never to mention any of this or the name, Geoffrey Parker, again you get to keep your houses and those signed resignation forms will remain in my folder.'

Each of them looked at the other but no-one spoke. Taking up the pens again they signed the agreements in front of them.

'Now get out of my sight. And if any of you even thinks about defrauding the bank again, I'll personally deal with you. Is that clear!'

The three virtually ran from the room in their haste to get away.

***

Roberts was summoned to Peter Christian's office and he didn't look happy; too many strange things were going on without his knowledge.

'Hello, Deborah,' he said without looking at her as he went through to the inner office.

Peter looked terrible. 'Sit down.'

Roberts did as he was told, his sinking feeling growing worse by the minute.

'Parker has dropped us right in it!' said Peter, dejectedly.

'What's going on?'

'Sign this and I'll tell you.'

Roberts took out his pen and signed the paper without even looking at it.

'By the way, that is a confidentiality agreement. After today you can't even mention the bastard's name.'

Not interested in Parker anymore, Roberts asked, 'Do I still have a job?'

'Yes of course you do: just not the same job.'

The relief on Roberts's face was too much for Peter and he took the signed agreement and put it in a folder to be sent up to the Head of Security.

'What's my new job?'

'They put you in charge of the mailroom. You stay on the same pay of course. At least you get to stay here; I'm being packed off to Perth.'

'I am sorry,' said Roberts, not caring. He still had a job and that was all he cared about.

'It could have been worse,' said Peter, feeling terrible he couldn't warn his old friend the mailroom was due for outsourcing in nine months. When that happened, Roberts's services at the bank would no longer be required.

Showing Roberts out, Peter turned to his secretary and looked at her properly for the first time in days. Forgetting his own problems for the moment, he asked, 'Are you alright, Deborah? You look dreadful.'

There were large dark circles under her eyes and she looked very pale. Deborah hadn't slept in days. Each night she went home and showered, then, leaving off her clothes, she waited naked for Geoffrey to come. 'I'm fine,' she said, more brightly than she felt.

'As you know, I am leaving to take up a position in Perth at the end of the week. I would like to thank you for all the assistance you have given me in my time here.'

Deborah looked at him blankly. This was news to her. She had been so wrapped up in her own problems she hadn't concerned herself with anything else.

'There is one last thing I need you to do for me. I don't know how well you knew someone called Geoffrey Parker. Anyway his name has become taboo around here these days. I need you to remove any mention of him from our files.'

Peter walked back into his office not ever realising how he had crushed her hopes. It seemed obvious now Geoffrey was never coming and she had been so looking forward to it. Most of her life she had fantasied about being treated the way he had offered, but she had been too cautious to do anything about it. 'I even bought that stupid whip!' she said out loud.

The mention of the riding crop brought a smile to her face. There was still that nice young man from the store. *I wonder?*

* * *

Mary and Nancy waited eagerly for Ricky to arrive home from work. The moment he walked through the door, Nancy pounced on him. 'Quick: in here,' she squealed excitedly.

Not knowing what to expect he followed his wife into the kitchen. Mary was sitting on one of the chairs with a number of piles of paper sitting in front of her.

'What are these? Do you know?'

Ricky picked up one of the bundles and fingered the heavy bond paper. He had a pretty good idea but there were too many of them to be what he suspected. All the same he felt the same level of excitement Mary and Nancy did. 'I don't want to get your hopes up without being sure. Do you mind if I show this to someone?'

'Do anything you want.' said Mary, trusting him to take one of the tightly bound bundles.

Ricky was gone for over an hour but when he arrived back he ran into the house.

'Do you know what they are?' Nancy demanded.

Ricky looked disbelieving at all the bundles on his kitchen table, before saying, 'These things are as good as cash. They're Government Bonds, redeemable at any bank, no questions asked.'

'How much is there?' asked Nancy, looking stunned.

Ricky collected his calculator, a pad and a pen before sitting down at the table.

'Don't forget this!' said Mary, handing over the package Sir Winstanley had given her. Opening it Ricky took out the cash and counted it first. Then tackling one bundle at a time he carefully counted and then re-counted each one. It took him a long time, while Mary and Nancy fidgeted.

Finally he was done and, rechecking the figures he had scribbled on the pad once more, he looked up at Mary and told her, 'There is exactly twenty-eight million, four hundred and twenty thousand, four hundred and ninety dollars.'

There was silence in the room for a few minutes before Mary broke it by saying, 'Twenty-eight million?'

'And four hundred and twenty thousand, four hundred and ninety dollars,' finished off Ricky.' As an afterthought, he added, 'Oh: and the deed to the house.'

'Oh-my-God, Mary, what are you going to do with all of it?' asked Nancy.

'Actually, I was wondering where it all came from.'

'Who cares? It's yours now,' said Ricky.

'But is it?' she asked. 'Geoffrey can't possibly have raised all this legally! Surely this must be the bank's money!'

'Sir Winstanley himself gave you access to Geoffrey's safety deposit box and he must have suspected what was in it. Otherwise they wouldn't have stopped you in the first place. So, if Sir Winstanley let you take it, it must be yours,' reasoned Nancy.

Mary gave her a look that said she wasn't so sure.

'I know her logic is a little twisted but I think Nancy's right,' said Ricky. 'Sir Winstanley, of all people, wouldn't have let you walk out of the bank with all this money if he wasn't happy about it.'

'It still doesn't feel right to me,' Mary said. 'Why would they let me keep it if it was stolen?'

'Maybe it isn't stolen,' suggested Nancy. 'Geoffrey did go on a bit about how clever he was. Maybe he did make it trading; it was his job after all.'

'Yeah, maybe all he did was use his insider knowledge or at worst use some of the bank's money to make this with. That would explain why they were interested in talking with him and why they let you keep it!' said Rick, searching for an explanation that would satisfy Mary.

Looking at all the money stacked up in front of her was beginning to weaken her resolve to do the right thing. After all, Sir Winstanley could have stopped her at any time, couldn't he? Only he hadn't. In fact, he had helped her and then offered to pay for Nancy's expenses; surely that meant he didn't care if she kept the money?

With a wink, Nancy asked, 'You're going to keep it, aren't you?'

Looking pleased with herself, she told her, 'What the hell, the bank knows where to find me. If they want it, I'm sure they'll ask.'

'And if they don't?' asked Nancy, a huge smile spreading across her face.

'If they don't, I am going to have some serious fun!'

***

Detectives Paul Pennin and Bruce Harrison were summoned to Captain Lewis's office once more. 'This case is turning out to be a real strange one but I think we are getting close to what happened,' reported Bruce.

'Forget it. The case has been closed.'

'What do you mean, closed? There are some really screwy things about this case that haven't been sorted out yet. For instance, where is Geoffrey Parker?'

'I understand the brother spoke to him,' said Lewis, looking at the report.

'That's what he said, but we didn't believe it for a minute.'

'Well, I am satisfied and so is the bank. The case is closed!' he said firmly.

***

The next weeks went by in a whirl. Mary's many bruises slowly healed with only a few grey shadows left to mark their passing. The house was on the market and all the contents had been given to a local charity. The only thing Mary kept was a small framed photograph taken by a fourteen year old boy with a disposable camera.

'When are you coming back?' asked Robert.

'I'm not sure. It might be just a holiday or it might turn out to be something more permanent,' said Mary, with a quaver in her voice.

Robert had his own scars from where Chantelle had clawed him. Noticing the direction of Mary's gaze, he gave her an edited version of what had happened when the Police interviewed them. 'I'm divorcing her,' he said simply, as he finished.

'Why don't you come with me?' she asked, in a deceptively quiet voice.

Robert looked at her and wondered what life might have been like if this had ended differently: only it hadn't. 'I told the police Geoffrey called me from Cairns, only we both know he didn't. That is why I can't. I'm not judging you but I can't go with you: not now.' He gave her a chaste kiss on her cheek, their tears mingling as he held his face to hers. 'Goodbye, Mary.'

'Goodbye, Robert,' she said mechanically, fearful this might be the last time she would ever see him. She stood on the front lawn and watched as his car disappeared. Nancy came over and put her arm around her. 'Come on. It's time to go or you'll miss your plane.'

Both the women were silent on the drive to the airport. Ricky was as nervous driving the BMW as Nancy had been. He didn't understand why Mary insisted they use it but he didn't argue. Parking the car he got out. Not sure what to do with the keys he offered them to her.

She smiled and told him, 'You keep them; it's yours now.'

'Mine?'

'It's my way of thanking you for everything.' Ricky had been such a help to her; he didn't have Geoffrey's flair with money but what he did do was find her people she could trust, people who had invested most of the money for her. The car was only a token gesture to her friends. She discovered she still had other friends, even after she had ignored them for such a long time. They helped her to secretly pay Nancy and Ricky's mortgage and to deposit five hundred thousand dollars into their account. Nancy and Ricky would only discover any of it once she was safely out of the way. She knew they would insist on her taking it back and she didn't want to. It was easier this way.

With a grin, she said, 'Trust me; you won't thank me. The registration and insurance will keep you poor.'

'Will you be back?' asked Nancy, with tears streaming down her face.

'Of course I will; I just don't know when. But I'll keep in touch. After all, New Zealand isn't that far!'

***

Mary was feeling a mixture of excitement and sadness as she took her seat on the plane.

'Have you been to New Zealand before?' asked the elderly lady next to her.

'No,' she replied politely 'But I'm really looking forward to seeing it!'

'You will love it, Dear. I go every year.' Looking down at Mary's hand, the woman asked, 'Your husband not coming with you?'

'No, he said he didn't think he would like New Zealand so I left him at home.'

'Well, good for you!'

A B Given

THE END

Printed in Great Britain
by Amazon